HIGH PRAISE FOR L. J. McDONALD

THE BATTLE SYLPH

"Lovers of *Stardust* and *The Princess Bride* rejoice! A must for every Fantasy library."

—Barbara Vey, blogger, *Publishers Weekly*

"Refreshingly different, with an almost classic fantasy flavor . . . an exceptional literary debut."

—John Charles, reviewer, *Chicago Tribune* and *Booklist*

"A fresh new voice in fantasy romance. . . . I loved the characters and mythology!"

—Alexis Morgan, bestselling author of The Paladins of Darkness

"A fabulous read, cover to cover."

—C. L. Wilson, *New York Times* bestselling author

"Unlike anything I've ever read. A brilliant adventure with tremendous heart. You'll love this book."

—Marjorie Liu, *New York Times* bestselling author

"A remarkable new voice and a stunningly original world. . . . An amazing start to what promises to be a truly engaging series!"

—Jill M. Smith, reviewer, *RT Book Reviews*

THE SHATTERED SYLPH

"McDonald is fast making a place for herself in the wonderful world of fantasy! . . . *The Shattered Sylph* draws readers further into a world where slavery and magic are intertwined. 4½ stars. Top Pick!"

—*RT Book Reviews*

"Fantastic books."

—All About Romance

"A smash hit."

—Fresh Fiction

A ROYAL THREAT

The assassin stared at Solie, eyes wide. He finally realized she knew what he was feeling. Or probably he thought she was reading his mind. She saw—*felt*—him shudder and try to draw within himself so as not to give any more away.

It was too late.

"How many?" Alcor had once sent two battlers to kill her, and when that hadn't worked, he sent three more and an army. What would it be this time? "Two? Three? Four?" She stared into their captive's ashen face. His brown eyes were dilated and wide, irises surrounded by white. "*Four* more assassins?" She glanced at Mace. "There are four more of them."

Other books by L. J. McDonald:

The Battle Sylph
The Shattered Sylph
"The Worth of a Sylph" in *A Midwinter Fantasy*

QUEEN OF THE SYLPHS

L. J. MCDONALD

Dorchester
Publishing

DORCHESTER PUBLISHING

Published by

Dorchester Publishing Co., Inc.
200 Madison Avenue
New York, NY 10016

Trade book ISBN: 978-1-4285-1216-0
E-book ISBN: 978-1-4285-1198-9

First Dorchester Publishing, Co., Inc. edition: September 2011

The "DP" logo is the property of Dorchester Publishing Co., Inc.

Printed in the United States of America.

Visit us online at www.dorchesterpub.com.

Dedication

To all the real friends in my life, only some of whom I have room to name. I hope that the rest of you know who you are. To my husband, Oliver, who is my best friend. To Andrew M, Andrew MJ, Amy, Blandine, Daniel, Ennien, Frank, Gene, Jane, John, Kelly, Perry, and always, always, to Eda.

Acknowledgments

A lot of people have said that even though it's the author who writes the novel, no book is written in a vacuum. That's true. I owe a lot to my husband, Oliver, who tossed ideas for the plot and the world around with me and suffered through reading my first draft. I owe my beta readers, Kelly Chang and Gene Kinney, who pointed out my periodic stupidities. Any errors still in there can be blamed on me of course, not them.

I also want to thank my agent, Michelle Grakowski at Three Seas Literary Agency for helping me navigate the bizarre world of novel contracts and publication. Along with her is my thanks to the great people at Dorchester, from the copy editor to the promotions manager and the cover artist, all of whom helped to bring the Sylph world to life. Most of all, I want to thank my editor, Chris Keeslar, who took a book I wrote purely because I want to write, and believed it was something that other people would actually want to read. It's because of him that you're holding this novel right now.

QUEEN OF THE SYLPHS

Prologue

The battle sylphs watched.

It was market day in Sylph Valley, and a large caravan had arrived with merchants from Eferem and Yed. There were several hundred new people in the town, all jostling and shouting their way through the myriad merchant stalls, and that had brought out the Valley's defenders. Above the crush, sixteen battle sylphs crouched atop poles bearing the Valley's unlit night lanterns, each perched like a giant blue and gold bird. Used to the outwardly human creatures, the people of the Valley went on their way, only glancing up periodically. The newcomers, however, gaped in amazement.

In turn, the battlers didn't appear to pay attention to any of the humans, but that wasn't true. They watched the outsiders with an intentness that bordered on obsession. They didn't like change and given their own way, no one new would be allowed into the Valley unless they were cleared first; but that would limit trade. Without commerce, the town couldn't grow, and if the town didn't grow, it wouldn't survive. They had no allies. Theirs was a settlement against the world.

Seated on his heels with his hands resting lightly on his knees, Mace studied the main street and considered their position. There were those who would trade with Sylph Valley, certainly, but other kingdoms who agreed with their queen's philosophy? So far, none even acknowledged her. The merchants who came to this place weren't the representatives of their kings, after all. In the case of Eferem, Mace had no doubt that they were coming directly against their king's command. The Valley was a good place to trade, for their queen made sure everything was kept fair. No one was cheated in the Valley. No one tried. Not with battlers watching.

Mace shifted on his pole, watching the crowd with more than his eyes. To anyone who saw him like this, he was a tall, heavy-boned man of indeterminate age with short, thinning hair and a face not given to smiling. His form held more power than beauty, he knew, but had a certain hard confidence that appealed to women. He never took advantage of that, not anymore. His loyalty was unquestioned—to the queen, who commanded him before all, and to the Widow Lily Blackwell, who owned both his body and his love. Each of the battlers had a woman, and they would take no other while that woman lived. It was for the women that the battlers guarded the Valley. For the hive.

As the day wore on, Mace studied everyone making his or her way down the street and felt their emotions. Amusement, contentment, impatience, worry: a tapestry of feelings. A thousand washed through him but left him unmoved. Empathy was something battle sylphs had in abundance. Compassion they had not at all.

Mace searched for anger, for violence and hate. A man about to cause harm would broadcast that, giving himself away to any sylph. The elemental and healer sylphs wouldn't react except to run, but battlers would attack. If a man felt rage, they came. If a woman felt fear, they came. Even the queen wouldn't deny them that, for it was their deepest instinct. Battlers protected their hive. It had always been that way.

Below, in an ordinary travel tunic with a pack on his back, a man passed through the market without noticing Mace's silent perch. The man felt . . . determined. He was eyeing the elemental sylphs who walked in the form of children. First came surprise, then contempt. He viewed with disgust the women who wore clothes like men and bartered or sold as equals.

Mace leaned forward, balanced unnaturally on his toes. He glanced over at the other battlers, who were watching the newcomer as well, their emotions interested. Mace nodded at the closest, a blue-haired and nervous creature named Claw.

We follow, he said silently into his fellow battler's mind.

Claw nodded spastically. He was a shivering, broken creature who'd been ruined by years of slavery. Mace would never send him on a mission alone, but even if Lily hadn't said to include him, Claw still had his uses. He was a battle sylph and nothing would change that.

Mace jumped down, landing easily before a woman carrying a basket of potatoes. She yelped and nearly dropped it, staring up at him in fright. Mace just nodded and set off, making his way through the crowd.

Whether they knew him or not, people got out of his way. The battlers here all wore the same clothes, a gold-trimmed blue uniform that made it easy for them to be identified. The queen felt it was kinder than the aura of hatred they otherwise projected, which she believed wasn't needed, not in the Valley. Mace wasn't inclined to argue, even if arguing with a queen or a master were comprehensible to him. People here knew what the uniforms meant. Those who didn't quickly learned.

Several passersby started to speak, perhaps to say hello, but they stopped when they saw the look in his eye and Claw at his heel. Mace felt their fear and kept going.

His mark was easy to catch, having to push his way through the crowd that parted for the battlers, but the sylphs held back, instead just following. It was not yet time. One of the queen's rules was that they not attack on instinct. They needed a reason. Not much of one, perhaps, but a reason nonetheless. The man reached the end of the wide road and headed into a square. Everything from food to tools to jewelry was being sold here, but the man didn't care. Mace didn't either. Above, a battle sylph named Wat perched on the edge of a building.

He feels like he's looking for something, Claw sent to Mace.

Yes. The man did, and it was nothing these merchants were selling. The stranger stared at the faces of the women he passed, and Mace could feel his annoyance: He wasn't finding what he wanted, and his determination was veering toward violence. He felt like a predator, and Mace let a low growl escape his throat.

A little girl toddled out of the crowd. She grabbed Mace's leg, beaming up at him. "Play with me!" she cried, her happiness a dizzying salve.

Mace scooped the girl up, tickling her under the chin. He passed her to Claw, ordering, *Take her to her mother*. The woman was not far away. She was one of the original Community members, there since the Valley was settled, and her emotions were content, trusting the battlers with her child.

As Claw hurried over to the smiling woman, Mace turned back to his target—and found him nowhere in sight, lost in the emotions of an excited, happy crowd watching a street performer with a dozen juggling balls. Mace snarled, looking around and reaching out with his senses. A moment later he glared up at Wat on the rooftops.

Where? he demanded.

The battler, dark-haired, slim, and gorgeous by any human standard, stared right back. *Huh?*

Mace growled and shifted, dropping the human shape he'd chosen years before and returning to his original form of dense black smoke. He had swirling eyes of ball lightning and teeth of pure electricity. Black, drifting wings spread out, and he rose dozens of feet in moments. People who saw him screamed in fright, even those who knew him. Some of those screamed even louder. Battlers only took this shape to travel long distances— or to attack.

Mace had no proof, but he knew exactly where his quarry was headed. Determined, violent, searching for a woman; not expecting to find her in the market but watching regardless, just in case . . .

He rose higher and confirmed his suspicion. On the other side of the square was another road that led eventually to a stone building, its walls as thin and delicate as candy floss, its windows tall with colored glass. It rose high in the air, a creamy white tower. Wide stairs led to great double doors, both open as they always were when the queen held court. Mace spotted the stranger already nearing the stairs just inside, since the building itself was nothing but a front for a grand stairwell into the underground complex below the town.

He roared. *PROTECT THE QUEEN.*

His call was a command to every sylph, whether battler or otherwise. The battlers answered, immediately taking to the air. The other sylphs shrieked, changing forms to escape, many dragging their human masters to safety. Those Valley dwellers without sylphs saw the others retreating, heard the battlers roar and fled themselves, all hurrying to stairwells at the corners of each square. These also led into the corridors below. Strangers to the Valley didn't know to follow, but Mace didn't care, not anywhere near as much as he cared about the safety of the human queen who was master to them all.

The interloper froze at the foot of the stairs, staring up at Mace in fear—at all of the battlers, while others rose behind him and created a storm many layers high. The doors to the tower closed, sealed shut by the touch of an earth sylph, and Mace opened his jaws wide, hissing. He couldn't speak in this form, could only project his voice to other sylphs, his master, or his queen. He projected to her now.

There is danger, Solie. A man has come to kill you. We have him.

Don't kill him, she sent back immediately. *Bring him to me.*

Mace hated it, but he obeyed.

Chapter One

She was a small, slim, redheaded girl only twenty-three years old, but as the queen of Sylph Valley, Solie was the most powerful woman alive. Most of the time, she didn't feel that way. She did feel like a leader, though. She spent her days doing paperwork, organizing the development of the Valley, and trying to convince the other kingdoms to get over their fear and enact formal trade agreements—or at least not go to war with them.

Dressed in a long gown of silk the same blue as the uniforms the battlers wore, she rose from her throne, shaped from stone by an earth sylph to be beautiful but still comfortable, and descended the dais stairs to the polished floor. Her reflection strode beneath her and Heyou bristled at her side, his feelings obvious even if she weren't able to feel them. His anger was no different than that of every single battler and elemental sylph in the room, or that of the humans here.

Heyou was specifically hers, the battler who bonded to her and made her queen. When they first met, he'd made himself look like a boy. As she'd aged, he'd aged his appearance as well. Now he looked very much like a man, though he was still not much taller than her own five feet two inches. And he was still the same Heyou: immature and devoted, and determined to protect her. Still, with twenty sylphs in the room, Solie didn't exactly feel any danger.

Her erstwhile assassin knelt on the floor, Mace twisting his arm behind his back. Solie didn't ask the battler to release his grip. Mace would be upset by that, and he wasn't actually hurting the man. She knew he wanted to. If it hadn't been for her order, the assassin would already be dead.

She studied the stranger. He seemed perfectly ordinary, sweat dripping down his dirt-streaked face. He smelled of travel, like many men who came to town, and he stared at the floor in silence. Once, she would have thought him an ordinary soul frightened into silence, but not now. Not anymore.

Solie was still human, for all her sacred status with the sylphs; she wasn't an empath. But one of the advantages of being a sylph's master was that she could feel the emotions they projected. And while a normal master could feel only what their own individual sylph did, Solie as queen could feel the emotions of any of her sylphs, and they could project to her anything they picked up from others. Thanks to that, she could nearly feel this man's mind churning as he tried to think his way out of his predicament.

He had indeed come to kill her. Once, that would have frightened her terribly, but Solie had spent six years as queen and she wasn't the naive little girl she'd once been. Neither circumstances nor her advisers had let her be.

She glanced over at Devon Chole, wishing that he wasn't the only one of her three advisers currently in the Valley, but Thom Galway was off in the woods, as he often was, and Leon was across the ocean, searching for his kidnapped daughter. Devon was far younger than either, being only five years older than herself. Still, he had a good heart and a great liking of people, and he'd been a true asset to her. He arranged her social schedule and audiences, somehow always able to figure out who needed to see her and when, and how to manage her time so that she was able to do all the things she had to. He also protected her time for herself and Heyou.

Devon wore the same blue uniform as the battle sylphs, but the gold piping on his coat was greatly diminished. The last thing Solie wanted was for someone to think he was a battle sylph and challenge him to a fight. It had happened before. The only reason anyone survived was because she'd ordered it.

Leon wore the same suit as Devon when he was working, but he could defend himself. Galway couldn't be bothered. The old trapper hadn't sworn himself to her like Leon and Devon had, either. Not that it mattered. However he'd learned what he knew, the man was a great source of information on how to set up an economy and make it work. He had seven children living in his house, three of them not his. He knew how to make successful compromises.

For now, though, however competent her other advisers were, Solie only had Devon and a great number of angry battlers.

"Do you recognize him?" she asked.

Devon eyed the man uncertainly, thinking. In the still air of the audience chamber, his hair moved as his invisible air sylph tossed it around.

"Do *you* recognize him, Airi?" Solie asked the playful little creature.

I'm not sure, the sylph sent. *I don't think so.*

"I don't think so either," Devon admitted, hearing his sylph as easily as Solie. "I don't think I've ever seen him before." He shrugged and whispered, "If he's from Eferem, Leon would know."

Solie made a face. Leon had been King Alcor's head of security and lead battler master. He'd also nearly been her assassin, himself. He'd got a lot closer to success than this one.

She stared deep into the assassin's heart. Seeing the resentment, she doubted he'd ever turn out to be one of her closest friends the way Leon had. Either way, she had to decide what to do with him. For the battlers, it was simple: kill him.

But Solie couldn't do that. It wasn't just that she'd been raised kind and nonviolent, killing him would be too easy. She didn't need Devon and the others to warn her that such methods led to corruption.

"Who are you?" she asked instead.

The man looked up at her. "N-no one," he stammered. "I'm just a traveler. I don't understand!"

He did, though. Solie could feel it. He knew exactly why he was there. He still wanted to see her dead, and the urge was only stronger now that he'd been taken. Too easily, he seemed to feel. He'd been taken too easily. He really didn't understand how battlers worked. No one who lived in a place that bound sylphs to slavery ever did.

Solie wasn't going to tell him. "You're lying," she snapped. "You're not a traveler, you're an assassin."

He gave no physical response, just stared at her in seeming confusion, but his insides flared with anger. Which just proved she was right.

She turned her gaze to Mace, who was watching her over the prisoner's head. He could hold the man forever, so she could take her time with this interrogation.

"You're lying," she said again. She looked back at the assassin. "Are you from Para Dubh?" It would be bad if he were. She really didn't want them to be enemies. The kingdom of Para Dubh on their eastern border had signed a trade agreement with them, encouraging the sale of certain goods in return for Sylph Valley's ore, but they hadn't officially acknowledged Solie. Yed, far to the south, still ignored them while trying to increase their army, even as merchants from there regularly came through. According to her battlers, most of them were spies. The kingdom of Eferem was right on their southern border, and King Alcor hated everything she stood for. She wondered if her would-be killer was from there. West were impassable mountains while north was nothing but ice and snow. Just worrying about the south and the east was enough for her.

No emotional reaction. The man was tense, waiting to see what she said next and still figuring a way out of this. He had no idea how much he was giving away.

"I've never been there," he said.

"What about Yed? Are you from Yed?"

He nodded, licking his lips in feigned nervousness. "Yes. I came up with a caravan. Is that illegal?"

He was lying. Solie's eyes narrowed. "You're lying again. You're from Eferem."

Fear shot through him, confirming her suspicions.

"You're from Eferem," she continued. "King Alcor sent you to kill me."

The more she spoke, the surer she was. She was also angry, if not surprised. Solie had actually been born in a hamlet only a few miles away from the capital, and she'd been taken for a sacrifice used to trap a battler. Her death had been meant to bind Heyou to Alcor's only son, but the prince ended up dead and Solie as Heyou's master—the first woman ever to link with a battler. It was when they'd become intimate that she'd become a queen. Alcor had tried to have her killed and lost five battlers. The only reason he hadn't attacked again was from fear. He had six battlers left; she had over fifty.

But, Leon had taught her that there were other ways to cripple a country than outright war. Whether he'd thought of it himself or someone finally suggested it to him, Alcor had just tried one.

"Are there more of you coming?" she demanded, her attention so focused that she wasn't aware of Devon watching her or the preening, proud looks of her battlers. She didn't want war with Eferem, but she wasn't so childish as to think she could ignore an enemy. Not anymore. If they didn't come after her again, who would they try to hurt next? How much damage could they do?

The assassin stared at her, his eyes wide. He finally realized she knew what he was feeling. Or probably he thought she was reading his mind. She saw—*felt*—him shudder and try to draw within himself so as not to give any more away.

It was too late. While sylph empathy could be fooled and someone with their emotions under control could slip by even battlers, it took tremendous skill. This man didn't have it. In moments, Solie knew there were more assassins coming.

"How many?" Alcor sent two battlers to kill her once, and when that hadn't worked, he sent three more and an army. "Two? Three? Four?" She stared into the captive's ashen face. His brown eyes were dilated and wide, irises surrounded by white. "*Four* more assassins?" She glanced at Mace. "There are four more of them."

Mace growled and she heard a call go out. Battlers roared outside and she felt their hate wash over the town. They were only allowed to do that in protection, but the hive was definitely threatened. Was she the only target?

"Who else are you after?" she demanded.

The power structure of Sylph Valley was no secret: Solie was queen. Mace directed the battlers. Devon was her secretary. Galway took charge of economics and trade. Leon governed just about everything else. Half a dozen others filled important, smaller roles . . .

"You're after the council," she realized. Leon and Galway were away, but Alcor didn't necessarily know that. "Send battlers to protect the council and their families." When Mace nodded, she knew it would be done.

Solie turned, eyeing Heyou by her side. To battlers in their own world, the oldest and most powerful usually won the queen—and the right to rule. Heyou had skipped around that, but only to a degree. He bowed to Mace as much as any other battler. She knew he didn't mind. He'd rather be with her than take on the responsibilities Mace carried.

Right now, however, there was something he could do that Mace couldn't. "Go to Galway," she told him.

Galway could be anywhere, but the trapper was his master. Heyou's pattern was bonded to him much like all the other sylphs were bonded to her, if in a lesser position. Galway could give Heyou orders and feed him his energy, and through that bond Heyou could find him.

Heyou nodded and leaned in, kissing Solie. Then he turned to smoke and lightning and was gone, hurtling out the door.

Solie eyed the assassin. All the resistance had gone out of him, and he stared at her in true bafflement.

"How do you know?" he whimpered. "How could you possibly know?"

"Because I do," she replied. When she moved closer, Mace tightened his grip until the man winced. "Now tell me exactly who we're looking for."

* * *

Heyou flew, ignoring the wind as he forced his way high through the air, his wings spread wide for steering. Below spread the Valley for a hundred miles or more, its lands verdant, its harvest healthy, its herds large. A lake stood in the center of the dominion, close to the town, and smaller farms stretched out from that, joined by clean white roads.

Beyond the canyon walls at the outskirts of the Valley, the Shale Plains were gray and dusty, all shattered rock and sand dotted by the gray tangled bushes that were all that would grow. The land had been a kingdom once, before an unrestricted war between battle sylphs destroyed everything. Uninhabited for centuries, this dead soil had been reclaimed by the settlement of Sylph Valley using elemental sylphs. Their hive would continue to spread life until all of these shale plains belonged to his queen.

Heyou didn't spare much thought for how long that would take; he rose high enough that the settlement was tiny and its inhabitants dots, higher even than the air sylphs liked to play. Hovering there in the bitter cold, he focused, reaching out with his senses.

Solie was easy to find. She was the queen, primary to them all, but Heyou also had that second pattern, deeper down. No sylph could stay in this world without a link to a mortal from it. Even if they could, without such a link they'd starve. Heyou would be poisoned by the energy of this world, except for that of the queen or Galway.

Every sylph had a master other than the queen. Solie didn't have the energy to support them all or give them the love they needed. Sylphs thrived on attention, and for the battlers, it was the attention of women they craved. Since Heyou already had Solie as his lover, he'd instead chosen a man he trusted—the first man he'd ever been able to trust.

He felt Galway to the east, in the mountains that marked the edge of the kingdom of Para Dubh. The man was wandering those forested peaks, hunting and trapping as he'd always done. Now it was more a hobby than a necessity, but Heyou didn't think the man would ever give the lifestyle up entirely.

He turned and set off, traveling as fast as the wind toward the mountains. The Shale Plains rushed by below, the elevation slowly rising until all at once the landscape completely changed. Pine trees covered the slopes, and Heyou arced over them, lightning flickering within him as he dove directly toward his master.

Galway sat by a small campfire, skinning a mink. He was a tall gray man, his long mustache thick but most of his hair gone. He looked up as Heyou dropped down across from him and resumed human shape.

"What's wrong?" the trapper asked, raising an eyebrow.

Heyou projected his emotions to Galway as much as he did to Solie, usually without thinking about it. The man remained calm, however, just like normal. Galway even went into battle calm, which was one of the things Heyou liked best about him. For himself, Heyou didn't quite understand calm.

"Someone tried to kill Solie," he crowed. "It was fun."

Another eyebrow rose. "Fun?"

"Well . . ." Heyou hedged. "Not for the assassin."

Galway rubbed his jaw. "I think you better explain this, and for once, Heyou, start at the beginning."

Heyou grinned. He loved to shock people, and the fact that he couldn't shock Galway just made the man more entertaining.

The news that the others might be in danger had gotten the trapper's attention. He straightened up and looked at his battler more intently. "Is the family safe?" he demanded.

"Sure," Heyou said. "Wat's watching them."

Galway looked unimpressed.

Heyou just grinned wider. Wat was the newest battler to the Valley, brought from Yed instead of being summoned by the Valley priests. He was known for being intensely stupid. Heyou liked him. He was easy to trick and never held a grudge.

"I hope that's not all," Galway said. "I wouldn't trust Wat to guard a chicken coop."

Heyou chuckled and shrugged. "Mace took care of things."

Galway nodded, more satisfied, and set his knife and the mink skin aside. Taking up a pan of water, he dumped it on the fire. Steam hissed everywhere.

"What are you doing?" Heyou asked.

"Going back to the Valley with you." The trapper looked around at the small collection of skins and drying meat he'd prepared, all stretched on racks made from saplings, and sighed. "It was nice while it lasted."

"Why bother?" Heyou asked him. "You don't have to come out here anymore."

"Why bother to guard the queen? You don't have to."

"But I want—" Heyou started to say. "Oh."

Galway smiled. "Nice to see you're not as dim as Wat."

"*Nobody* is."

Heyou sat, grumpily watching his master break camp and arrange gear on his horses. If Galway hadn't brought the beasts, Heyou would have just carried him home. Now it would be several days of travel back and he missed Solie already.

Galway let him sit for a minute before kicking him off his seat to come and help, never quite giving an order that he would have no choice but to obey. Still, Galway got what he wanted, just as he always had. Heyou liked that about him, too.

An hour later they were on their way. Galway sat astride one horse and led the other, which carried all his skins and meat. In his natural form and guarding him, Heyou floated happily alongside.

Chapter Two

The hive was quiet, and she, nameless—she would always be nameless, names being reserved for the queen and her lovers—slipped down through the corridors and into the egg chamber, flowing along the ceiling so that she wouldn't get in the way of the lesser sylphs who tended the translucent globes. Dozens of these sylphs worked carefully to sort through the eggs, putting them in groups based on their pattern and moving them to cubbyholes where they could gestate. The nameless sylph looked at what they were doing, checking the eggs herself for any that were damaged, and then continued on farther into the chamber.

Deeper inside, newly hatched or hatching eggs were already in their individual nests, watched over by attendant sylphs. Looking into each, she made her way through and recoiled in pretend fear as a baby battler aggressively lunged at her, still too small to do more than bristle.

Silly thing, she told him. *There'll be enough of that later.*

Too young to understand words, the baby battler rolled in on himself, tendrils flapping uselessly, internal lightning spurting in little pops.

An air sylph moved between the newcomer and the cubbyhole, emotions annoyed. *Don't wake him. I just got him to settle down. He keeps trying to escape.*

Sorry, she replied, moving out of the way and shimmering across the chamber. She liked to see the babies and did so whenever she could, but she really was getting too big to fit in the chamber anymore. She felt the disgruntlement of the nannies, despite her attempts not to bother them.

Sighing, she left the nesting chamber and went down a connecting corridor on the other side, flowing up and over a battle sylph guard as she did. He turned his lightning-formed eyes upon her, and she hurried on, a little uncomfortable. The baby battlers were adorable, but their older brothers weren't. They stared, more now than ever.

Hurrying down the corridor, she turned a corner so that the young guard couldn't see her anymore. The passageways here were many thousands of years old, but the hive was still growing, as did the fields that supported it. This hive was huge and ancient, the walls of the corridors shiny from the passage of thousands upon thousands of sylphs.

It was the queen's chamber she was going to now, to rejoin her sisters. It had been a long time. She'd been sent with a raiding party to a distant nest, and they'd been gone far longer than expected. The whole trip had been strange. Healers weren't usually sent away from the hive, and she'd felt terribly exposed. She'd been itchy as well, as she'd gone into a growth spurt she wasn't expecting that nearly doubled her size. Still, the raiding party were all back and safe. None of them was lost—thanks in part, she hoped, to her own efforts.

She moved into the queen's chamber, passing another battler as she did. Like the other one, he stared, but his regard wasn't quite so uncomfortable—though it was no less unsettling. He was big and mature, his energy levels impressive enough that she wondered if he'd drawn the attention of the queen yet. Probably not. The queen had more than enough lovers as it was.

She turned and sidestepped, skittering out of his way. As she passed, he formed a tentacle out of his mantle and stroked it along her belly. Sucking her own mantle upward, she shot through into the queen's chamber and left him behind.

Her six sisters looked up, all of them white and gleaming, their half dozen eyes swirling patiently. They were smaller than she, but they made room willingly as she settled down and stared up at a sylph still far larger than herself, glad to finally be back.

You've returned, the queen said, voice rumbling in her mind. The queen stretched herself, nearly doubling in length. Her latest mate nested against her—a battler she'd named some confusing combination of sounds on a whim—his red eyes taking in everything.

Yes, my queen, the returned healer answered. As she did, she wondered fleetingly if that was imagined disgruntlement in the queen's tone.

* * *

Leon Petrule stood on the deck of the *Racing Dawn*, watching for any sign of land on the endlessly blue horizon. For two days the ship had been flying, carried through the air by the power of an ancient air sylph, but even at her speed it would be another three days before they reached their destination.

It was better than the trip out had been. That voyage had taken weeks, for the ship they were on stopped at every port during its sea voyage south, picking up passengers, dropping them off, and risking pirate attack at every moment. This ship didn't have that problem. Pirates didn't have air sylphs to carry them above the clouds, and even if one did, they wouldn't have battlers. Leon glanced a few feet over to his own battle sylph. Ril wasn't as powerful as he'd once been, thanks to an injury, but he still had the strength to wreck any ship that might threaten them.

Right now, the battler didn't look threatened by anything at all. In his human form, the blond-haired sylph leaned against the railing and the woman beside him, his arm encircling her waist. Lizzy Petrule in turn leaned back.

Lizzy. His daughter. She now shared Leon's battler, though her relationship with Ril was vastly different. Leon pondered that with a bit of amusement and still a touch of shock. The amusement was at the idea that the battler might want a physical relationship. The shock came from the fact that he'd found it with his master's eighteen-year-old daughter.

Not that he should be *that* surprised. Battlers were highly sensual creatures, as interested in physical love as they were in fighting. But Ril had always seemed immune to that, staying as he did with a male master that he never touched. Not that Leon wanted any kind of physical relationship with the battler. Apparently, Ril had just been waiting for the right woman.

Lizzy. Leon shook his head. He had no idea how her mother was going to react to this little revelation, but he didn't think he wanted to be in the room when it was announced. He was a brave man, but he wasn't stupid. Betha didn't dislike Ril—not exactly—but she'd always been of the quiet opinion that she had to share rather too much of her husband with him. Now she was losing a daughter to the battler as well.

Still, at least Lizzy was alive, and there was no doubt she was happy. Leon was overjoyed that they'd been able to find her. She'd been kidnapped off the docks of Para Dubh, taken to Meridal and sold as a concubine to a battle sylph harem. Bound to her since she was seven years old without anyone knowing, including Lizzy, Ril had been able to track her, and he and Leon had gone to bring her home. It hadn't been easy. Now, Lizzy was safe and they'd found an ally in the new queen of Meridal.

The importance of Meridal was something Leon needed to impart to Solie as soon as possible. Sylph Valley had fifty battlers and still feared attack if the other kingdoms should band together. Meridal had *seven hundred*. Because of that, a friendship with them was vital. Leon had to get his family home and arrange for a diplomat to return to Meridal to make sure that Eapha didn't forget her new friends in the face of all the changes she'd gone through: from harem girl to queen in an instant.

Eapha didn't just need allies, either; her entire country was still reeling with shock. She needed advisers, the same as Solie had when she first became queen. Leon's first task would be to find them.

It just couldn't be him. Not this time. Such a position wouldn't work without leaving Ril behind, and he couldn't do that to his sylph or daughter. He would not leave the battler torn between two masters on different sides of the ocean or away from his queen. The adviser would have to be someone else, and it would have to be decided soon. Leon already had a few ideas, if he could be convincing enough. Those ideas would wait, though. For now he was just happy to be reunited with his daughter.

Ril looked over, and Leon nodded in response. Surprised about the new relationship or not, Leon had to admit it was good for his battler. Before, Ril had hidden most emotions from his master, but now he seemed to revel in sharing them. Leon felt his battler's happiness. Almost he could be jealous of that, but Ril sent him a flicker of annoyance as he turned back to Lizzy and Leon had to hide a smile. The very fact that his battler projected his emotions to Leon at all meant he wanted him to feel them. Leon was just glad he didn't project *everything*.

Ril glanced toward him again with a start, then past him, his lip curling in a snarl. Lizzy gave him an elbow.

"Behave!" she snapped.

Surprised, Leon looked behind him. A few feet back, a young man had stopped at the top of the stairs that led to the upper deck. He glared at Ril angrily, even as his throat moved in convulsive fear. Ril stared back, and Leon felt the battler's hatred.

"Easy, Ril," he soothed, still looking at the boy. "Do you need something, Justin?"

Justin turned, though his eyes didn't leave Ril. Leon could tell what he was feeling. Ril couldn't project the emotions of others to him, but he didn't need any such help. Justin was a very angry young man. He'd come with Leon and Ril when they'd gone to rescue Lizzy, intending to announce his love and take her to wife. Instead, he'd ended up captured and turned into a feeder, a human bound to Ril as his master, but with his tongue cut out so he couldn't give any orders. Ril had fed from him, while Justin sat like an animal in a cage barely five feet across. He'd been rescued and his tongue regrown, but he hated Ril for what had been forced on them, as well as for Ril taking Lizzy.

Ril hated Justin in return. The boy now had the ability to give him orders he couldn't disobey. The boy had been warned, though: he was never to give the battler any sort of command.

Leon walked forward. "What is it?" he asked, putting a gentle hand on the boy's shoulder.

"Lunch is ready," Justin said. He dragged his eyes away from Ril. "I thought you and Lizzy would want to know."

"Thank you." Leon turned. "Lunch, Lizzy."

"Great." She came hurrying by, running down the steps and not once looking toward Justin. For all he'd come to Meridal to help rescue her, and suffered, she hadn't forgiven him for abandoning her when she was first caught.

Ril followed a moment later. He did look at Justin, his smile smug, and Leon knew somehow that he'd let the boy feel his flash of victory. Leon swore, and the battler blinked, his smugness faltering before he continued on.

Leon turned back to Justin, not knowing what he could say that would make this better. He didn't think there was anything. Justin was breathing hard, his face flushed and angry.

"I hate him," the young man gasped. "I hate him. I hate him."

"Let it go, Justin," Leon urged. "Please. For your own sake. It's not worth it." He tightened his grip on the boy's shoulder.

Justin turned and followed the other two. He had to work through this on his own, Leon knew. The best he could do was make sure Ril didn't mock him anymore. If he had to, he'd order it. Justin deserved a little peace. He needed it, too. The boy had to figure out what he was going to do with the rest of his life.

* * *

Gabralina had come to Sylph Valley without ever hearing about it. Born far to the south in the humid kingdom of Yed, she didn't mind the change. Even if this place was far to the colder north, she could be with her battler Wat here, and no one threw vegetables at her or called her whore and murderer. She wasn't one. She really wasn't.

They liked her in this town, and the people were kind. Gabralina had found work, too: helping the Widow Blackwell take care of the Valley orphans. Wat helped guard. She had been rescued in more than one way by Leon Petrule and Ril, not just from a trap for a battle sylph.

She tried not to think about the past now, or about the reasons why she'd been set to be killed, but she did think about her dearest friend back home, whom she still missed. Once, she'd hired a scribe to write to her, telling her of her new life and love, and sent it in the mail that was just starting to deliver to the Valley. Every day afterward she checked for a reply. To her disappointment, no answer came.

It was a long way to Yed, she had to remind herself, and her friend must have been in hiding after she left. The letter might never be read. It could also take months to get there.

Gabralina walked toward the Widow's house along the sidewalk from her tiny underground apartment, her fingers twined together before her. She was a stunning woman, her hair long and shiny as polished gold, her face round and smooth, her eyes seductive.

Though she wore a simple brown dress, men stopped to stare. None of them approached her, though. She also wore a rawhide string around her neck, laced through a large stone ring. Like the battlers in their blue and gold uniforms, female battler masters wore necklaces to identify themselves. Gabralina was still taken aback by men not trying to get her attention, but she'd been told it had to be that way. Wat would be desperately jealous of any man who approached, and a jealous battler was a very dangerous creature. This necklace was to protect everyone else.

Gabralina wasn't so sure. Wat was a sweet thing and wonderfully energetic in bed, but he wasn't really smart enough to get jealous. He did love her, and Gabralina was blissfully happy to have him. She had been used to men always telling her what to do, not the reverse.

Ahead, the lane she'd been following turned through a gate toward a large stone house. It looked as though it had been there for centuries, but the surrounding trees were small and young. Gabralina walked up to the front door, already hearing the excited shouts from the children inside.

As she reached the doors, they were flung open and a trio of boys ran out, bolting past her and laughing as they headed around the side of the house. Gabralina spun to watch them, smiling and reaching up to brush her hair out of her face. They were all good boys, if rambunctious. Once, boys like that tried to get her behind the stable, and she'd often let them. Now she felt positively adult while watching them play.

She entered the house. To her left was a doorway into a wide chamber used as a playroom, the floor meticulously clean and the toys all in their boxes under the window. To the right was the Widow's sitting room, where the children weren't permitted to go unless they were very good. There was no one in either room, and so Gabralina continued down the hallway, following the sound of voices.

A huge kitchen took up most of the back of the house. There, a massive harvest table stretched for nearly twenty feet, children of all ages crowded on the benches to either side. In the cooking area of the chamber, older children helped the Widow prepare porridge in a great pot on the wood stove or cut bread and cheese. She directed them like a general, allowing laughter but keeping the chaos under control.

Mace stood nearby, presiding in his trousers and shirt, his coat nowhere to be seen. He held a baby in his arms and was patiently spooning mush into her mouth. She kicked her feet at him and spit onto his shirt. Mace merely raised an eyebrow. Cleaning off her chin, he offered her more. She smiled toothlessly.

The Widow Blackwell looked up. Gabralina didn't know the woman's first name; she was just the Widow Blackwell to the entire Valley, despite the fact that she was Mace's master and they were clearly together. She still wore black, and Gabralina had to think that the color of mourning rather suited her. She couldn't wear black herself; it made her look washed out.

"Did you see Moran, Gilter, and Pel?" the Widow asked.

Gabralina nodded and reached for one of the aprons hanging by the door. "Yes, ma'am. They passed me."

The Widow frowned, making lines appear all over her face. "I warned them. They better not complain to me later if they miss breakfast!"

Gabralina just smiled and went to take the large wooden spoon from the oldest of the orphans. She edged past Mace, who eyed her impassively and moved back to give her room. She quickly started to spoon porridge into bowls, and the girls carried these to the younger children at the table. There was a lot of giggling and chattering, but under the Widow's watchful eye everyone stayed in their seats and ate politely. At the last moment, Moran, Gilter, and Pel reappeared, grinning at the Widow, who immediately sent them out to wash their hands at the pump in the backyard.

Gabralina moved around, helping the children get more food and to use their napkins and utensils properly. She was a bit hungry herself, but she'd eat later, along with the Widow. The older woman circled the table as well, keeping everything under control.

Mace joined them at the table, still feeding the baby. There were twenty children in the Widow's house, all between the ages of seven months and seventeen years. Gabralina had tremendous respect for the woman, and she loved that she could help out. She'd always adored children, but she couldn't have any of her own now; not with Wat. Still, helping with these was enough, and she was still smiling when the children finished eating and were sent off for their lessons. Everyone in the Valley was supposed to learn to read and write as well as to do math, but that was the job of someone else, and Gabralina went to clean the kitchen.

She proceeded upstairs to tidy the great long rooms the children slept in; the Widow's room in the attic she left alone. She was on her knees scouring the floor when a great black cloud drifted through the window, sparked with sparse, slow lightning. Gabralina looked up and smiled.

Her battler re-formed himself into human shape and flopped down on one of the beds, twisting around to leer at her. "Hi," he said, rolling over the sheets she'd just straightened, apparently not caring how much he wrinkled his uniform. "Are you done yet?"

Gabralina giggled, happy to see him even if she knew his being there would get in the way of her work. Wat almost always showed up at some point during the day. She straightened and tossed her brush back into her bucket. "Aren't you supposed to be guarding the market this morning?"

"Maybe. I forget." Wat crawled off the bed and toward her. He really was beautiful, and it made her breath catch in her throat. Battle sylphs could look like anything they wanted, and he was everything she'd ever found attractive in a man all at once.

When Wat crawled into her arms, she forgot what she'd been supposed to be doing as well.

* * *

"He's back, isn't he?" The Widow Lily Blackwell looked up at the ceiling as a faint giggle sounded, and then at her battler.

Mace was looking at the ceiling as well, a stern line between his brows. He growled, and the baby he was diapering whimpered. Immediately, he returned his attention to the infant and cooed. Little Gila giggled and tried to put her foot in her mouth.

It was a rhetorical question. Wat was incapable of leaving his master alone for even half a day. Granted, all battlers were like that, but Mace's needs certainly didn't get in the way of work. Not for either of them. Responsibilities always had to come first, and Mace's strong recognition of that was one of the things Lily was fondest about. He was a good man, and theirs a good match. It was just too bad Gabralina didn't have the same work ethic. She was a sweet girl, but she was flighty, and her battler was next to useless.

The Widow helped Mace finish pinning the diaper around Gila and pulled a pink shirt on over the child's head. They were in the playroom, the other toddlers who were too young to go to school playing around them. "Try not to break anything," she said as she picked up the baby and rocked her.

"Yes, Lily," Mace promised, and leaned in to kiss her.

She let him. He was a very good kisser, and she sighed against his mouth before lifting a hand to his cheek. It was smooth. Mace would never think to appear before her unshaven.

"Dinner is an hour before dusk. We're almost out of potatoes."

"I'll bring you some," he said, and he reached into her apron, taking out a few coins for the purchase. Transferring them to his pocket, he kissed her again.

The Widow, who'd been called that for so long that only Mace knew her by her first name, let herself feel the deep, powerful, and extremely private love she had for him. Her partner relaxed into it, taking it into his being. Battle sylphs craved love; they even deserted their own world to find it. Silly young girls like Gabralina and her Wat upstairs thought the only way to show that was physical. Lily was hardly celibate, but moments like this were so much purer.

"Lily," Mace whispered, his lips brushing hers. Another giggle sounded from upstairs, and the big battler sighed. "Anything else?"

"A good-sized goose if you can find one. I'd like to cube it for stew with the potatoes." She stepped back and cuddled Gila. "Only if it's fresh, mind you."

"Of course."

The battler shimmered and became smoke and lightning, flickering out of the playroom and down to the stairs in a corner of the kitchen. Seconds later, Lily heard him roar. A girl screamed, followed by a frightened, inhuman wail. Turning to the window, the Widow watched a black cloud shoot over the front yard and away, pursued by a much larger one. Lily humphed and turned back toward the kitchen.

"Gabralina!" she called as she entered and herded several children before her. "Come on down, dear. It's time to make bread."

* * *

Gabralina hurried down the lane, shivering, her heart still pounding from the fright Mace had given her. She'd been in a very compromising position when he burst in, and Wat almost dropped her on the floor before he fled out the window. She was just glad the Widow hadn't said anything. She liked the work and needed it. The Widow fed her, but Gabralina also liked to buy clothes and other nice things.

She kept up a hurried pace toward the town center, a basket in her hand. In it were three loaves of bread. She would trade the loaves for a basket of eggs, which was part of an arrangement that the Widow had with a neighbor. Gabralina supposed that was better than having to clean out a chicken coop every day.

She reached the main lane and trotted down it, staying to the side where she was out of the way of traffic. There wasn't much today, but she could see a transport coach moving quickly toward her, drawn by a team of six horses. As it rattled past, Gabralina waved the dust out of her face and checked that none got on her bread. None had.

Tucking the cloth more closely over them, she looked up. The coach was slowing in the middle of the road, the driver shouting at the horses. Gabralina blinked, recognizing the style of it from her time in Yed. A moment later, the door opened and a woman leaned out. A plain, brown-haired woman in a low-cut red dress.

"Gabby? Is that you? I *knew* it was you!"

Gabralina gaped. "Sala?" she gasped. "Sala!" Dropping her basket, she ran forward with a happy laugh. It was her oldest and closest friend.

Chapter Three

Rachel had never thought that, in the twilight of her life, she would end up a schoolteacher. Once, she'd been a rich man's wife, but when he died, her sons took over the business and lost their use for their poor old mother. At first she'd been bitter about that, but no longer. Life was too short—and far too beautiful. Being a teacher, she supposed, made sense. She was educated for a woman of her birth and had learned how to be patient. More importantly, she didn't have much else to do with her time and she liked to feel needed.

She looked over her class. The children were all under the age of ten, none terribly interested in what she was trying to teach but required to sit there anyway. All children were obliged to attend school until they were at least twelve or proved they already knew what was needed. It was a rule unique to the Valley, and the children from other places weren't used to being in the classroom. They fidgeted endlessly.

"Quiet," she ordered, tapping the board with her pointer. "Eighty-six plus four hundred and twelve. Who knows the answer?" She looked over all the silent faces. "Surely someone remembers this. We worked on it all last week. Come now. We're not leaving until someone gets it."

Up near the ceiling came a shimmer, an air sylph taking on the translucent form of a young girl so that she could speak. "Four hundred and ninety-eight?" she asked, her voice a throaty whisper. The rule about education applied to the sylphs as well. In some ways, they were better students than the human children. In others, they were far worse. At least they didn't squirm in their seats waiting for recess.

Rachel beamed. "Excellent! Thank you, Current." She tapped the board for the next question. "Three plus three hundred. Anyone?"

A bell sounded. Immediately, the sylphs hovering around the ceiling and walls of the room were gone, and the children all broke for the door to join the mass exodus from the other classrooms. Lunchtime. Rachel sighed. So much for the great process of learning.

She quietly set down her chalk and went to close the classroom door, and the sound of children galloping along wooden floors was immediately deadened, or most of it. She crossed the room to the last desk in the corner at the back of the class and crouched down, her knees protesting a bit, and looked up at the blue uniformed man who sat there, staring at his clasped hands on the desk. His hair was as blue as his uniform, and he looked to be a young man in his early twenties, but Rachel knew that was only an illusion.

"You didn't participate in class today," she said in a gentle tone. "Why not, Claw?"

The battler hunched down, his shoulders up around his ears. "I didn't know the answers," he said.

Rachel smiled and set a wrinkled hand over his. "That's why you're here, sweetheart. So you can learn the answers."

Claw looked up, miserable and unconvinced.

Rachel's smile softened, and she reached out to lay her hand on his cheek instead. This battler had all the power of any other, but he was an emotional wreck. He had been for years, since long before she'd been asked to be his master. He'd been abused by his former master, used as a slave for decades like Mace, but unlike Mace he'd been broken by it. Claw had no faith in himself and a terrible fear that Rachel would decide he was useless and desert him. Telling him she'd never leave was useless. Claw wouldn't believe her. He couldn't.

Wincing a little, she rose and unbuttoned her dress. Claw watched as she did, watched as she took the garment off and laid it gently over the back of a chair. She was old and fat and wrinkled, but he didn't care. She was his master, and that was all that mattered to him. Someday, she hoped she could get him to understand that he mattered as well.

She opened her arms.

"Come here," she called to him, and with a sound nearly like a sob, he did.

By the time lunch was over, the classroom was returned to perfect order and Rachel was back at the blackboard. Claw answered two of the questions that afternoon, and to her mind that was a success.

* * *

Solie stared breathlessly up at her lover, her hands clasped behind his neck and tangled in his long hair. Heyou grinned down at her.

His skin was dry, unlike hers. Unless he thought of it he never sweated, and she was so used to it that she rarely noticed anymore. She didn't now. Instead, she tugged on the back of his neck and Heyou sank down next to her, pressing soft lips against her mouth as he gently rocked against her. He could project his lust at her if he wanted, driving her absolutely wild and making their bodies desperate and violent, but this was in her mind more enjoyable. She felt more like a participant this way instead of just a passenger.

For six years, Heyou had been her battler, her best friend, and her lover. Her dearest confidant. He remained the best thing to happen in her life. She still reacted to his touch with the same ardor she'd felt the first time, still loved his sometimes crazy company. His being gone for even a few days had left her lonely, and she'd pulled him into her room the moment he got back. Galway would be busy with his family for a while anyway.

They rolled across the wide bed, Heyou pulling her up and over him so that her long red hair framed his face. She sat upright, his length still deep inside her as he reached to caress her breasts. Solie sighed, leaning back and baring her chest for him, staring without seeing at the stone ceiling. He stroked her nipples and she cried out, the fire he always brought building in her belly. She let it carry her along, the muscles in her thighs flexing as she rose up and down on him, biting her lip to keep herself from screaming.

Not that it would matter if she did. The stone walls were too thick to let sound travel through, and even if it did, there was only a battler on duty outside. Even before the arrival of the assassins, three more of whom had already been captured, battlers were her guards. They were out there whenever Heyou made love to her. There was a battler wherever she went except for her toilet.

Solie leaned back farther, spine arching, and cried out after all. The joy inside her exploded free, rushing as a wave through her entire body. Empathically linked, Heyou cried out too, stiffening and filling her, his own pleasure reflecting back and increasing her own.

Sitting up, he wrapped his arms around her waist and nuzzled her neck, kissing her gently. Solie relaxed against him, smiling, enjoying him just holding her. She loved him *so* much, loved everything about him. If there was one thing he couldn't give her, she just had to live with it.

* * *

Heyou knew something was bothering his queen. He couldn't read her mind, not quite, but he could interpret her emotions thoroughly enough that it was the next best thing. Today, though, she was hiding it well.

At first he'd thought it was the assassins. They'd picked up three more, finding them easily because of their hostility. All of them were locked up, waiting for Solie to decide what to do with them. But it wasn't fear he felt now, which was what he would expect if the problem were the assassins. Instead he sensed sadness, a feeling of something missing. He didn't know what to do about that.

He would have asked her, but she was the queen. Battlers didn't question queens. Moreover, he was afraid what the answer might be. Solie was everything to him. He didn't want to take the slightest chance that he wasn't everything to her in return.

* * *

Gabralina and Sala walked hand in hand through the marketplace, Gabralina's mission for eggs forgotten. Sala had been her best friend since childhood and the force behind all their plots and plans. Having her now in the Valley felt like everything was right again, and Gabralina couldn't wait for her to meet Wat.

"I was so worried about you," she confessed. "When I was arrested, I didn't know what happened. I thought you were in the house, but then they only took me, so I guess you left just before they got there. You're so lucky."

Sala smiled, squeezing her hand as they walked. "No one bothered me. Thank you so much for not saying anything. You're a true friend." When Gabralina beamed, Sala added, "I wanted to help you, but there was nothing I could do."

"I know. It all turned out for the best, though." Gabralina

giggled. "I have Wat now! It would never have happened otherwise. It's so wonderful. Everyone is nice here, too, and I have a job."

"A job!" Sala laughed. "That's a bit of a drop from being a magistrate's mistress."

"Maybe." Gabralina shrugged. "But I was bored there a lot of the time, and he was old and fat. I get to take care of children here. I love it."

Sala smiled. "Whatever makes you happy, dearest."

They wandered through the busy morning crowds. Gabralina wanted to show her friend everything, hoping against hope that she would stay.

A group of air and fire sylphs soared overhead. Sala was watching them in wonder, her eyes shining. "Is it true what you wrote about anyone being able to have a sylph here?"

"Yes," Gabralina said. "Well, they're picky about who can have one, but it isn't like back home in Yed. They don't care how rich you are or anything."

"So, anyone can have a sylph?"

Gabralina frowned, remembering what she'd been told when she first arrived. "Unless the sylph picks them, they have to be fairly old. At least, the women with the battlers are older. I'm not sure why. I think it has to do with them not being able to have babies or something. But the other kinds of sylphs have masters as young as me. I'm sure they'd love to give you one."

Sala smiled. "That sounds nice. I think I might ask for a sylph. It would be lovely to have a friend like that. To feel a bond and . . ."

"Oh, it is," Gabralina assured her. "It truly is." It would be wonderful for Sala to have a sylph of her own. "Does this mean you're staying?"

"I was thinking of it. When I heard you were here, I had to come. It just wasn't the same without you back in Yed."

Overjoyed, Gabralina hugged her. She would have stayed

a simple field hand if Sala hadn't found her so long ago and introduced her to the city, to all of the rich people who lived in it. And Sala was always so much fun.

In the center of the marketplace, a roar suddenly sounded, echoed shortly thereafter by others. Both women jumped as cloud-shaped battlers descended, smoky shapes surrounding a screaming man in worn leathers.

"What?" Sala gasped. "What's going on?" She clung in horror to her friend.

Gabralina held her just as tight, trying desperately to think. She'd heard Mace talking to the Widow about this earlier. She hadn't really thought about it further, but she remembered now.

"There are killers after the queen," she explained. "The battlers have been trying to flush them out for a week."

"How?" Sala asked.

Gabralina paused. What had Mace called it, evil intent? "They . . . they can tell when someone wants to do something bad."

"Oh," Sala whispered, her face pale. Her eyes were bright.

The market cleared. Both women watched as the battlers' target was apprehended, smoky tendrils wrapping around him and lifting him up into the air. Gabralina wondered if Wat was among the group, but the sylphs' lightning flashed much quicker than his ever did. They carried their captive away toward the underground, and Gabralina turned back to her friend, her heart pounding.

"Sorry about that," she said. "It's normally very peaceful here."

"I'm glad," Sala replied. "I don't think I could take that much excitement on a regular basis."

The two shared a smile and they continued walking, here and there, just enjoying the day. It wasn't until hours later that Gabralina remembered the eggs.

* * *

Sala shivered, rubbing her arms.

Her friend's home was an underground apartment near the center of town. It was small and plain, just a front salon and a bedroom with a bathroom down the hall that Gabralina shared with everyone else on the floor. There were no windows, but a series of narrow slits in the ceiling let in daylight. It didn't cost Gabralina anything, as earth sylphs made enough apartments for everyone in the Valley, but to Sala's mind there wasn't much encouragement for anyone to want to stay.

That was probably the point, she decided, looking around at her friend's tiny space. A small table and two chairs in the front room took up nearly half the area, and she'd already seen that the bedroom was mostly bed. Gabralina had offered this place for her to stay, but the minuteness of the apartment felt like it was closing in on her. It was a huge change from the plantation where Gabralina had been living as the mistress of one of the most powerful magistrates in Yed. That house had eighty rooms and forty servants. The magistrate had given her gowns and jewels and brought her into the highest circles of society. Naturally, Gabralina brought her oldest friend Sala along for the ride.

Sala sighed, still processing how her friend's life was reduced.

Behind her, the door opened. She turned, expecting to see Gabralina, but instead she found the most beautiful man she'd ever seen. He was flawless, even more gorgeous than Gabralina herself.

The man entered and stopped, staring at her. He was dressed in a blue uniform trimmed with gold, but for all his beauty and splendor his eyes were vapid. He blinked, his hand still on the door handle. He tilted his head to one side.

"You feel funny," he said.

"Do I?"

"Yeah." His head tilted to the other side. "Are you in there?"

"I would assume so . . ." She laughed. "Are you Gabby's battle sylph?"

"Gabby?" he repeated.

Gabralina appeared, pushing through the door and against his back until he got out of the way and she could pass with an armful of blankets. Sala found herself backed into a corner, feeling more claustrophobic than ever.

"Hi, Wat," Gabralina said, beaming at him before putting the blankets on the table and turning to Sala. "Have you two introduced yourselves?"

"We were about to," Sala said.

Wat glanced between his master and Sala, and he put his arms around Gabralina, staring at Sala as he did. "This is Gabralina," he said, pronouncing her name slowly and carefully.

Sala smiled as her blonde friend giggled. "I'll remember that," she said. Glancing at Gabralina she asked, "He's a sweetheart. I have a few things to bring in. Can you tell him to obey me so I can ask him to bring them in? Some of them are heavy."

Gabralina shrugged. "Sure. Wat, obey Sala, okay?"

"Okay," he said.

"Are all battle sylphs like this?" Sala asked. He was staring up at the ceiling for no reason she could determine.

"Oh, no," Gabralina said, leaning back against him. Her battler forgot whatever had drawn him to the ceiling and started to nibble on her neck. "Wat is unique."

Sala was somewhat glad to hear that.

Chapter Four

When the main settlement of Sylph Valley was first created, a lot of thought went into how it should be laid out. Buildings were planned that wouldn't be needed for years, as well as an underground maze of apartments and storage areas that the town could retreat to in case of severe weather or attack. Every building that existed was thanks to the sylphs, from the huge warehouses to the single homes and cottages. Even the henhouses had been made by sylphs, shaped from the earth and rock itself.

At the same time the sylphs built the rest, they made the land fertile again and brought in water for drinking and sanitation. Along with the buildings, they'd also put in greenery. Where earth sylphs were passionate about building, shaping rock as though it were merely clay, water sylphs were fascinated by things green and growing. Often with the help of masters who'd drawn them through the gate by being just as passionate about gardening, these sylphs helped restore life to the Shale Plains. In the town center, they took that passion further by creating elaborate gardens.

Today, Solie didn't see the elaborate, always-changing glory of the park, a pet project of three particular water sylphs and their masters, so beautiful that already it was being spoken of in other kingdoms and people were starting to travel to the Valley just to see it. Not caring about the explosion of endless colors or the rich scent of healthy earth, she sat on a wide stone bench, her head resting on Heyou's shoulder. She watched a trio of small children play on an expanse of green grass, screaming and yelling. A young woman with a little baby sat on a bench directly across the grass from them, discreetly nursing her child. Back in the hamlet where Solie was born, everyone would have been disgusted with the woman for feeding her baby publically, but if anyone so much as looked at her funny in this place, Heyou would react. So would any of the other half-dozen battlers spread throughout the garden.

Solie glanced around. They didn't know for sure if they caught all the assassins yet, no matter how much she trusted her reading of the first. She hadn't been able to take being locked inside and guarded anymore, but now that she was outside and guarded, she couldn't stop herself from staring at the young mother and wished she hadn't bothered.

Heyou's emotions spiked toward true alarm. "Why are you crying?" he asked.

Solie put a hand to her cheek, surprised to find it wet. She stared for a moment at her hand, her head still resting on his shoulder. The fabric of his blue coat was scratchy under her skin.

"It doesn't matter," she said at last.

Confusion washed through him, along with something else. She could feel it, a growing need to know. Heyou wasn't the type to question, but she could feel it was going to happen anyway. Even as she cringed, she wondered how he waited so long.

"You're upset. You're sad all the time. Why? It's worse now. I don't understand." He glanced around, searching for something to attack, something from which she needed defense. Other battlers appeared, drawn along garden paths by his distress. Solie recognized Dillon, Claw, Hector, and Blue, and she hoped they wouldn't come closer. She didn't want their scrutiny. They thankfully held back, sensing her reluctance.

Heyou was a very young battler, inexperienced and likely to defer to older battlers like Mace, even if he was the one who slept with the queen. He wasn't stupid, though, and his gaze finally settled on the playing children and the mother with her baby. He couldn't help but notice. Solie couldn't stop staring.

"You want babies?" he asked in a whisper.

Solie took a deep breath. "It doesn't matter."

"Oh," he managed, and she heard a world of hurt in his voice. She put her arm around him, hugging him, and he held her back, his emotions as sad as her own. That just made her feel worse, for there was nothing he could do about it. Heyou couldn't give her children, and she didn't want to be with anyone else, not even if he would allow it. She could order him not to mind, but to do that to a battler would destroy him. She couldn't be so cruel. Not even to gain a child.

A noise sounded: battlers tense and suddenly roaring, flashing into the sky as smoke and lightning. The playing children froze in fear. Others ran, the new mother joining them. She looked back fearfully over her shoulder as she did.

Solie started to rise, all thoughts of children gone. Heyou's arms went around her, his upset trumped by the urge to violence. He didn't shift form, though. He stayed to protect her.

More battlers flashed upward, rising over the town and moving to the east. Solie saw the big cloud that was Mace fly overhead, and she looked at Heyou in surprise. "What is it?"

He stared after the others, his body tense. "An air ship."

Solie was confused. Air ships were an uncommon form of transportation, being expensive and requiring enough air sylphs to carry the load, but they did exist. Battlers didn't normally react so badly to them.

Heyou picked up on her confusion. "The air sylph carrying it. She's from a hive." He frowned. "She has a queen."

Solie gaped. A queen? How was that possible? Sylphs who

crossed through a gate from their old world lost all connection
to their original queen. They took masters in order to stay in
this world and feed, but they were generally singular in their
connection. The only way to turn a woman into a queen
connected to many sylphs was for a battler to take her for both
master and lover. The Valley was the only place in the world
where women were allowed mastery over any kind of sylph, let
alone a battler. That truth was also something they kept very
secret. There wasn't anyone outside the Valley who knew how
Solie became queen.

"Are you sure?" she asked, suddenly frightened at the
possibility.

In the distance she could see a wide-sailed ship heading
toward the Valley, still tiny against the mountains behind it. A
dozen battlers circled it.

"Yes." Heyou tilted his head to one side, his emotions turning
speculative. "But Ril's on that ship. He says it's okay."

"Really?"

Solie focused on the vessel again, concentrating. This would
never come to her as easily as Heyou; she might be queen, but
she was still human. Faintly, though, she could hear the call of
Ril, one of the first battlers to join her hive, telling her they
were back, that they'd succeeded in what they needed to do.
That—

"They found Lizzy!" she crowed. She was so glad to hear it.
When Lizzy Petrule was kidnapped, Solie never thought she'd
see the young woman again. She'd never hoped to see Leon or
Ril again either. Not really.

Heyou hugged her. "Do you want me to ask Leon to come
see you?"

Solie shook her head. "He'll want to see his family first."

She felt the longing again. Heyou's grip around her shoulder
tightened.

* * *

The *Racing Dawn* slowed near the warehouse district. The sylph who'd carried it from Meridal was a placid shimmer overhanging the entire ship, barely visible to the humans. Her original name was Forty-seven Air, but now she was called Ocean Breeze and her master Kadmiel, once a feeder, sat beside her. Both were guarded by a half dozen Valley battle sylphs. Her master seemed scared, but he drew strength from Ocean Breeze while he waited.

Leon nodded reassuringly at him. Kadmiel was a good enough fellow, and he was in remarkable mental shape given what had been done to him. He'd be all right—which was good, as the last thing Leon wanted to deal with right now was anything that would keep him away from his family. It had been months, and his heart pounded at the thought of seeing his wife and daughters again.

Nearby, Lizzy clung to Ril's arm and waved down at people she recognized. Given the reaction of the Valley battlers to the ship's arrival, there were a lot of people down there, all gathered to see what was happening.

Leon glanced at the big battler standing next to him. "I'll need to see the queen in the morning," he said. "First thing."

Mace nodded. Her calendar wasn't his responsibility, but he would make sure Devon knew to arrange a meeting.

"Tell her that Meridal now has a queen, and that she is interested in a formal alliance with us. I'll want to go over the options."

Mace regarded him steadily. "It is strange to make arrangements with another hive."

Leon slapped his arm. "A lot of things must be strange to you here. Trust me when I say it'll be worth the effort."

Lizzy grabbed her father's arm. "Look! It's Mother! Mother!" she shouted. *"Mother!"*

Leon turned, Mace and Solie forgotten. Hurrying forward to the rail, he could see a dark-haired woman in a long, pale dress, hair bound up on top of her head. She carried a four-year-old in her arms, and three more girls ran after her, ranging in age from seven to ten to thirteen. The family's neighbors followed, but Leon had no eyes for them. *Betha.*

Lizzy giggled excitedly beside him, and once the ship was settled, she ran for the ladder. She got there just ahead of Justin, who'd been looking over the rail at his father. The boy jumped as he nearly walked into her, but Lizzy didn't spare him a look. She scrambled over the side.

Ril looked at Justin, baring his teeth in a silent warning before following Lizzy. Leon sighed and went over the side as well, clapping the boy on the shoulder in silent sympathy before climbing down to the street.

The ground felt odd under his feet after so long on the ship. Leon looked over his friends and neighbors, Galway with his wife and many children, Gabralina with a strange woman at her side. Devon with his air sylph playing with his hair. Dozens of others. He only processed his wife and family.

Lizzy was throwing herself at her mother, sobbing. Ril ducked forward, collecting Mia into his arms, and Betha hugged her daughter tightly, crying. The other girls crowded around, only Cara leaving them to run to her father. Leon hugged her, luxuriating in the feel of his thirteen-year-old child before setting her down.

"Have you been good?" he asked. "Listening to your mother?"

"Of course, Daddy. It's so good to have you home!"

Leon just smiled.

Done hugging their sister, Nali and Ralad came to him next, and he hugged them as well before turning to his wife. Betha stared at him with tears in her eyes before rushing into his arms. Everyone cheered as he kissed her.

"I was afraid I'd never see you again," she cried. "Oh, Leon, I missed you so much."

He hugged her close. "I missed you, too. I never want to leave you and the girls ever again."

She wiped her eyes. "Careful. I'll hold you to that."

A thin and balding, nervous-looking man with dark circles under his eyes pushed through the crowd, followed closely by an earth sylph that looked like a child made entirely of mud. It was Cal Porter, and he eyed them for a moment before his entire face lit up. His only son had returned.

"Justin!" he cried, meeting the youth with a hug. "Oh, my poor, dear, brave boy. It's so good to see you again. I thought about you every day, I really did. It just wasn't the same, not having you around. Surely it wasn't. I don't ever want to go through that again."

He pulled back, grinning at Justin before looking to Leon and Lizzy. "And you found Lizzy! I knew you could do it! When's the wedding?"

Ril immediately stepped between Lizzy and the Porters, Mia still in his arms. Lizzy's lips tightened, and she looked away. Leon opened his mouth to try and explain, as much as he could. This wasn't exactly the place.

Justin beat him to it. "There won't be a wedding," he said bitterly, loud enough to be heard by everyone. He jerked his chin toward Lizzy, who went white. "They turned her into a whore over there." He stared at Ril. "She's fucking that monster."

The only thing that saved Justin's life was Solie's rules. Ril growled but didn't move. He couldn't without more provocation.

In the sudden silence, Leon stepped forward. "Go home," he told the boy. Justin flinched.

Turning, Leon saw his wife's shocked gaze. Lizzy was still white, staring at the ground, and Leon ached for her.

"Let's go home," he said aloud, and led his family away from the air ship. Behind them, the people who'd arrived to welcome them back could only watch them go in silence.

* * *

Gabralina pressed her hand against her heart as she watched the Petrules leave. She wasn't entirely sure what had happened, but they looked beaten where they should be victorious. Leon had been so kind to her when he brought her to the Valley, and in a little tiny way she loved him. This wasn't fair.

She glanced at Sala, who was watching the boy with the big mouth being shaken by his father while the man demanded answers. Gabralina saw the speculative look on her friend's face. She felt a familiar chill.

"Interesting," Sala said before they continued on the tour of the town. "So, tell me. Who was that blond man with the beard? He's cute."

* * *

Devon Chole watched the two women stroll off, Gabralina chattering about how Leon had saved her life and how he was chancellor for the Valley. The beautiful blonde and her much less attractive friend were soon out of sight, and he shook his head with a sigh. Gabralina was definitely not available, even if she'd had anything to her other than looks, which he doubted.

Turning back, he saw Justin Porter storm away from his shocked father. It wasn't often that Cal Porter was rendered speechless, but the man gaped after his son while the crowd murmured about what they'd just seen. Devon wondered how serious this was going to turn out. In the city he'd been born in, what Justin said would have ruined Lizzy's life. Here, women were less restricted. Lizzy had every right to be with Ril and, crippled or not, the battler was no one to mess with.

It was still sad. Until now, none of them had known if Lizzy would come back. Here, in the first moment of her return, Justin had hurt her as much as anyone could without touching her. All because he hadn't gotten what he wanted. To Devon's mind, that showed a lot more about Justin's quality than it did Lizzy's.

Airi ruffled his hair, constantly blowing it up and smoothing it back down. Devon kept it just long enough for her to be able to do so without it getting in his eyes. He felt her attention turn to the boy and heard her sigh.

He's angry, she said.

"I'd imagine so," Devon murmured. "Still, I guess that was the worst he could do, and he only managed to make himself look like an idiot."

I guess, Airi replied.

Devon turned, intending to head back to the queen's hall. Given the recent problems, Solie was staying away from crowds and had sent him to find out what was going on. Heyou might have come instead, but sylphs didn't always give human descriptions of events. Heyou was one of the worst culprits.

Completing his turn, Devon came face to chest with Mace. Heart pounding, he glanced up. Even six years after this place was founded, he was still terrified of battlers. He'd been raised to fear them, those bound by Eferem's masters, and by the terror brought by their projected hate. He'd also seen them fight, which still brought nightmares. Mace was at the forefront of those nightmares, tearing men apart around him while Devon tried to flee. It didn't help that Mace could feel exactly what Devon felt and didn't care at all.

He felt Airi press against his back, sharing his fear even

while she tried to comfort him, and Devon swallowed. "What is it?" he managed to ask.

"Arrange for the queen to meet with the chancellor first thing in the morning," the big battler said. A moment later he vanished, swirling into smoke and lightning and then soaring away over the crowd.

Devon sagged, exhaling heavily. "Right," he muttered. "Whatever you want."

Chapter Five

For the nights he wanted it, Ril had a room in the Petrule house. A proper bedroom had been set up in the attic.

It was better to have a room of his own, though he'd never admit to anyone that he appreciated having his own space. It still felt unnatural. He was the only sylph who needed to sleep on a regular basis, though, and he didn't much care to do so lying on the floor. He was now of the opinion, however, that the bed was too small.

Shifting and nearly falling off the edge, he snapped awake, lying on his side with his arm over Lizzy. She'd crept up the ladder to join him after her parents and sisters went to sleep, probably without her mother knowing. After Betha's reaction, he hadn't been sure he'd ever be let near her or Leon again. He was glad Lizzy had taken the initiative, but the bed was definitely too small. The wooden frame was pressing into his back.

Ril kissed his lover's bare shoulder and rolled off the mattress, catching himself on the wooden floor with a wince. Achy and out of sorts, he stood and headed down the ladder, needing to move these human muscles he'd given himself. More, he needed to go to his original shape and rest, but he couldn't do that without dying. Not unless Luck the healer sylph helped and another sylph held him together. The same injury that made him need to sleep now kept him from changing shape without agony and from changing to his original form at all. Normally that didn't bother him so much, but he and Leon had been gone looking for Lizzy for a long time, and just being home made him itchy.

Ril climbed down the ladder and then the stairs that would take him to the main floor. Everyone was asleep. He could feel Leon and Lizzy most clearly, but he could sense the others as well. Not wanting to wake them, he went into the kitchen. He didn't need to eat human food, but the chairs were comfortable. He sat in one and looked out the window at the night sky.

There were sylphs out there, none of them needing sleep. A few humans as well. Ril sensed their emotions and scanned them by instinct, looking for hostile feelings that might be a threat. He was just turning toward one, a snarl on his lips, when he heard footsteps in the hall. A moment later, Leon's wife appeared, dressed in a long nightgown with her dark hair braided and hanging over one shoulder.

"Betha," he said. His snarl was gone.

The woman stared at him, her lips pressed tightly together, fine lines stretching out from the corners. She'd been part of his life since he first came into this world, trapped in the body of a hawk. At first she'd been the only woman he'd seen on anything approaching a regular basis, and then she'd been the mother of all the girls and his beloved Lizzy. Finally, once he gained his freedom, she'd allowed him to live in her house. They'd never been close.

Ril felt her anger and frustration, and he glanced down at his hands on the tabletop. While Betha resented that she shared too much of her husband with him, she'd never been cruel. They'd had a quiet sort of coexistence where Ril did what she asked and they tried not to get in each other's way. That peaceful truce was ended. He was sleeping with her daughter.

She had no control over him; she wasn't his master the way Lizzy and Leon were and she couldn't order him. While battle sylphs were subservient to females, Ril was different in that aspect as well. To save Lizzy, he'd killed a lot of women in Meridal, yet he would never hurt Betha. She was no threat to Lizzy, only to him.

"I looked in Lizzy's room," Betha said, standing on the other side of the table with her hands on the back of a chair. "She's not in there."

Ril watched her evenly. He might never hurt her, but that didn't mean he wouldn't fight back. "She's fine."

Betha's lips tightened even more. "Where is she? In your room?"

Ril nodded, his tension increasing. He had to calm himself or wake his masters. He felt a sudden urge to lash out with his hate, but he suppressed that as well.

"She's sleeping," he said.

"I'm sure she is. Do you have any idea of what you've done to her?"

Saved her from being raped by dozens of battlers, he didn't say. If he hadn't already made Lizzy his master, she would have had a much harder time in Meridal in that harem. But all of them had decided not to tell her mother about that.

"What is it you think I've done?" he asked.

Betha yanked her chair out so that she could sit down. She flattened her palms against the table. "She'll never be able to marry now," she said. "She'll never have children. Or grandchildren. You took that from her, didn't you?"

Ril glared back, forcing himself to think through the anger that was filling him. He was a battle sylph and Lizzy was his master. He knew her feelings, just as he knew those of the woman seated across from him.

He snorted. "Took it from her or took it from you? Lizzy doesn't want children. She never did. *You* want grandchildren. Well, the rest of the girls can give you some. If they want to."

"How dare you?"

"I love her! I'm not apologizing!" he roared. Then he paused. "Leon's waking."

Both he and Betha were silent, staring at each other while they willed Leon not to wake. Ril felt his master stir, roll over in bed, and then drop back into a deeper sleep. He gave an internal sigh of relief.

"He's asleep," he said.

"Isn't it bad enough I have to share my husband with you?" Betha hissed. "Now you take my daughter?"

"I never took Leon from you," he replied, "and I haven't taken Lizzy. At least you know I won't leave her, or betray her, or run off and leave her to be kidnapped from a stinking dock."

Betha looked away. She said nothing.

Ril stood, leaning over the table toward her. "I may not be able to give your daughter children, but I can promise you this: I'll give her everything else."

Then he turned and went out, not wanting to be there anymore. Betha would either hate him or get over it. There wasn't much else she could do. He was what he was, and he couldn't change that. Nor did he want to.

He walked out the front door and into the darkness, still too restless to go back to his room. He felt hungry as well, but he was more in the mood for Leon's heavy warm energy than Lizzy's light sparkling kind, and it would cause all kinds of hell for him to go into Leon's bedroom right now. He didn't really need to feed anyway. It was just part of the itchiness.

He let the energy of the night flow over him instead, trying desperately to relax. It was poisonous to him, but the breeze was cool on his bare skin and the clear sky vaguely hypnotic overhead. Not so hypnotic that he didn't pick up the emotions coming from beside the rock wall that separated the front garden from the street. He'd felt them earlier, before Betha came in for her little confrontation, and he recognized them now as easily as he would from any of his other masters.

"You're not welcome here, Justin," he said.

The youth stepped out from the shadows, glaring. Ril glared back. Even before the last few months he hadn't liked him. As a child, Justin had been needy and obsessive. Cowardly. Since he'd been turned into a feeder in Meridal, he'd become bitter and angry as well. Right now he was outraged.

Ril held his emotions under control. He couldn't help but project anything strong he felt to his masters, and he did *not* want Justin knowing what he was going through. Nor did he want to wake Lizzy or Leon.

"Go away," he repeated. "Lizzy doesn't want to see you."

Justin sniffed, ignoring Ril and walking forward. A growl finally stopped him a few feet away.

"I realized something tonight," the young man said. "You know what it was?"

"I don't care."

"You should," Justin snapped. "It's your fault. I went home with my father tonight, and you know who I saw? I saw Stria, my father's earth sylph, and I realized that I'm stuck being master to *you*, so I'll never be able to be master to *her*."

"I sure she's relieved to hear that."

Justin's face went red, obvious even in the darkness. "I wish you were dead. You took everything from me."

Why was it that everyone was thinking that tonight?

"I didn't take anything you actually had," Ril pointed out.

Justin's rage exploded inside of him, flashing out so brightly that Ril snarled at the feel of it. So did other battlers. Ril heard a distant roar and sent out his thoughts. *I can deal with this.* He didn't want anyone believing he needed rescue. Not from this pathetic human.

"Go away," he repeated. "I mean it."

"Why didn't you die?" Justin raged. "You bastard! Just die already!"

Ril flinched, the absoluteness of that order rocking through him along with a sudden fear. Whatever else he might be, this youth was his master and no sylph could disobey. Leon had bound Ril in Meridal to obey only him, but he'd given that freedom back when they left. That had once again granted Justin the ability to hurt him. And while Leon had warned Justin never to take advantage, the boy didn't seem to care anymore.

Ril felt his rage, and he felt his order, but the order had no direction. He bucked anyway, instinctually trying to obey.

"Justin."

Startled, the youth looked up. Betha stood on her front porch, her arms crossed under her breasts.

"Mrs. Petrule?"

"Leave my husband's battler alone."

"But . . ." He gestured impotently at the shaking Ril. "But—"

"Leave him alone, Justin. He's a member of this family. Go home. Now."

Justin glared at her, his lip trembling. Then he turned and stormed away.

Betha stared at Ril. Walking down the steps, her arms still crossed defensively in front of herself, she approached. Staring him right in the face, a moment later she sighed. "Come on, Ril," she said. "Let's go inside."

She had no control over him, but Ril obeyed her anyway. Neither of them spoke about that night to anyone.

* * *

Half a block down the street, attracted by the shouting and now hidden in the deeper shadow of a home, Sala paused. She hadn't been able to sleep and had been out walking, thinking about what she'd do with herself here. This was a nice little place with a lot of potential. She really couldn't have stayed in Yed, anyway. Not after what happened to Gabralina.

She watched Justin storm past, angry and hurting, and she sighed. In a lot of ways, Sylph Valley was a great deal like Yed. She studied the house she'd been watching and turned away, wandering back to her friend's tiny, unappealing apartment. If she was lucky, she supposed she'd find some sleep.

* * *

Solie sat in the conference room and listened with amazement to Leon's story. The romantic heart in her fluttered at the thought of Ril and Lizzy finding each other as they had, in a land far away, and the part that wanted to be a mother could have wept at how far Leon went to find his daughter. She needed to swallow a lump in her throat. Under the table, Heyou gripped her hand.

The political ramifications of his voyage were what really sank into her mind, forcing out thoughts of romance and family. Leon laid everything down very clearly, and the people around the table reacted so that Solie would have been able to tell their shock even if she hadn't had their emotions projected at her by each of the present sylphs.

Leon was dressed again in the blue and gold uniform that both he and Devon wore to show their service to her. Ril's garb was far more ostentatious—there was more gold, more ornamentation—but he slouched in his chair, not appearing to pay attention. Solie didn't really mind; she'd brought Heyou, after all, and he wasn't paying attention either. From the way he and Ril were looking at each other, she suspected the sylphs were having a silent conversation.

Mace, however, was paying attention. He sat on Ril's other

side, and he was the only battler there without his master. He frowned as he listened, no doubt weighing the danger of making an alliance with a country that had more than seven hundred battle sylphs, all with their own queen.

Beside him, Galway also leaned back in his chair, the tips of his fingers pressed together. Unlike Leon and Devon, he wore plain clothes; his beard was shaggy though clean, his bald head gleaming. Devon was beside him, scribbling furiously onto parchment, while Airi sat in the chair between him and Heyou. It was one of the few times Solie had seen the air sylph in solid shape, and she'd made herself appear a young woman, probably in honor of the seriousness of the meeting.

Solie shifted in her chair, sucking her lips into her mouth as she thought. "How much of a risk are we taking of a couple hundred battle sylphs showing up and conquering us?"

Leon shook his head. "Logistically speaking, little. It wouldn't be worth their while. It's an incredibly long distance for them to come; they'd have to set up a supply base on this continent first, and honestly, we're not big enough to be worth it. Politically, it's not worth it to Eapha, either. She's in the same situation you were six years ago." He gave a brief smile. "Only, she has a lot more sylphs backing her and a human population that doesn't even know what's happened. Their system is completely gone. Smashed." His smile faded, and she could tell he had no regrets.

Beside him, Ril growled. "Good. They were worse than the masters in Eferem."

Heyou didn't react, but there came a strange energy from Mace and Ril. Solie knew how bad it had been for Claw, also, having come from Eferem. Ril had been blessed to end up bound to Leon, but he'd still been a slave for his first fifteen years in this world.

Solie felt a flash of Leon's eternal regret. His battler didn't react. While Mace's and Claw's original masters were both dead, Leon wasn't. The very fact that Ril was sitting beside him showed he'd been able to forgive.

Still, murder was murder. Solie didn't want to think about a floating island filled with an emperor, his family, and who knew how many officials, guards, servants, and slaves drifting out over the ocean and being dropped. Nor did she want to imagine the hundreds of officials who'd survived that fate only to be hunted down in the city streets by battle sylphs. Did the many thousands of men and women who'd been locked in cages as feeders with their tongues cut out justify that? These were the new sylph masters in Meridal, and she wondered how many of them were even sane.

No, she truly didn't envy Eapha, forced to come out of a harem where she'd been a slave and become queen. At least the girl was safe, what with all those battle sylphs to protect her. Solie glanced at Heyou, who gave her a strained smile in return.

"She must be lonely."

All three present battlers stared at her in bafflement.

"She has Tooie," Ril said. "What more does she need?"

Airi giggled, pressing a hand to her mouth. Her master watched her out of the corner of one eye.

"Maybe . . . someone who knows how to run a kingdom?" Solie pointed out.

"Precisely," Leon agreed. "I thought about staying there myself to help her."

Very slowly, Ril straightened in his chair. He turned his entire torso to stare at his master, his hands gripping the chair arm until the wood creaked. "Pardon me?" he said with tremendous indignation. "You thought about *what?*"

Solie saw Leon fighting not to smile and had to bite down on a laugh herself. Leon lost his battle, but he suppressed the grin just as quickly. "I won't do that to you," he promised. "We're not going anywhere."

"Good." Ril glared a moment longer and then returned to his slouched position. Behind his back, Leon chuckled.

"Who are you sending?" Mace asked. "I assume you plan to send someone."

"Yes." Leon's eyes sought the end of the table. "I want to send Devon."

Devon, who'd been in the process of putting more ink on his quill, started and knocked the bottle over. That led to a frantic scramble to try and sop up the spill with parchment, but he finally gave up and stared at Leon, his stained fingers crushing the pages.

"Me?" he squeaked.

"You have the experience Eapha needs," Leon said, and Solie found herself agreeing. From the emotions of the others, they agreed, too, but Devon felt terrified. Airi stared at him in shared fear, shimmering back and forth to invisibility.

"You can guide her through this and make sure that she remembers us as her friends," Leon continued.

"But . . . but . . ."

"I've trained you for six years," Leon said. "You can do this."

"But, I can't! I wouldn't know where to start!"

"At the beginning. You'll see what needs to be done when you get there, and you'll be able to tell her."

"No, I won't!"

"Devon," Leon growled. "There's no one else. I gave that woman my word, and it has to be you. I'm sorry, but you *are* the best choice, whether you believe it or not. You and Airi both."

Devon glanced at his air sylph as though he'd never seen her before. She gaped back at him, and Solie felt both her trepidation and intrigue.

Leon was right. Devon was the only one left in the Valley with the experience to help create a new society. Neither

Leon or Galway could go without splitting or relocating their families. Their battle sylphs couldn't go without angering the battlers of the other hive. While the battlers could be ordered not to attack, the tension would make the whole situation next to impossible. Ril had likely needed to leave Meridal as fast as he could.

Solie would have liked to meet Eapha, but she already knew that was impossible. She'd never be able to leave the Valley. Nor could Eapha leave her home.

Devon could. Airi wasn't of Eapha's hive, but air sylphs didn't stress battlers the way other battlers did; and she would give Devon the company he needed as well as the ability to know what others were feeling. Her insight would be valuable.

"It won't be forever," Solie promised. When Devon turned, she added, "You just have to go long enough to help Eapha figure things out."

"It shouldn't be more than a year," Leon clarified. "We want her strong and friendly, not reliant on us or resentful."

Devon sagged in his chair. Airi reached over to squeeze his hand, her gaze never leaving him.

"I have to think about this," he managed. His face was still pale.

Leon nodded. "I can't ask for anything more—but don't take too long to make up your mind. She needs help *now*."

Devon shuddered and stared down at his ruined parchment. "Who'll take my job here?" he whispered. "I mean, do you have someone in mind for that, too?"

"As a matter of fact, I do," Leon said.

Slowly, Ril turned to look at him again.

Chapter Six

There was something wrong with the queen.

Yes, wrong. The recently returned healer just didn't know what it was. She'd tried to talk to the others, but none of them wanted to listen, perhaps for fear they would also become a target. The queen was growing sullen and short-tempered, lashing out with a tentacle whenever she came near. The queen hadn't laid an egg in days, either, and she wouldn't let her close, though the other healers still lounged contentedly nearby. The one time the unnamed healer dared ask if the queen was feeling unwell, she'd been chased out of the royal chambers, her hindquarters stinging from a slap.

She hurt. Not her hindquarters but her heart. It felt like the link between her and her queen was being stretched thin, pulled taut until it was about to snap. That made her feel itchy all through herself where she couldn't scratch.

The queen's chambers were the deepest in the hive. Above were the egg chambers and hatching rooms, and above those the chambers dedicated to food. The healer slipped into these, flowing through a crowd of chattering air sylphs, and she looked down at those that handled sustenance. There were more than two dozen, eyeless and fat, their cloud shapes a soft blue-green, though most were solid right now, forms that were all mouth, stomach, and udders.

The food sylphs ate, devouring the purple crops brought in by the air sylphs and drinking deeply of the funnelled-in water. In turn, they were milked of pure energy, balls of light that were packed into storage rooms for the rest of the hive to eat later. Any sylph could eat the plants outside, but except for the food sylphs it was a wasteful effort with far less return. The amount they'd need to consume would rise exponentially. A food sylph could drag out every bit of energy.

It didn't make the creatures intelligent, which the healer supposed was a blessing. She flowed over them, looking for any sort of illness. Food sylphs didn't speak, didn't move, didn't even feel. They just lay where they chose and ate, only rolling over so that they could be milked.

It was a peaceful place to visit. Food sylphs knew their place in the hive, and they didn't have to be concerned with anything else. The healer floated over them, wanting their peacefulness to soothe her as well, but it wasn't working. The queen was still snappish and angry, and she didn't know where she fit in the hive anymore.

The itchiness grew inside her, and the healer scratched, shook herself, and continued on. Restless and not knowing what to do about it, she knew only that for no reason she could fathom, her queen was starting to hate her.

* * *

Galway sat patiently through the long meeting, putting in comments and giving his analysis of economic reports regarding the Valley. The situation wasn't too bad, but without more trade they'd have to start imposing taxes. It would be easier if their fledgling government didn't pay the sylphs even the pittance they did—the sylphs would have worked for free, anyway, and most didn't know what to do with their admittedly tiny salaries—but Solie wouldn't want to concede the point. Only slaves worked for nothing.

The possibilities inherent to forming a trade partnership with Meridal were immense. The old empire was already known for its luxury goods, and Eapha had inherited everything.

Galway made a few notes about the ways she could get her manufacturing base working again; he'd have to discuss them with Devon. Providing the man intended to go. Galway looked over to see him sink down in his chair as the meeting ended, his air sylph invisible and playing with his hair.

But, Devon and the Valley's economic future weren't his most immediate concerns. He'd sat through the entire meeting feeling his battler's emotions jumping around like a swamp bug. Solie hadn't seemed to pick up on it. She could feel the emotions of everyone in the room, so he had no doubt that Devon's near hysteria was swamping her.

She left ahead of the others, with Mace following. Devon hurried out almost on her heels. Galway gathered his notes and traversed the hallway behind Leon and Ril, right after Heyou. When the young battler made as if to follow his queen, Galway put an arm around his neck and pulled him aside.

Drawing him close, he steered the battler across the main audience chamber and back toward the more public area of the underground complex. Heyou looked surprised, but he didn't pull away and let himself be guided. They walked in the same direction as Ril and Leon.

"So, what's wrong, boy?" Galway asked, careful to keep his voice low. Ril could probably hear him, but the battler wouldn't care. The chancellor shouldn't know Heyou's issues, though. This felt like a private matter.

"Wrong?"

Galway tightened his arm around the battler's neck. Heyou made a fake gagging sound but pressed closer, suddenly burying his face against the trapper's chest. His aura sad, he stopped walking.

Galway stopped, too, worried. Ahead, Ril and Leon vanished through the main doors, leaving them alone. "What is it, Heyou? Tell me."

The battler wrapped him tight in his arms, standing very

close. He wasn't tall in this chosen form, and his face pressed into Galway's collarbone. "It's Solie," he said, his voice muffled. "She wants to have babies. I don't know what to do."

"Ah. I see."

Galway brought his free hand around and laced it through Heyou's long, dark hair. To him, Heyou being a battle sylph didn't mean much; the boy was just like any of the other children he and his wife had taken in over the years. Not all of them were blood, but all of them were family. His wife felt the same.

"Come on," he told the battler. "Come home with me. We'll talk."

He ruffled Heyou's hair and started walking, dragging the boy along behind him. Heyou sighed, but he came along obediently enough. Galway felt a spark of hope flare through the battler and that was good enough for now.

* * *

Ril yawned as he and Leon walked down the wide, well-lit corridor that formed the main throughway of the hive's underground complex. The ambient light came from a lattice of crystals in the ceiling and walls, lit by a single fire sylph in a central location who illuminated the entire network of corridors and rooms.

The corridors were all clean and easy to navigate, but there were still few humans to be seen. Most still found the idea of living here too alien, and they stayed aboveground when they could. Sylphs liked it more. There were a lot of those in the halls, and at night, while their masters slept, there were hundreds enjoying the camaraderie of a proper hive.

Leon looked over appraisingly at his battler. "Do you want to go to the nest?" he asked. "I can do this without you."

Ril shook his head and yawned again. "No. I can manage."

Leon just nodded. Once this was done, Ril was going to the nest, the chamber by the main audience and throne room that the battlers had taken as their own. They congregated there in their natural form, relaxing, and Ril slept in it, the other battlers necessary to hold him in his original shape. He'd fall to specks of light anywhere else. He still sometimes needed to take that shape and rest that way, but it was usually his choice about when.

"Have you thought about what you're going to do?" Leon asked. They headed down narrower corridors that led deeper into the hive, and then down more stairs.

"Do?"

"With Lizzy."

He saw Ril's puzzled look and felt the battler's uncertainty. Ril was apparently still afraid of his reaction about his daughter. The battler had made Lizzy his master long ago, secretly, and Leon's discovery had been an accident. He knew Leon could still change his mind and not allow Lizzy to be with him. Leon could order him away and Ril would have to obey.

Leon had no intention of doing that. The situation couldn't go on the way it was, though.

"In every way that matters, you're married to Lizzy," he told the battler. "Usually when two people get together, they move into a home of their own."

Ril frowned, blinked, and frowned again. "I don't want to leave you."

Leon smiled. He didn't particularly want Ril to leave, either, even if they'd still work together. The battler hadn't been too keen on the idea of becoming Solie's majordomo and social secretary, taking Devon's place, but the job would be good for him. Thanks to his injuries, Ril couldn't fulfil the usual duties of a battle sylph, but he was still immortal. If he was going to survive the centuries to come, he needed a purpose. Leon intended to give him one.

He also wanted to make it easier for Ril to keep all of his masters close. At least until he outlived them.

"You don't have to move out," he suggested to Ril, "but I think it's a good idea to give Lizzy a place that she knows is her own. It's good for both of you." When the battler looked suspicious, Leon added, "We have that barn at the end of the garden we use for the horses. The neighbors down the road have said we can put those in their pasture. They won't even charge us except for feed. That means we can replace the barn with a cottage. That way you'll both be near the family but able to get away and be together."

Ril tilted his head to one side, pondering. "That sounds all right."

"Good." Leon grinned. "I'll see if I can get an earth sylph to change the barn. It's all stone anyway."

Ril nodded and yawned again, but Leon felt happier. His battler's emotions were content and relaxed.

Ahead, doors were spaced along the corridor. Claw slouched outside one, staring at his hands. He glanced up as they approached, and the battler, who had blue hair for some strange reason, looked almost frightened. Not that Leon doubted his ability to act as guard; the sylph would destroy whomever he had to. Still, Leon spoke gently to him, knowing how long Rachel had been working to build up his shattered confidence.

"Good morning, Claw. I need to see the prisoners, please."

The battler shivered, glancing from Leon to Ril. Ril stared back with understanding. The two were unique among sylphs: Ril was crippled in body, Claw in spirit.

Claw nodded shakily. "Okay." He turned and pulled a key out of his pocket, using it to unlock the door.

"Thank you," Leon said, and passing the battler started down another set of stairs.

Ril paused, eyeing Claw. "How's the reading coming?"

"Um, good," the other battler said. "I read a story to Rachel last night."

"Nice," Ril said.

Claw sagged. "The math is hard, though."

Ril clapped him on the shoulder. "I *hate* math," he confessed. Then, without another word, he followed his master down the stairs.

Claw locked the door behind them, and quietly Leon and Ril descended. The stairs opened onto a section of the hive that had been intended for storage, though, like much of the rest of the complex, it wasn't actually in use. Not yet. The earth sylphs just liked to create things, even far beyond the needs of the population.

The light was much dimmer here, the reflective crystals transmitting illumination from the on-duty fire sylph more sporadically placed. Leon and Ril moved without concern through the shadows, coming at last to another door, one of many, that was guarded by a large, prone mountain lion. The beast lay right before them, tail flicking.

"Good morning, Dillon," Leon said.

The transformed battle sylph looked up and yawned, showing a massive array of teeth. Most battlers stayed in one preferred human shape when they weren't in their natural form, but Dillon liked to experiment. The big cat rose and revealed a key. He padded out of the way, moving to the other side of the corridor where he sat down again, shifting into the shape of a large brown bear. He didn't say anything, not bothering to form vocal cords, but watched placidly as Leon bent to pick up the key.

Leon unlocked the door. Ril stepped up beside him, just in case the men inside were stupid enough to try and attack. Inside was a single storage room, lit by a lone oil lamp suspended from the ceiling. Cots had been brought in, and there was a pitcher of water and some towels beside a large basin. There was even a curtain covering one corner where the captives could relieve themselves. The room smelled of sweat and fear, but at least it was clean.

Five men sat on the floor or on cots. Each glanced up as Ril and Leon entered. They all had been taken easily, which was hardly a surprise. There were ways to get by a battler, but not many men knew them. Leon had learned them by observing Ril over the years and he'd used several of those tricks in Meridal. Battlers reacted to emotion, and if a man didn't feel the emotions they were seeking, they ignored him.

The five assassins stared at him, their faces impassive. They looked as calm as a group of men sitting around a tavern, but he had no doubt their emotions were revealing themselves to his battler. He felt Ril's amusement.

Leon crossed his arms, not really needing his battler's perceptions. "Borash," he said, nodding to the closest. "Mikel, Deel, Randel, Erry." All were soldiers, men he'd known in King Alcor's army. They returned his look with expressions not of surprise, since his betrayal was already known, but disgust.

"Traitor," Randel hissed. He was the first captured, Leon had heard, though he hadn't given his identity to anyone. He matched Solie's description.

"Mmmm." Leon regarded him for a moment. "I suppose I'll dispense with the questioning. The reasons why you're here are plain. If it wasn't Alcor's idea to send you all, it was Umut's."

Umut Taggart was Leon's replacement, and this felt like something he would try. He likely wouldn't be surprised by his assassins' failure, either. Nor would he be regretful.

"I need to decide what to do with you," Leon announced.

"You don't have the right to do anything," snapped Deel. "Just surrender yourself and come back to Eferem for your trial."

"I . . . don't think so." Leon glanced at Ril. The battler looked bored. "My fate isn't in question here."

"Are you going to kill us?" Erry asked. He was the youngest of the five, and he looked the most uncertain. Leon didn't have any sympathy, not considering his intended crime.

Still, there was no reason not to be honest. In the long run, compassion would also work better than violence.

"No. If the battlers didn't kill you already, I certainly won't. But I have to decide whether to let you go or keep you here. Or, rather, *you* need to decide that. All of you."

"What do you mean?" Erry asked.

"If you carry a message to Alcor and swear never to come back, we'll take you to the border and let you go." It was Solie's decision, but Leon had seen its merit.

"That's all?" Randel looked dubious.

"That's all. We know why you came, and we know we caught all of you."

Leon turned and headed back out into the hall, Ril beside him. He had only needed to confirm where these men had come from, and he'd done that. Now they could carry a message back to Alcor, hopefully dissuading Eferem's king from sending assassins or spies ever again. He'd be a fool to try. At least, they had to convince him of that. No matter how paranoid he was.

None of the people in the Valley wanted to go to war, Solie especially, but they wouldn't risk her life either. Solie was a good queen, but even if he weren't fond of her, Leon wouldn't have wanted to see her hurt. If Solie died, the Valley battlers would go mad until another queen was chosen, and it would be far too easy to end up with the wrong one. The first battler to have sex with his female master after Solie passed would make her the new queen. There were women here Leon could see as queens, but others only had a battler through necessity.

He walked out past Dillon, Ril still following. "Wait!" one of the prisoners shouted, but Leon didn't look back. These men could stew for a while. He had other work to catch up on.

* * *

Claw stood guard, not moving. He wasn't bored; he could stand forever just waiting and watching. He felt the emotions of the prisoners below, and he sensed Dillon, too, shifting from one form to another and just enjoying himself. Back in the hive, Claw could have stayed an eternity wherever he was put, watching a single spot for what in this place would be years. Here, though, the masters became unhappy if they didn't see their battlers for too long, so his shifts were amazingly short. In only a few hours he'd be relieved. Then he would see Rachel again.

He thought of her, of the woman's soft skin and her wonderful emotions, of how kind she was and how incredible she felt; about the classes she'd been giving him, and of the comfort she gave. He loved her so much that he thought he'd go mad if she left him.

There were older memories: the girl he'd seen for only an instant and come through the gate for, only to watch her killed. His mind had fractured in that moment, and the man who'd held him, Boradel, only laughed. The agony of his amusement, the horror of his taunts and mastery, it all came back to Claw again, just as it always did. Claw flinched, hands clutched defensively to his chest as though he was about to be struck. Just as he'd been struck so many times before.

Rachel. She always told him to think of happy things when these memories came, to remind himself of all the good in his life. He tried to think of her now, but Boradel was laughing again, ordering him to cut himself so that he could watch, to throw himself off cliffs or onto swords. To feel the master's pleasure at his battler's pain. Claw whimpered, not knowing how to get past this no matter what Rachel said or did.

"Hello?"

Claw started, his form shimmering into the hideous, fanged creature that was the shape he'd worn when he belonged to Boradel. He spun, hissing, and saw a woman standing only a few dozen feet away. She watched him down the corridor.

She certainly didn't seem afraid. Her emotions were placidly calm instead. He stared back, resuming his human form, not understanding how she'd managed to get so close.

"You're a battle sylph, aren't you?" she asked. "Gabby said you wear blue and gold all of the time."

Claw blinked, not sure what to do as she came closer. He was supposed to guard this door, but she didn't feel dangerous to him. Women were calming instead, and he took a deep breath as the memories of Boradel faded.

She didn't even look at the door, instead focusing on him with that endless, soothing calm. She was much younger than Rachel, her soft brown hair bound back in a long braid. She wore simple clothes and a plain shawl, though Claw was no judge of fashion. Like all battlers, he just liked women, and the urge to violence didn't exist in him near her.

"What's your name?" she asked. She was only a few feet away.

"C-Claw," he stammered.

"I'm Sala. It's nice to meet you."

She smiled and glanced up at his wild blue hair. He'd made it that way, not remembering at first that humans didn't have blue hair, but Rachel had told him it was all right. If he liked it, she liked it, she'd said, and it didn't matter what everyone else thought, even if he knew they thought him crazy.

"I like your hair," she told him.

"Oh," he whispered, shivering. "Thank you."

She smiled. Her emotions never flickered.

* * *

Galway's household was a huge, sprawling manor created by an overly energetic earth sylph named Stria, who was a friend of the family. Having been restricted to simple, ordinary houses for most of her work, she'd been given free rein here and turned the dwelling into a melange of stylistic elements, rooms, and hallways that reached as far underground as they did into the air. Embossed on every wall were images of whatever interested Stria at the time she'd shaped the rock; the furniture was part of the floor and there were windows everywhere. It was strange, but the family had grown used to it, and here everyone had their own room. Before the Valley they'd been crowded into a single cottage.

Heyou and Galway walked up the front path, making their way through the hazards of wooden children's toys and tools left scattered everywhere. The grass was long and the garden unkempt. The family wasn't the neatest, but none of the neighbors complained, not with the thick hedge of lilacs that had been encouraged to grow during the last six years to hide the mess, and especially not with the frequent visits of a battle sylph who considered himself one of them.

The two arrived just before lunch, entering a foyer with a ceiling thirty feet high and made from a kaleidoscope of colored glass. A massive, curving staircase led to the second and third floors, while others passages split off as well. It was completely silent, Stria having managed to design the dwelling so that sound didn't travel. That sometimes made it hard to find whomever you were seeking, and it definitely made it hard to get everyone to the dinner table.

Right now, however, most of the family was gathered in the dining room at the center of the house. It had a stream flowing down one side, filling a deep channel in the stone floor before it vanished again on its way to the bathrooms where it fed the tub with continuously fresh, if cool, water. A huge harvest table made of solid malachite rose out of the floor. Five people ranged around it, all of them talking at the same time they grabbed the food Iyala had prepared. She stood in the doorway to the kitchen, eyeing her husband and Heyou as she brought in some potatoes.

"I didn't expect you," she said, setting the bowl down and opening her arms.

Heyou immediately launched himself at her. She was a large, immensely broad woman, and he wrapped himself in her hug, his head nearly vanishing between ponderous breasts.

"Ah now, *you* I can hug without worrying, my duck!" she exclaimed, squeezing him with a strength that probably would have broken a human boy's ribs. Heyou just made a happy exclamation, lost to the depths of her bosom. Galway laughed and headed to the table.

Several of the young people sitting there had been born to the couple, but there were others that he and Iyala acquired over the years. They ranged in age from twelve to twenty-two, and Galway never bothered to remember which were biologically his; he'd picked up the rest from the towns and hamlets he visited during his travels. Iyala called him a soft touch, but he wouldn't leave an abandoned child to suffer. She'd never turned down any of the boys or girls he'd brought, and she hadn't turned down Heyou either. Her only comment had been about not having to feed him.

It had taken the rest of the family longer to adapt. The fights between the boys had been, as Heyou put it, "Wonderful." No one got seriously hurt, and once all of the boys' courage and status was established, Heyou had become family.

Right now, he was content to be hugged to death by his adopted mother and the rest of the children were happy to let the battler take the brunt of her affections. Galway used the opportunity to fill his plate, and he settled down like everyone else to eat. Usually he took a cold meal to work with him, and he was glad of the opportunity for something better.

Nelson, his oldest son, sat right across from him. "Why are you here, Pop?" Nelson asked. "You never come to lunch."

"I had some business in the area."

Galway saw Nelson look at Heyou. He was not a foolish young man. He'd first met Nelson in an alley in the Eferem capital. An eight-year-old at the time, the boy had tried to mug him. But that was long ago.

"You're not working?" he asked.

Nelson shook his head. "Cal and I brought in all the cattle this morning. We'll start gelding the calves this afternoon. I wanted a full belly for that."

"I don't blame you," Galway said. Cal's herd was up to a hundred animals, which at least kept him in the Valley instead of driving carts all over the place and babbling things he shouldn't to anyone who might listen. Galway liked Cal, but the man had no concept of discretion. "Did his son help out?"

Nelson shrugged, chewing and swallowing before he answered, just in case Iyala was watching. "He was there, but he didn't help all that much. He spent most of the time bitching about how his fiancée was stolen."

Galway had to smile. Nelson's expression said it all. He'd known Justin for years, and he never would have spoiled the boy like Cal had. Justin thought he was entitled, which none of Galway's children did. Then again, many of Galway's had been disabused of the notion before they even joined his family. The rest had learned fast. Including Heyou.

Behind him, Iyala finished mauling her newest, strangest son, and she let him go with a final kiss and a mad tousling of his hair. He reeled back, grinning, and flopped into a chair beside Galway. He looked like he'd been through a windstorm.

"You better bring Solie around to dinner soon," Iyala warned him, her stern tone belied by her twinkling eyes.

Heyou's grin faded. "I guess."

Everyone glanced up in surprise. He stared down at the table.

Galway sighed. "Keep eating, you lot." He looked at his wife before his eyes shifted to Heyou. She nodded and moved to pile another helping on the youngest children's plates, whether they wanted it or not.

Nelson eyed Heyou suspiciously, like he suspected one of their infamous fights. Nelson was a peaceful sort now, but that hadn't stopped him from hitting Heyou with a chair once while they were still working out their differences. "What's wrong with you?"

"Nelson," Galway cautioned. "Finish your lunch."

The young man processed that and sighed, digging back into his meal. He was done in minutes, and when he left, most of the other children followed. Heyou without a grin was an unusual thing, but they wouldn't bother being worried until they had to.

The two adults weren't quite so complacent.

"What happened today, Thom?" Iyala asked.

Galway shrugged, pushing his bowl away and regarding Heyou. After decades of everyone calling him by his last name, it still felt odd when his wife did otherwise. "It seems Solie wants to have children."

"Ah," Iyala breathed. "I see. So you're going to be a father, Heyou? That's a big responsibility."

Heyou froze, incredulous. "Be a father? How do I do that? I can't have human kids."

"So?" Iyala started to clear the table, piling bowls so she could carry them to the kitchen. "I've only borne two of my children. The rest just showed up."

Heyou blinked. He looked deep in thought.

"That doesn't mean you just go and find a child to take home," Galway pointed out. "That sort of thing tends to irritate a parent."

Heyou smiled, his eyes twinkling, but his mirth didn't last long. "She wants a baby *inside* her. I can feel it. I can't give her that."

"Do you want to?" Iyala asked.

"Yeah. I want Solie happy." His response was immediate and he shivered. "I don't want her to think about leaving me."

"Well," Galway said, with a speculative tap of his finger to his lips. "There is a way to get her pregnant, given a little intervention."

"Intervention?" Heyou asked.

Galway gave a small smile. "Do you know how human women get pregnant?"

Heyou shot him a look. "Yeah—unless it's different than cows."

Iyala gave a hearty guffaw. Galway laughed, too. It was apparently considered a spectator sport among battle sylphs whenever the bulls were released into a herd.

"Well, if you know that, do you know what they do when they have a cow that's especially reluctant?"

Heyou blinked.

"Don't tease the boy, Thom," Iyala said. "Just tell him."

Heyou's eyes got huge as Galway explained.

Chapter Seven

Solie sat in an opulent private garden created by her friend
Loren and Loren's water sylph. Shore was someone Solie
considered a friend as well, though the little sylph had only
spoken to her once and was obviously still nervous around
her.

It had been Shore's idea, actually, to make the garden,
and the space was beautiful, with trickling streams and richly
flowering bushes. The area was small, only a few hundred feet
across, but it lay directly through wide doors that led from her
bedroom, and her view of the growing settlement was cut off by
an encircling wall, making a serene retreat for Solie whenever
she wanted to get away. Also, thanks to the addition of wind
chimes and the artful arrangement of the trickling streams,
most of the noise of the town was blocked as well. Solie could
pretend she was miles away from everything, safe in her own
private little haven.

Unfortunately, too many people knew about it. Solie saw
that such feelings were uncharitable, but this was the only
time this morning she'd had a chance to sit and have some tea.
Loren didn't *need* to be sitting here. Not like Solie did. She had
a talent for gardening, and with Shore to help her she could
make as many private gardens for herself as she wished.

Well, maybe it was the dynamic between Loren and Lizzy
that was making Solie twitch. Lizzy had been kidnapped off
the docks and sold into slavery because Loren convinced her
to come along to Para Dubh. Loren hadn't been kidnapped at

all. Thanks to Shore, Solie could feel the girls' tension far more clearly than she would have liked.

Loren was twenty, older than Lizzy but younger than Solie. She was attractive, but the only thing in her life that she took responsibility for was Shore. The little water sylph sat beside her, looking like a younger version of Loren, her hair only a little damper. There was no sign of Lizzy's sylph, but Solie had to wonder how long it would take Ril to decide to show up, given how tense the girl felt.

Seated in one of two chairs nearby, Gabralina chewed on a biscuit with great enjoyment, oblivious to what else was going on at the table. Her friend Sala sat beside her. Until Lizzy arrived, Loren had been regaling Sala with the story of how she became Shore's master after the sylph's original master died.

Solie almost groaned. Why had she decided to let all of them into her garden in the first place? It hadn't even occurred to her that Loren and Lizzy wouldn't have already talked. But Lizzy looked ready to dive over the table at her friend. She sipped her tea and licked her lips, not turning away from Loren at all. She was clearly furious.

Sala turned to Solie, one eyebrow raised. The young queen glanced away, giving a brief shudder. The tension was ratcheting up even more between Loren and Lizzy, and Sala's calm placidity felt cloying in comparison.

For her part, Loren looked guilty. She felt remorse as well, along with fright. Faced with something she couldn't hide from behind her usual shallow chitchat, the girl didn't know what to do. Solie sighed inside and wondered if she should just call Mace and ask him to bring the Widow. Lily Blackwell would knock the two girls' heads together and be done with it.

Lizzy continued to glare, and Solie tried to hide another sigh. This was supposed to be her break! For half the afternoon she had meetings with merchants wanting to set up permanent shops in the town, and then others with the local planning committee about the next phase of reconstruction to bring more arid land back to life. After that was Petr the priest, and they would decide how many more people to train to utilize the gate, as well as how many sylphs they would invite through this year. She also had to sit with Devon, who was understandably nervous at the prospect of going to a foreign kingdom.

She did hope he agreed. Devon was a dear man and a gentle person, and she couldn't imagine anyone she'd trust more to do this job. Well, other than Leon, Galway, or the Widow Blackwell, none of whom were in a position to go. But she had no intention of forcing him.

Her mind was turning more and more to the things she wished she could have, and her hand pressed against her childless belly for a moment. She then took control of herself and turned back to see if she could stop this silliness before broken crockery started flying.

"So," Lizzy said, her teeth gritted so tight she could barely speak. "How have you been, Loren?"

"Good," the girl replied. "I've moved out of the hive apartments. Stria made me a cottage on the lake in return for Shore making Cal a vegetable garden." Then, realizing perhaps that discussing her own good fortune and the Porters' earth sylph might not be the best move, she fell silent, her throat moving convulsively.

Lizzy's teeth ground loud enough that Gabralina finally looked up from her plate. Sala said nothing, just continuing to watch everyone with that surprisingly flat gaze.

Solie was just lifting her hand, not able to stand any more, when Shore spoke. She'd moved from her chair to stand beside Loren, her small fingers appearing over the side of the small round table next to her childish face. "I'm sorry," she said in her light, bubbling voice.

All five human women stared.

The little sylph closed green eyes with endless waves of ocean in the iris. "I left you there. I'm sorry. Please forgive me."

The little sylph's distress and regret were so great that none of them could help but feel it, and the anger and resentment that had been building among them collapsed. Loren threw her arms around the water sylph, hugging the small creature to her and telling her how wonderful she was, while Lizzy dropped to her knees to hold them both, telling Shore that it wasn't her fault, that no one could have known what those men on the docks would do and that Shore should be proud of saving Loren from the same fate. Somehow, in reassuring Shore, the words became true, and the two friends-cum-enemies ended up sobbing in each other's arms, everything forgiven.

It was infectious. Gabralina watched for a moment, eyes brimming, then dove herself into the pile with an unladylike wail. Solie was just about to join them when she saw Sala. Gabralina's friend continued to watch without any emotion. None at all. There was nothing wrong with that, exactly, but still Solie felt a chill.

A step sounded behind her, and she turned to see Claw peering out into the garden, on guard and drawn by the morass of emotion. Solie smiled, seeing as she did the reflection of the table and her friends in the glass doors he'd pushed wide. Behind her, Sala was beaming at the battler, her face transformed into something almost beautiful. Claw stared back, entranced.

Sala's emotions didn't change, however. Still placid, still calm—and Solie spun to see her face had once again gone blank. The girl sipped her tea and watched the three women and the water sylph untangle themselves, saying nothing, feeling nothing.

Solie turned back to the battle sylph. "Thank you, Claw," she said, suddenly wanting him to leave for reasons she couldn't explain. "Why don't you go see if Rachel needs your help?"

Claw gave a convulsive swallow and nodded. Another battler was summoned to take his place as guard, and Solie felt him move inside the house almost immediately, but this one ignored the women as much as they ignored him.

Solie turned back to Sala, but the woman didn't meet her gaze, smiling at Gabralina instead. The queen took another sip of her tea, wondering what it was that had her spooked. Maybe her fears were just a woman's vapors.

Such thoughts reminded her again of what she wanted and couldn't have, and she sat in silence and tried not to sigh.

* * *

Justin trudged homeward, tired from his day and bitter about it. Nelson Galway seemed to have an unreasonable expectation of him, considering the man worked for his father. They'd been friends while growing up, but it wasn't Nelson's place to hint that Justin wasn't working hard enough. Justin worked plenty hard. And he'd just gotten back from a terrible trip.

Ahead, the road branched off toward several different houses, one of them his father's. Justin had planned to be moved out already, but of course that hadn't happened. Not without a wife. He could still have a home of his own, but he didn't want to live alone.

His father was still finishing up with the cattle, along with Nelson. At least he understood. Seeing those calves being gelded and listening to the screams . . . it was all too much a reminder of Meridal, where his tongue had been cut out. That had been the worst pain in the world, and he couldn't ever forget it. Even with his tongue restored, he carried too many other scars.

Justin shuddered and went inside. He headed into the kitchen, where Stria, his father's earth sylph, was playing with the marbles Cal was always making for her. She had thousands of them, and she never tired of the stupid things. Seeing her just brought the anger back. She was supposed to have been his, just like Lizzy. Justin was supposed to inherit her, along with this house and all the cattle, and he would have been rich, for Stria was an old sylph and powerful. Some of her marbles were made of ruby or emerald, brought up from diving expeditions. His father didn't do much with them other than turn them into marbles. As far as he was concerned, they didn't need a lot. Stria had made their home and they owned a large herd. They didn't need more.

Justin would have put her to work. He stared at the little mud-covered, squat, doll-like creature. He would have been rich enough to give Lizzy a home that everyone else envied; only now that was impossible. Stria could have a hundred masters, but a human could only have one sylph, and thanks to Meridal, Justin was bound to Ril. He could feel the battle sylph in the back of his mind like a vague itch. He didn't get more than that and didn't want it. Ril ignored him, and Justin was glad—or he would have been if the damned battler hadn't stolen his future. Both Stria and Lizzy.

He'd come home feeling hunger. Now Justin just felt sick to his stomach again. He turned to go to his room, but halfway across the kitchen, his foot shot out from under him and he had to grab the counter to keep from falling. Stria turned her broad, flat face toward him, her chinless mouth hanging open. He'd slipped on one of her marbles, he realized, and he saw her swallow convulsively.

Justin's anger surged. She'd never be his, and all she cared about were her bloody marbles! "How can you be so stupid!" he shouted. "Are you trying to kill me?"

Stria cringed, mumbling an apology he couldn't really hear, then plopped out of her chair and shuffled hurriedly across the floor to recover her errant toys. She left dirty footprints as she went. She was always tracking mud into the house.

"You're making a mess!" he screamed, truly wanting to hit her in that moment.

A shadow fell over the kitchen window, and Justin heard a low growl. A quickly there, quickly vanished surge of hate flashed through him, the emotion of another, and he spun, his bladder nearly letting go. Swirling, ball lightning eyes glared in through the window.

"I wasn't going to hurt her," he gasped, his hands raised as he backed away. He nearly tripped over one of Stria's marbles again, but he regained his footing and kept retreating, reaching the doorway at last and running to his room.

* * *

Stria watched her master's son run out the door, taking his panic with him. She glanced next toward the window, where Blue's swirling eye still regarded her.

Thank you, she sent.

You're welcome.

He moved away, continuing his rounds, and Stria slowly moved to collect her scattered marbles, checking them meticulously for damage. Cal would be home soon, but she wouldn't tell him about this, not wanting to see him upset. She was glad, though, that Justin would never be her master.

* * *

Devon wandered his small underground apartment, digging through his belongings and wondering what to take, what to leave behind, and if he was losing his mind for even considering the trip.

Do you want to go? Airi asked, floating around his head and ruffling his hair.

"Yes. No. I don't know." Devon turned and sat down on his bed, his hands dangling between his legs. "Oh, stars, why me?"

Because you can do this? I think it would be fun. I'd like to feel the winds of a new place.

He stared up at where he knew she floated. "You want to go?"

Yes. Coming here was wonderful. Now we have a chance to make friends with another hive. That never happens back where I came from. I like it.

Devon frowned. He appreciated her point of view, but he was terrified of leaving. More than just about anything, he hated change. Yes, he'd brought Airi here to a new place, but that hadn't exactly been planned. He hadn't actually had a chance to really stop and think until he was a full-fledged member of Solie's hive. If he had been given a choice, he would have been too afraid to get out of bed that morning.

Turning, he opened the top drawer of his nightstand and pulled out a wooden flute, an instrument nearly as small as a whistle. He felt Airi's excitement, and he raised it to his lips to play.

His fingers flashed. The music was sweet and high, filling the small room and causing his air sylph to dance happily above him. She loved this, was drawn to music as all air sylphs were, and though she'd have been his whether he had talent or not, Devon's family had insisted he learn to play before his father transfered mastery. Devon had chosen the flute because it was portable and he could carry it anywhere, but playing the instrument calmed his mind as much as it made Airi happy. He never went a day without playing, and as his fingers danced over the holes, he felt his tensions ease.

He didn't really think as he played, but he knew suddenly that, whether he wanted to or not, he would go to Meridal.

Leon had asked him, and Solie was in agreement, and he owed them both more than he could ever admit. He'd been just an air sylph master in Eferem, little better than a laborer. Airi hadn't even had the right to speak. Now they both had their freedom. And more than just his debt, he wanted to help the others. Their position here was precarious if the kingdoms around them decided to join forces. With Meridal on their side, they were far more secure.

Devon finished his song much more content with the world, even though he knew he'd be panicked again at some point—likely when the sheer distance he'd be traveling and the enormity of his task next occurred to him. For now, though, he and his sylph were at peace. That was all that mattered.

A knock sounded at the front door, hurried and hard. Devon felt Airi's sudden recognition and alarm just before the knob turned violently enough to break the lock. The door swung wide.

Heyou stood there, in human form, grinning in a way that would have terrified Devon even if he didn't already instinctively fear battle sylphs. He knew he shouldn't, that none of the Valley battlers had any reason to hurt him, but he'd experienced their hate aura too many times and had even seen this particular battler fight. The town of Devon's father had nearly been decimated in the process.

And, Heyou's grin had far too many teeth. Airi pressed herself against the back of Devon's neck, a freezing chill, just as frightened as he.

"Hi!" Heyou said, probably knowing exactly what Devon was feeling but not caring. "Since you're leaving and everything, I was wondering if you were interested in being the father of my baby?"

* * *

Rachel sighed wearily as she swept the floor of the classroom. The children were restless, and it had been a long day. More, her arthritis was acting up and her hands ached where they held the broom. Tonight she'd have to ask Claw to make dinner and then rub some ointment into her hands.

She smiled slightly. He was wonderfully adept, and in many ways she preferred that kind of intimacy to his making love to her. It wasn't that she didn't like his more physical attentions. At her age, she hadn't expected to have any kind of man's touch again, and Claw did make her feel very young. And he was doing so much better now. He was still shy, but he was trying harder and his confidence was building. When she could draw him out of his shell, which was happening more and more frequently, he was a wonderful conversationalist. Overall, Claw was a good soul, and he didn't deserve what had been done to him.

"Let me do that . . . for you." Slimmer, younger hands reached for the broom. Sala, her new assistant, smiled and started to sweep the floor. "There's tea in the back room for you. Rest. I'll finish up here."

Rachel gave the young woman a grateful look. Most of the sylphs took classes at night while everyone else slept, but some preferred the day, and there were so many students who needed to learn. Children, adults . . . And there were just so few teachers available. When Sala volunteered to help, it had been a blessing. The young woman didn't seem to have the compassion needed to be a good instructor for the little ones, but she controlled the older children with ease. None of her classes were unruly. All Sala's students were quiet and well behaved.

"Thank you, Sala," she said. Slowly making her way out of the classroom and down the dark hallway to the tiny kitchen at the back of the school, Rachel rubbed her sore hands.

Everyone was gone now, and the halls echoed strangely, the soft susurration of Sala's broom in the classroom behind her the only accompaniment to the shuffling of her feet on the polished wood.

The kitchen was a spare room overlooking the back garden, with a fireplace equipped with a pole that a kettle could be hung on. The windows were large, and Rachel sat down in the light of the setting sun, reaching for the fat pot of tea that had been left to steep on a tray in the middle of the small staff table. Sala had even set out a mug and a pot of honey, along with a small plate of cookies. Thanking whatever kind deity brought the woman, Rachel poured herself a mug and added a dollop of honey. Sitting back, she took a relishing sip and sighed.

* * *

Sala could have arranged to have her own apartment, but it suited her to stay with her friend. She arrived back at Gabralina's shortly before dark. Letting herself in, she found her roommate wasn't back yet. She put down her bag and went into the back room. Wat was sprawled across the bed, his legs and feet up against the wall, his head hanging over the side. He turned toward her. His coat was unbuttoned and wrinkled.

"Hello, Wat," she said. "Where's Gabby?"

He shrugged slowly, watching her upside down. "Working. Something to do with food. She'll be back later." He looked bored.

"And you're not supposed to be somewhere else right now?" she clarified.

"No," he said.

"Good," she told him. Undoing her dress she said, "Service me."

What Gabralina would think of Sala having sex with her battler, Sala didn't know, but given how Wat had been ordered to obey her, she didn't need her friend to find out. Conveniently, she'd learned that Wat could be ordered to forget whatever she asked. And, coitus with a battle sylph was too good to pass up. No worry of pregnancy, no bother with commitment, and her pleasure was paramount. Most interestingly, since battlers could change shape, they were able to provide all sorts of simultaneous stimulation that Sala was pretty sure the boring women of this Valley never thought of.

Wat worked every erogenous zone Sala had at once, leaving her shuddering with pleasure and him with a somewhat lost look. Sala didn't care what he thought, any more than she worried about Gabralina coming back at an inconvenient time. When the girl got close, Wat would warn her, and once they were done, he'd forget. That was tremendously useful.

It also wasn't enough. Not after hearing what having a battle sylph of one's own was like. Still, she had a lead on getting one, and from there, getting more control in the Valley. It would take a while, but her plan was doable, and thanks to Gabby's foolishness, she was already directing one battler. She had potential links to another, and in time she'd have one of her own. From there, she just had to remove a few human obstacles.

It would be hers—all the power and wealth she'd worked for in Yed, using Gabby to get into the coffers of the magistrate before she finally poisoned the man, expecting Gabralina to inherit his estate. That had been her one mistake, because Gabralina fell under suspicion for murder instead. That's how she'd ended up on the altar as a battler sacrifice. Sala had cut her losses at that point, but that letter from her friend had been a gift from the heavens. The potential here was so much greater, and she wouldn't make the same mistake twice.

Sala screamed under Wat's weight. He filled every part of her that could be filled, his body distorted and ugly to do so but perfect for what she wanted. He was part of her plan. So were a lot of other people, whether they planned to become traitors or not. By the end of it, Sala would be queen and finally have everything she was entitled to. She just had to get rid of all the people on the council first, and of course, her precious majesty Solie as well.

Chapter Eight

The healer didn't know what to do. The queen recoiled from her, snarling and ordering her away, forcing her out of the ruling chambers even while the other healers curled up around her, staring. She felt a terrible despair at that, and since it started, the mild itch in her body had slowly grown worse, spreading into her very core.

Was she sick? Was that why the queen was rejecting her? If so, it was no sickness she'd ever seen, and the other healers didn't understand it either—those who were still talking to her, anyway. She couldn't affect the feeling inside her, not even using all her healing skill. The itch just kept burrowing deeper, spreading until it felt like even the pattern that bound her to her queen was beginning to break.

To a sylph, that was the most horrifying destiny possible. Was she going to be thrown out of the hive? Was that to be her fate? Only, healers weren't banished, no more than elemental sylphs were. In her entire life, she'd never seen a female sylph banished. Only battlers were banished—for being too weak or too crippled, or for being unappealing to the queen. They were thrown out, forced to live as exiles with no pattern in them at all, scavenging from other hives if they managed to survive at all. But, she wasn't a battler. This shouldn't be happening!

Frightened and cold despite the warmth the fire sylphs brought to the hive, the nameless one made her way down a twisting corridor toward the chamber of the food sylphs, wanting to soothe herself with their calm. But halfway there she passed a storage room, and the battler on guard there snapped out at her, hate flaring.

The healer recoiled. He was small, young, nothing the queen would ever look at, but his hate aura still blasted through her and sent her recoiling with a surge of terror. Other battlers arrived, attracted by her fright, but they didn't try to comfort her. Those who didn't ignore her growled as well.

Get out! they snarled.

Why? she wailed. *What have I done?*

A battler half her size lunged forward, and she twisted over herself to get away. *You make the queen angry,* he said.

But I've done nothing!

They didn't care. The queen was inviolate though the queen be cruel.

Not understanding, the nameless sylph fled, flitting down a corridor past dozens of sylphs content with their work, all of them knowing just what was expected. The nameless one didn't know that anymore. She was supposed to heal, but she couldn't heal the itching inside of herself, and no one else would let her touch them. Maybe there *was* something wrong with her. She was over twice the size of the next largest healer and faster by far.

She passed another group of battlers, fleeing before they could react and racing outside into the golden light that shone gently down on the hive and its crops. The worst of this was that she could still feel the queen; the pattern link between them was strong, but it felt like it was twisting, distorting. That had to be true, since there was no reason for the queen to ever fear her. What was going on?

Alone and depressed, she made her way across the fields toward the outskirts of the hive territory, just wanting to get away for a while. She wouldn't travel beyond these fields; no sylph did if they could manage it, save battlers on raids, but the borders weren't visited much.

The hive was halfway up a mountain in a mountain range that stretched from end to end for the length of the world, it seemed. The plateau the hive sat on was immense all on its own, enough that she could travel without leaving it until the hive had shrunk in size and was obscured by a faint haze. There the nameless sylph settled down between rows of tall purple plants. Their fruit and leaves were lush and healthy. Moaning miserably, the sylph formed a tentacle and reached out to touch one's smooth surface. Ah, to be a plant. They just got to be what they were, and if they grew larger than everything else, that was seen as a reason for celebration. She moaned again, wanting to go home.

Past the edge of the field, the ground of the plateau turned rocky and sharp, strangled black plants and mosses growing there instead. It dropped with increasing abruptness toward a chasm, a gash in the landscape only a few thousand queen-lengths away. Sometimes *things* crawled out of that chasm, things that hunted sylph energy. Battlers often went in to kill them before they did. Not all of them came back. Beyond the chasm, the mountain dropped down to distant, forested plains and lakes that were no safer.

No, this wasn't a safe world. Everything out here seemed to want to eat either the sylphs or their crops, and even with their battlers a hive couldn't be sure something wouldn't destroy them. They shouldn't be fighting among one another. The nameless sylph stared at the wild landscape beyond the haven elemental sylphs made so long ago, pondering. If they made her an exile, how was she supposed to survive?

They wouldn't, she told herself. They wouldn't make her an exile. She was a healer, and she'd done nothing wrong. She wouldn't leave!

Something moved among the rocks. The nameless sylph froze, terrified, even more so at the sudden realization that battlers might not come to help at her screams. A shadow slid between two jagged boulders, moving toward her, and she shivered, the itch inside suddenly a hundred times worse.

She braced herself to flee. She was fast after all. More than anyone else in the hive, she was fast.

Lightning flickered, and she blinked half a dozen eyes, partly relaxing, mostly confused. A battle sylph slid out between the rocks, floating slowly toward her. He was big, certainly as large as most of the queen's subordinate lovers, but he hunched low to the ground as though he were trying not to attract attention. His energy pattern was hidden, like a newborn hatchling or . . .

She jumped in realization.

Hello, the exile cooed, *beautiful*.

* * *

Adjacent to the queen's underground throne room was a chamber a hundred feet across. The ceiling soared up so high that it erupted out of the ground as a dome of ornate, colored glass ribbed by arching stone. Sunlight made an interesting ripple effect of glowing hues that shone down into the deepest corners of the chamber, entertaining most of the battle sylphs who currently floated there.

The room was big enough to hold them all, with space for more to come. In their natural shape, clouds of battlers would group up here, enjoying the camaraderie and relaxation in a place where they didn't have to worry about frightening any people or being bothered. Each of the sylph breeds had a chamber like it, a place where they could go and just be together, with no need to do anything in particular. Most of these sylph chambers were inaccessible to humans, but the battlers preferred a central location and proximity to the queen.

At the moment, ten of the Valley's fifty battlers floated in the chamber, drifting about halfway up in a mass of cloud and lightning so dense it was hard to make out individual creatures. The closeness was comforting and, in its own way, as important to them as the touch of the women who were their masters.

One sylph floated near the bottom of the mass and under the shadow of the others, his middle distended by the smaller battler he carried within him. Ril was in his natural shape inside Claw's mantle, kept from unraveling by Claw's energy. Even with his injuries, Ril needed to take this shape from time to time in order to relax, just like all the sylphs, and Claw shuddered at the unwilling memory of decades spent in a single form, not allowed to change until the itch threatened to drive him mad. The discomfort made the sleeping battler inside him shift without waking, so Claw wrapped himself more carefully around Ril, frightened by the thought he might drop his friend.

Half dozing beside him, though Ril was the only one of them who truly needed sleep, Dillon flickered his awareness at Claw.

What? he asked in a grumpy tone.

Nothing. Just a bad thought.

You have too many bad thoughts, Dillon said, though there was no real censure and the battler pressed closer against his flank. Above, other battlers pressed down, all of them warm and content. Claw sighed, his turmoil fading more quickly than it ever did when he was alone. Ril's torpor was soothing to them all.

A footstep sounded on the stone floor below, and all of the battlers turned their attention to the door. This room wasn't off limits, exactly, but the only ones to visit were the queen and their masters. There were benches down there so that the women could sit and visit while their battlers floated, and Claw had a sudden, hopeful thought that it was Rachel come to see him. She did from time to time, though the stairs were very steep and hard for her.

It wasn't Rachel. Sala stepped into the room, looking up at the cloud, and he felt a sudden fear/excitement that was different from his reaction to Rachel, or the queen, or anyone else.

Sala walked underneath their cloud, a shawl wrapped around her shoulders, and stared around at the sleek walls. When she turned her head upward, Claw felt another surge. She looked directly at him.

"Claw?"

He shivered, suddenly realizing that he couldn't talk to her in this form, even though he wanted to. He could only speak mentally to other sylphs, the queen, or his master, and he would need to change shape to have vocal cords. To do that, he'd have to drop Ril, who couldn't change from this shape at all without their healer's help. Claw felt a sudden desperate panic that Sala wouldn't understand, that she would leave thinking he didn't want to speak to her.

Dillon pressed close. *Give him to me,* he said.

Thank you!

Dillon rolled upside down underneath him. The other battlers watched, rapt. Like some sort of bizarre mating, Claw pressed against Dillon as they both opened their mantles at the same time, and Ril slid limply from one down into the other.

Zzwha . . . ? Ril managed, not really awake.

Shh, Dillon soothed, wrapping his mantle around him as gently as Claw would have. *Go back to sleep.* Then he turned over and rose back up into the cloud.

Claw flashed down to the floor and shifted into human form. Sala regarded him evenly, her head tilted slightly to one side. The foam green of her shawl brought out sparks of emerald in her eyes, and colored light from the dome shifted across her body. Her emotions were calm as always, and her smile was friendly.

"I thought that was you up there," she said. "What were you doing?"

"Oh." He looked up at the cloud to see eight pairs of ball lightning eyes looking down. Feeling suddenly self-conscious, he guided her out into the hall where it was quieter. "I was holding Ril," he said. "I had to give him to Dillon before I could talk to you."

"Why?"

"Oh. Um, he lost part of his mantle." When her eyebrows rose, he had a sudden, panicked need to explain. "Another battler tore it off. He can't change shape without it hurting, and he can't take his natural form without the healer's help."

"I didn't realize battle sylphs could be hurt so badly."

"Oh, yes. Um, I guess we can hurt each other. Not that we would! Hurt each other. Or anyone. Um."

Sala smiled, turning and leading the way along the wide corridor to the auxiliary stairs that led aboveground. Almost no one used the grand main stairs, which had been designed mainly for dignitaries, though these were narrow and steep.

"I was in the area, so I thought I'd drop by and say hello," she admitted. "I can't stay long, I need to get to the school before class starts. I'm helping Rachel again today. She's such a sweet woman, I absolutely love her."

Claw smiled, happy to hear that she adored his master as much as he did.

"You're very lucky to have her," she went on. "She must be wonderful to you."

"She is. I was a little crazy when they gave me to her." He shrank into himself. "I'm not, though. Crazy, I mean. Really." He winced, feeling stupid.

She laughed as they climbed the stairs and came out into a square behind a stable. "I know you're not. I'd like to hope we can all be friends," she added. "Me, you, and Rachel."

Claw beamed. "Of course!"

Sala left him there at the top of the stairs, hurrying off to help Rachel set up for the day, but not before she gifted him with a final smile. Claw watched her until she was out of sight, his usual nervous turmoil eased. Someone other than his master seemed to like him just for being him.

* * *

Though normally it didn't matter apart from giving a heads-up as to when they were likely to be cranky, battle sylphs could tell when their mortal masters were fertile. Their scents changed in ways that were fascinating, and the battlers stayed close, despite the women's moods. Heyou especially hated to leave Solie when she was fertile, particularly since she didn't turn into a crazy person.

This time, he did.

"Hurry up!" he shouted through the door to Devon's bedroom. "I don't like leaving her alone!"

"Why don't you try leaving *me* alone?" the man shouted back. "I don't do well under pressure!"

Heyou snorted, pacing across the small apartment. Devon had never bothered to have an earth sylph make him a home aboveground, since he really only used the place to sleep.

Hovering in the air by the window, Airi watched. *You frighten him*, she said. Heyou frightened her as well. If she had her way, she and Devon wouldn't have anything to do with battlers.

"So?" Heyou couldn't think of anyone more perfect for this than her master.

Galway had reminded him that there was only one thing that could make a woman pregnant, but he also pointed out that there was no rule stating the donor had to deliver the goods personally. Given Heyou's ability to shapeshift, he just needed to get some male seed, and he could perform the conveyance himself. All he needed was a donor.

Devon Chole. Young, healthy, even-tempered . . . and completely terrified of battlers, which meant he wouldn't be sniffing around for any parental rights. Besides, he was leaving in a very short while, and if he was especially thoughtful, he'd never come back. Solie was going to have a baby, and Heyou fully intended to act as the father. He'd seen fathers with their children. They didn't seem to do much, so how hard could it be?

He might not be able to do this if you frighten him too much, Airi supplied.

"What's to be scared of? Hurry up!" Heyou shouted through the door.

The air sylph sighed. *Devon doesn't want to be a father.*

"Perfect. He won't be. I will."

Are you ready for that?

"Sure. All fathers have to do is yell at their kids and bitch about how they don't behave. Oh, and scare away any suitors who come after them. I'm looking forward to that part."

Oh, Airi said. *There was more to it when Devon was a boy.*

Whatever. Heyou just wanted Solie to be happy. She wanted a baby, so he'd give one to her.

Does the queen know you're doing this? Airi asked.

"No. She likes surprises." Heyou grinned. "I can't wait to see the look on her face." The smile dropped. "How long does it take for women to figure out they're pregnant?"

Weeks? Maybe months?

"But that's forever!"

An inarticulate sound came from the bedroom, and a minute later Devon opened the door. His hair was a mess and he looked exhausted. "Here," he groused, handing over a clay mug.

Heyou looked inside. "That's it?"

Devon slammed the door.

Heyou shrugged and headed outside. He had what he wanted; now he just had to get to Solie and sweep her off her feet.

Airi watched the sylph go, waiting until he was out of sight before going to console her master. Briefly she thought about warning the queen, but there was a simple rule both she and Devon tried to follow: never to get in the way of a battler that wanted something. It made life much easier.

This also solved any last lingering doubt about going to Meridal. Suddenly, neither of them could wait to leave.

* * *

Heyou burst into Solie's garden to find her having biscuits and tea. Lizzy, Loren, and Shore were also there. Solie looked up and gave him her beautiful smile.

"Hi!" Heyou said to her. He looked at the other two women. "Get out."

"Heyou!" Solie protested, but her friends hurried away, sniggering. Heyou's words clearly hadn't offended them. "What's got into . . . ?"

He pounced.

Five minutes later, Solie stared at the ceiling in her bedroom and frowned. That had been very . . . short. Heyou lay lower down on her, his ear pressed against her belly. It was strange.

"Heyou . . ." she began.

"Shh. I'm listening."

Solie lifted her head and looked down past her bare breasts at him. "To what?"

He blinked and winced. "Um, it's a surprise."

Solie stared. What possible surprise could involve her

stomach and such a crazed libido? The possible answer came a few seconds later.

"HEYOU!"

* * *

Solie stood in her living room, her shirt pulled up to expose her stomach. She could barely breathe as Luck ran soft hands over her skin.

Despite their best efforts, Luck was the only healer sylph in the Valley, and she belonged to the most neurotic hypochondriac Solie had ever met. Zem fascinated Luck. No matter how hard she tried, she couldn't put him right. Apparently, that was an attractive trait for a healer sylph's master and there was no doubt that Zem loved her desperately. In every way but the physical, Luck was his wife.

"Am I pregnant?"

Luck straightened. For whatever reason, she had the shape of a softened wax image of a woman. Her features were barely defined, and she glimmered translucently even out of the light. Her voice was clear as she answered her queen's question. "Yes."

"And the baby's healthy?"

"She is."

Solie's breath caught. Her eyes filled with tears. "She? She's a girl?" She turned and beamed at Heyou, who sat on the edge of the dresser against the wall. He returned her smile, and she felt a wave of happiness and love for him that made him croon. He didn't have the faintest notion of what he'd done; she had no doubt about that. He didn't exactly think long-term. But just the fact that he'd done it for her and that she'd have a baby of her own when she'd already given up all hope . . .

She ran forward to hug him, and he dropped to the floor just in time to catch her in his arms. He hugged her tightly as she pressed herself against him and sobbed, "I love you, thank you, I love you!"

She'd have to have a nursery built, knit some clothes. She'd need to send a message to her parents and aunt as well. None of them could read, but she'd have one of the drovers deliver a message as he went through. She hadn't seen them in years, and none of them had accepted her invitation to move here, but she received word and harvest presents from them each year. Maybe if he knew that she was going to be a mother, her father would forgive her for running off with a battle sylph.

She'd have to tell Leon and Galway about the baby, too, and make sure they could take on more of the workload as she got close to giving birth—and when the baby was born. Ril would be able to keep most people away; he'd only been on the job for a few days, and already the foreign ambassadors were terrified—actually, she needed to speak to him about that . . . She'd talk to Rachel and Iyala as well; both of them had been mothers and could tell her most of what she'd need to know.

Behind her, Luck turned and half walked, half floated to the door, her feet hard to see beneath a sweeping floor-length dress that was actually part of the form she'd chosen. She found her master waiting nervously in the hall. His energy was skewed, warped and abnormal, and she reached out, putting a hand against his cheek and focusing. His energy smoothed out, the turmoil fading, but once she drew her hand back, it started to twist again. The experience was fascinating.

"That took longer than I thought," Zem whined. "What about me? Do you have enough left to heal me?"

"Always," she assured him.

Zem sighed, fidgeting as he ostensibly led the way back down into the underground complex. In actuality, he followed her. "I hope she thanked you. You don't have time to spend on just anyone. They don't appreciate us here. Not the way they should. I mean, you're unique. There are hardly any healers anywhere, so you should get paid lots for what you do." He frowned. "We should be rich."

Luck didn't say anything. Zem liked to rant and wail about his lot in life nearly as much as he liked to complain about his health. She couldn't fix that any more than she could his body. It fascinated her, though, and she partially followed but mostly led him toward home without saying anything in response. Zem didn't mind, just going on despite that. He was used to it. Only a few would listen to Zem's constant complaints, and of those, only one person actually agreed with them. Luck sensed her ahead, waiting with a constant, unwavering placidity that Luck couldn't affect any more than she could her own master's illness. She was waiting for them.

* * *

At Leon's request, the *Racing Dawn*, the air ship upon which he and the others had returned from Meridal, had postponed its departure. Its air sylph Ocean Breeze and her master Kadmiel were now waiting to see who they might be taking back to Meridal.

Devon rubbed his arms, standing by his luggage. The bags were filled with his clothes, and also with something more precious: a copy of the treaty Leon drafted before he left Meridal. He'd brought two back with Eapha's signature. One was returning with Solie's.

It'll be okay, Airi whispered, though Devon could feel her nervousness like his own. It was time to leave. A week's flight to Meridal and he'd start his new life. He took a deep breath. It wasn't a new life. It was just a year or so.

"You're not thinking of coming back, are you?"

Devon jumped at the voice, and Airi shrieked silently in his mind. He spun and nearly ran when he saw it was Heyou standing only a few feet away, grinning. Every terror he had about battle sylphs rushed through him, and he had a panicked second to think that his heart might just stop, followed by another when he was afraid it would never stop. Heyou's grin widened.

"Devon!" From behind the battler Solie hurried forward, beaming. She put a hand on Heyou's arm, and the sylph stepped aside with a worried look. She didn't notice. Devon was her whole focus, her entire being aglow. He swallowed, a little bit afraid of what her battler might do to him.

"Ma'am," he managed.

"Oh, don't you ma'am me!" she cried, and she threw her arms around him, hugging him tight. Her soft breasts pressed against him, and Devon tried to feel nothing. "Thank you," she whispered. "Thank you so much. Heyou told me it was you."

Probably not willingly, Devon thought. If the battler had been given a choice, he never would have told anyone. Not how he'd made Solie pregnant. She would have insisted, though, and she seemed so happy.

Devon sighed and put his arms around her, careful to place his hands on her shoulders. "You're welcome," he told her honestly. He hadn't been given a choice in the matter, and having a child he couldn't ever acknowledge if he didn't want to become a pile of ash had never been in his plans. He wasn't really even sure he'd ever wanted a child. But seeing her happy made this meaningful, if not quite worth the terror.

"You're welcome," he told her again, patting her shoulder awkwardly.

Solie giggled and squeezed him for a long moment. Then she let go, stepping back to smile up at him. Tears sparkled in her eyes. "I'll never forget this," she said. "You've given me a gift I can't ever repay."

Devon managed to return her smile. "I'm just glad you're

happy." And, he was. Solie was a kind woman, and she deserved every good thing. His smile widened. "I really am."

"Good," she said. She stroked his cheek, her eyes damp and shiny. "Be safe, Devon. Promise me that, will you?"

"I promise."

She looked over his shoulder. "And you, Airi. You be safe as well."

Oh yes, my queen. I will.

Solie smiled again at both of them. "I should let Leon talk to you. I think he has a few more instructions." She wiped her eyes. "Thank you both for everything!" Then she turned and ran away, going to Heyou and pressing her face against his chest. He took her greedily into his arms.

I don't understand why she's crying if she's so happy, Airi said.

"I think I do," Devon whispered. Turning, he found a somewhat bemused Leon.

* * *

Rachel stirred the soup in the big pot while Claw set the table behind her. He didn't eat food the way she did, but he sat with her for meals whenever his schedule allowed. For him, she'd discovered, her willing presence was the greatest indication she could give of her love. She enjoyed his company, so it was easy. And when they were alone, he wasn't nearly so nervous.

Carefully ladling soup for herself, she turned and carried it to the table. Claw held her chair out, and once she sat with the bowl, he helped push the chair in. Grabbing the big bread knife on the counter, he started to carve the loaf of bread that Sala brought earlier. It was still fresh enough that steam rose from its insides, and he spread butter on top just the way Rachel liked.

Happy. Claw felt happy. Rachel sensed his emotions refreshingly clearly, and he hummed under his breath a lullaby she had sometimes sung to him when he first came to her. That had been back in the days when he was too terrified to even come to her bed for fear she'd hurt him. She'd had troubles herself. Being able to share emotions with him had been hard, but no harder than she was sure it had been for him; and by forcing herself to project emotions that wouldn't make him cringe, she'd made it so that she started feeling those emotions for real. In healing Claw, Rachel found she conquered many of the demons arising from her husband's death and the betrayal of her children.

She smiled at him and accepted the bread he offered. "I gather you had a good day?"

He nodded and sank into a chair. He'd taken off his jacket when he came home, and his hair was shockingly blue against the white of his shirt. "Sala came to visit me."

Rachel beamed. "She told me. I was so pleased."

It was good to see Claw making a friend. The battle sylphs were closely knit, but Claw had few human connections. Those who could get past the fact that he was a battler were often frightened by the belief that he was crazy, and Claw's strong reactions to negative emotions didn't help. Sala had been able to see through that, and Rachel reached out to grasp her battler's hand.

"I'm so glad you have a friend," she said, picking up her spoon.

"Me, too," he admitted, ducking his head. "Do you mind at all?"

"Of course not." Rachel swept her wrinkled hand across the table to indicate the soup and bread and steaming tea. "She came by and brought all this food. Said she couldn't imagine leaving someone who reminds her so much of her own grandmother to cook for herself." Rachel laughed. "Silly girl. Her grandmother! Still, her heart's in the right place."

She took a sip of the soup. It had a bitterness that she didn't quite like, but she wasn't one to turn down a free meal. She'd just have to find out what particular spice that was and ask Sala to use a little bit less.

"Are you all right?" Claw asked, sensing her dismay.

"Of course, love. Be a dear and pour me some tea."

He did so, and Rachel finished her soup. She started on the tea next, which had the same odd taste, but a dollop of fresh honey took care of the bitterness and she settled back in her seat with a contented sigh. "Yes, her heart's in the right place, even if her cooking isn't."

Though he still couldn't voice it, a flicker of Claw's need came to her. She extended an arm. "Come here."

He immediately shuffled his chair closer. Leaning forward, he laid his head against her breast. She wrapped her arms around him and closed her eyes, listening to his breathing change to long, deep inhalations and exhalations. There was hardly ever a pause.

He was feeding; she knew that. She couldn't feel him draw off her excess energy, but they had formalized the process and she was always aware when he did. Most of the other battlers preferred to go to their masters for energy several times a day, but Claw came to her only once, drawing everything he would need. It generally left her sleepy, which was convenient given her chronic insomnia.

Claw finished and shifted his arms around her, slipping out of his chair and lifting Rachel in his arms. Knowing her usual reaction, she'd put on her nightdress, and he carried her into the bedroom now and settled her on the bed.

"Sweet boy," she murmured, reaching up to cup his cheek. Then she pulled him down for the last of their nightly traditions.

"I love you, Claw," she murmured a while later, worn out but sated. She dozed off in his naked arms, nestled in the warmth of the many blankets.

Feeling that she was asleep, Claw kissed Rachel's forehead and settled down beside her. She hadn't heard his answering words of adoration. Though he didn't need sleep, he had no intention of being anywhere else for the night. He didn't have to leave until the next morning.

There came a distant crash and far-off screams of pain. Stiffening, Claw felt both the terror and pain of others. Roars followed, battlers being summoned, and he felt them moving, their rage washing over everything.

Claw glanced down at Rachel. She was still asleep, her wrinkled hand lax on the pillow beside her equally wrinkled face. He swallowed. He had to go; the hive was in danger.

Gently he leaned down and kissed his master, feeling so much love that he didn't want to leave. But the others needed him. That was absolute. The hive needed him.

He kissed Rachel one more time and slid out of bed. Scooping up his clothes, he flashed into the shape of a lightning-streaked cloud, his uniform inside his mantle, and flew out of the cottage toward the threat.

Chapter Nine

The largest warehouse in the Valley was one of the crowning glories of the town. It rose four stories into the air, the roof made of translucent colored glass that let in sunshine and reduced by far the number of lamps or fire sylphs that were needed. Heavy metal shelving was stacked in dozens of rows, all packed with goods either brought to the Valley or meant to be exported.

With the majority of townspeople still rising at dawn and going to bed with the sun, most of the work here was done during daylight hours. Sylphs were active at night, of course, but they were mostly left to their own devices. This sometimes resulted in people waking up to find that groups of sylphs had become inventive during the night and created something. Occasionally, it was something huge. The warehouse was just such an event. So were enough stables to house a thousand horses, and one building with a pointed roof that reached nearly a hundred feet in the air. No one had figured out what to use it for yet.

When a caravan arrived, though, no one went home early. Well after dusk the warehouse was still full of people and sylphs working to unload, unpack, set up. Dozens of locals labored to move goods from the wagons and pass them to air sylphs who carried them up for storage on the higher shelves. While this happened, the wagon masters argued with the warehouse mistress.

Today they'd been in disagreement over where the wagon drivers were going to sleep and who was supposed to pay for their rooms. It was at the peak of this fight that one of the huge shelves lurched forward. It shuddered at first, no one even noticing, but then slowly tilted and began to tumble down, the beams screaming as they twisted and tore, showering bystanders with lumber, wool, metal, and more. All came crashing down, for the first shelf slammed into others, creating a cascade of destruction like collapsing dominoes.

It lasted only seconds. For a moment there was nothing but the sound of debris rolling across the uneven floor, as well as the wails of injured men and frightened animals. Then a roaring started, distant but growing louder.

Before the survivors could even fully grasp what had happened, battle sylphs were there, thunderous and raging around the warehouse as thick, flickering clouds. They didn't use hate auras, but their presence caused some to flee in fear. Others tried desperately to dig free those trapped beneath debris.

Frantic, the woman who ran the warehouse and the caravan master struggled to move a huge pile of sawn lumber from a man whose outstretched hand was all they could see. It clutched the floor by their feet. Moments later, Mace pushed both mortals aside and grabbed the edge of a log. Hauling it up, he tossed the entire piece to Heyou, who caught and threw it to Dillon, who carried it away.

More battlers crowded around, some acting as guards, others helping remove rubble. Other sylphs joined in, hundreds of them, many hysterical about their now-trapped masters.

Panting through gritted teeth, Leon sprinted down the street toward the accident. He had his pants and shirt on, but his jacket was at home and his suspenders flopped around his waist as he tried to get them back over his shoulders while he ran. He'd been getting undressed for bed when he'd heard the crash, and he'd barely got out of his room in time to see Ril shoot down the stairs. The battler was well ahead of him now, still in human shape but immensely faster.

All around him, Leon saw people standing on their porches, staring in fear and confusion toward the black dust rising in the distance but doing nothing. He even saw Wat flicker past in the wrong direction, his lightning sparkling more slowly than usual.

Footsteps sounded behind him, and Lizzy pulled abreast. Her face was red, for she ran nearly flat out, her skirts raised in both hands. She looked like she was floating in the layer of froth around her knees. Her hair was down and streamed behind her like silk.

"What are you doing?" he panted, hating how he sounded. He was in better shape than this.

"Helping," she grunted, and she put on speed, leaving her father behind as she raced after Ril.

Leon swore under his breath, but he also grinned, and chasing his daughter became a race between them to the accident site.

Mace directed the sylphs silently and the humans aloud, bellowing orders to get debris moved and the wounded found—and to watch that ceiling. He wasn't so sure it wouldn't come down as well. Stria, one of the earth sylphs who'd erected the building, stood beside him, wringing her hands and moaning.

The big battler wasn't sorry to see Leon arrive a minute or so after Ril, who was put to work moving rubble; he didn't much care to be in charge of humans. Most were men, and he didn't have any interest in those. Women he wouldn't send anywhere there was danger. Mace nodded to the chancellor and leaped into the air, shifting to cloud form and rising up to the glass ceiling. Fire sylphs floated there, giving illumination to those below.

Keep that light up, Mace told one as he heard Leon start barking different orders below. *Get close enough so they can see but be careful not to set anything on fire*. He didn't know for sure what was stored in this place, and he berated himself for his lack of knowledge.

Yes, Mace. The fire sylph shot downward, moving closer to some of the human and sylph rescuers. The sylphs were doing most of the heavy lifting, but humans did their own part, mainly moving the dead and wounded.

Below, Leon found Ril. He grabbed the battler's shoulder. "Has Luck been called?" he asked, already coughing from the dust that had been kicked up.

The battler peered over his shoulder at his master, then pushed him out of the dust cloud. Glancing up and contacting Mace provided a quick if silent answer. "Yes," he relayed. "She's on the way."

"Good." Leon sighed, staring at the carnage. There was no telling yet how many wounded or dead were in the wreckage, and without Luck most of them wouldn't have a chance.

Even with her, it looked like it was going to be a long night.

* * *

It was. Solie arrived soon after Leon, and she labored all night long with the others, setting up rubble removal stations and places for the injured to be brought. Galway directed the latter area, along with his wife Iyala and older children. Lizzy, too; and while her father might have preferred to spare her the sight of injured and dying people, he never refused her the right to make up her own mind.

At the Widow Blackwell's suggestion, Gabralina spent the night scurrying through the chaos carrying a bucket of water and a dipper to the workers. The men and women were thirsty from their efforts, and they thanked her for the relief she brought. She smiled but kept moving, feeling scared and restless at the same time.

Wat. He was confused. That was hardly unusual for him, but the battler felt off-kilter where he resonated in the back of her mind, and she'd started to worry that he had been hurt somehow in this accident. She didn't see him anywhere, and she'd know if he was in pain—wouldn't she? Leon said he knew whenever Ril was hurt.

She eyed the bearded man, who was busy directing the last of the wounded out of the warehouse. She wished she had his confidence. She knew she'd been a trial for him when he and his battler brought her and Wat to the Valley, but she hadn't meant to be. She hadn't even thanked him for saving her. She should have, certainly. She'd been in a terrible situation when he came, and if he hadn't come to her rescue, she'd have been killed and her poor defenseless Wat someone's slave. She knew that, and yet she still hadn't thanked him. She hadn't even told him she was in love with him a little.

She just didn't ever want to think about her past. One moment she'd been the somewhat bored and periodically beaten mistress of Yed's head magistrate, the next he was dead and despite all her protests she was being charged with murder. She'd been so terribly alone.

Gabralina swallowed and walked over to him, filling her dipper with water and holding it up. "Thirsty?" she asked.

Leon glanced down at her and smiled, his face tired and dirt-streaked. "Thanks," he said and took it. After draining it, he handed the empty dipper back and clapped his hand on her shoulder. "Good work."

Gabralina sighed as he turned back to his task. According to the sylphs, the wounded were all out now, and most of the remaining debris could wait for daylight. Already Solie was sending people and sylphs home. A few moments later, Gabralina was one of them.

She left with another sigh, her bucket abandoned and forgotten. She still hadn't thanked Leon, she realized as she trudged off to her empty bed. And, Wat. Where had her battle sylph gone to?

* * *

Claw let himself back into Rachel's house as quietly as he could. Shivering slightly, he latched the door and pulled off his boots, setting them neatly by the coatrack where he hung his jacket. It was filthy. He hated it when it got filthy, because Rachel had to clean it. He'd tried to do laundry himself, but he always shrank everything. Rachel suggested he got the water too hot, but that didn't make much sense.

Twenty-three people were dead in the warehouse accident, along with seven sylphs and a dozen oxen. Claw didn't know for sure how many were injured—that was Luck's job—but he'd seen how exhausted she was when Mace finally sent him away.

He crossed the tiny sitting room and entered the back bedroom. He was tired himself after so long lifting rubble; he just wanted to curl up and maybe even go to sleep for a little bit himself.

Able to see through the darkness, he moved toward the bed. Rachel lay there, curled on her side with her face turned toward the door. She seemed almost to be looking at him. She lay very still, and he realized for the first time that he couldn't feel her presence, not even the little tiny bit she normally exuded when asleep. Claw paused, puzzled, then moved closer.

She didn't look like she was asleep.

Claw whimpered, suddenly shaking so badly that he nearly

fell. *Luck*. He needed to get Luck. Only, Luck was exhausted and working on a dozen people who would die without her, and she was on the other side of the town, and he knew already that . . .

The blue-haired battle sylph climbed gently into bed, careful not to disturb Rachel as he crawled over to her side and lay down, arms around her. She might be cold, he decided. She liked it when he lay with her, especially when he was there when she woke in the morning.

He whimpered one last time, a sound like no creature born of this world, and then was silent again, lying with his master in the dark.

* * *

Mace made his rounds with a dozen other battle sylphs. The warehouse was now secure. Well, the building was too dangerous for humans to enter, but everyone was out.

He didn't like this. Such disasters were never supposed to happen in a hive, and the fact that the queen wasn't blaming any of them only made it worse. So he searched for threats he could stop before they threatened the hive, tracking negative emotions throughout the entirety of the town. There were many. People were scared by what had happened, upset. Almost everyone seemed to know someone who had died or been hurt, and the town resonated with their collective pain. The big battler was looking for more, though. Some emotions alerted him to danger. Those always gave humans away.

Mace found an angry little boy planning to leave home because his parents wouldn't give him a puppy; a single glare through the window dissuaded him. He tracked down a woman furious at her husband for being late, her house on the far side of the town where she hadn't heard about the accident. Mace told her the situation and she was gone, running to look for her husband at the warehouse. Mace had seen him up and mobile, but that didn't matter; Mace let the woman run off, knowing she'd be safe.

Next he found Justin Porter glaring hatefully at the Petrule house from the shadows. Mace knew the story of what happened between him and Ril, but even if he hadn't, he would be drawn to that hate. Other battlers were as well. Justin had almost daily encounters with battle sylphs now, all due to his temper, which was only making matters worse. Mace didn't care. If it weren't for the queen's rules, Justin would already be dead.

Ril wasn't home. Leon, either. The house was full of females, which set off Mace's protective instincts. The big battler started to move forward as one of the females passed the lit front window: Lizzy, back from her efforts at the warehouse.

Justin's anger immediately changed to a helpless, hopeless love. He watched Lizzy moving through the house, pacing back and forth, and Mace stopped unnoticed behind him. Justin loved the girl. Mace didn't really care about that; Lizzy was Ril's master and he'd gone through worse than hell to get her. Justin had no place in any of that. But love was an unthreatening emotion, and so long as Justin didn't try to force himself on the girl, he could continue to feel it. Mace would warn Ril that the boy had been there, but otherwise he'd do nothing.

He slipped away without Justin ever realizing he'd been seen. But the battler had been distracted by other things, and in return he hadn't felt how that love overlaid a subtle additive of obsession.

* * *

Mace continued his sweep, checking on the queen and marveling for a moment at her sleeping, pregnant energy. Heyou lay in bed beside her and looked smug. That little donor trick the young battler pulled would make things very different for battle sylphs in the future. They wanted to fight, they wanted to mate, but in the secret silences of their minds, many of them wanted to be fathers. Heyou had first given them a queen. Now he'd given them a way to be parents as well.

He nodded at the young sylph, sure Heyou would be insufferable about this, and slipped away from the window, not wanting to wake the queen. Slipping down into the underground hive where classes had been canceled for the night, he saw almost no one at all. The corridors were empty, and at last he floated down to the holding cell used for the assassins. The door was unguarded. Only one battler had been assigned, but there was no sign of him.

Mace wrenched the door open and snarled his way down the stairs, his hate flaring out as he reached the lower level. This door was unguarded as well and wide-open. Mace stopped in the archway, seeing the abandoned cots, the empty privy, and some tossed-aside blankets. Furious, he roared, broadcasting his rage to every battle sylph in the Valley. They in turn began roaring, rising, ready to hunt and do battle. The assassins were free, the queen was threatened, the hive in danger. A battle sylph had failed in his duty.

Mace backed out of the cell, his lightning swirling in a maelstrom of rage. Heyou was head battler as the lover of the queen, but Mace made the rules and assigned the duties. He thought back to the schedule he'd made for all the battle sylphs, all of it kept in his head instead of on paper. He knew exactly who was supposed to be watching this cell tonight.

Wat.

* * *

The battle sylphs all gathered high above the clouds, where the air was cold and clear, the dawning sun still hours away from topping the mountains. Heyou had been granted permission to stay back, but that was strictly so he could guard the sleeping queen; when Mace left, he'd been growling with suppressed anger. Even Ril had come, a red-feathered hawk circling among them, his eyes still a little red from the pain of his change.

Where's Claw? someone asked.

YOU! Mace thundered, flaring out at a much smaller, slower battler. *WHY DID YOU LEAVE?*

Wat squealed in terror, trying to run, but the battlers were everywhere, suddenly closing around him, blocking him in. They pushed him back toward Mace, who hit him with his hate. Wat squealed again and tried to flee, tried to hide from all of their anger. There was no way out.

WHY DID YOU LEAVE THE ASSASSINS UNGUARDED?

I don't know! the young battler wailed. Even terrified, his energy flickered slower than everyone else's. *I forgot!*

You forgot? How could you possibly forget?

Circling above, Ril screamed. Dillon hissed, lashing out with a tentacle at the ignorant Wat, who squealed again and tried to present himself as a smaller target.

I forgot! There was the accident! I came to the accident!

I didn't see you at the accident, Mace thundered.

I-I realized then that I wasn't supposed to be there! Then I didn't know what to do.

So, he'd been too stupid to go back to the cell. Ignorant, foolish, idiotic . . . Mace roared and delivered Wat a blow that would have torn him in two if he hadn't pulled back at the last moment. Wat still tumbled away with the force of it, squealing in terror.

Useless, stupid reject. He would have been killed in the home hive. Inferior, foolish . . . The queen had her rules, though. Much as he wanted to, Mace couldn't kill Wat. From the rage of the others, they agreed, but none of them moved against the idiotic creature. Wat whimpered brokenly, too stupid even to realize that he wasn't going to be destroyed.

No more, Mace growled at him. *You'll guard no more.*

Wat looked at him without comprehension.

You won't wear the uniform, you won't stand guard, you won't come to any calls. You're not a battle sylph to us anymore.

Wat shivered, not really getting it, not understanding that he'd been ostracized by his brothers and what it really meant. He did grasp that he wasn't going to be murdered, and after a frightened hesitation he flickered downward, racing away from them as fast as he could, returning to his master.

Mace watched him go for only a moment. He turned to the others and said, *Spread out. Find those men.*

He didn't need to say anything more. The battle sylphs vanished in every direction, sweeping low to the ground in a crisscrossing pattern as they searched for the five escaped assassins. Only one stayed behind, circling Mace, wings beating against the still cold air.

Where's Claw? Ril asked again.

* * *

The sun was coming up, lighting the room through the lace curtains Rachel knitted so patiently during the evenings of one long winter, working by the light of an oil lamp while Claw watched; he'd been nearly hypnotized by the motion of her hands as she produced yards of airy material from what looked to him to be string and two sticks.

The early morning light glistened off the edges of her hair, though most of her still lay in shadow, blocked by his body lying next to her, pressed against her back. She was cold. Despite his attempts to keep her warm, she was cold and still. Lifeless.

Claw whimpered again, shivers running through him. He cooed, trying to communicate with her but not able to form words.

Footsteps sounded in the room outside. Mace and Ril appeared in the doorway.

Claw screamed, his voice shrill and inhuman. He could feel the panic that caused throughout the town, other sylphs echoing his cry, humans starting in fear, but he couldn't stop. He could only shriek his agony, terror, grief, horror. He kept on screaming as the other battlers descended on him, not sure he'd ever be able to stop, only knowing that Rachel wasn't answering him in her soft, gentle, loving voice, knowing that no matter how long or loud he screamed, Rachel would never answer him again.

Chapter Ten

Solie was carried in Heyou's mantle from her palace to Rachel's home. She was worn out from the accident the night before, and she'd woken early to be told that the five assassins escaped. Now this.

She could feel Claw's pain and hysteria beating against her with all of the battle sylph's strength. The other sylphs in the Valley had picked up his distress and were wailing as well, though their screams were nowhere near as fierce. He felt like a creature about to go mad.

"Oh, Heyou," she whispered. Poor Rachel. Poor dear Rachel. Poor Claw.

Don't get too close to him, Heyou cautioned.

He wouldn't have brought her anywhere near this place if he'd had the choice, Solie knew, and she shared his fear. Battle sylphs could go crazy, and Claw had always hovered near the edge. Without Rachel, Claw was totally alone. Without Rachel, he could only feed from Solie, his queen. She put a protective hand over her belly. She hadn't needed Luck to warn her not to spend any energy on sylphs during her pregnancy. Claw would need someone new. Only, who? And how could they do that to the poor creature so soon after losing Rachel?

Heyou dropped to the ground and released her. Solie stood on the street in front of a row of small, bizarrely organic-looking houses that looked like round puffballs given windows and chimneys. A dozen battlers stood in one front yard, staring at the open door.

Crashing crockery and furniture sounded from inside. Claw's screams were nonstop, piercing her ears until Solie had to stick her fingers in them. A flurry of sylphs hurried through the air farther down the road, including a few battlers in their natural form, and the neighbors gathered on the road itself, murmuring and looking nervously at the house. Solie didn't blame them. A single battler could destroy the entire Valley if they weren't stopped.

"Will he be okay?" she whispered to Heyou.

"I don't know. None of us who had masters before ever cared when they died."

He stood close to her, partly to protect her and partly, Solie suspected, out of the nervousness that she might die and leave him the way Rachel left Claw. It was inevitable, of course. Sylphs were nearly immortal. Humans were not. Quietly she reached out to take his hand, and his answering squeeze was almost painful.

Another crash sounded from inside the house, and Ril suddenly stumbled out. He was dragging Claw, his arms wrapped around the frantic battler's body. Claw was still screaming, his eyes wide and crazed, but he made no attempt to fight back. The screaming didn't stop, not even as the pair tripped and fell, landing on the front lawn and rolling, Ril still hanging on to Claw. Mace stepped out of the house next and looked straight at Solie, his face impassive. His emotions felt disturbed. No sylph was unmoved.

Solie hurried forward, Heyou still holding her hand and keeping himself between her and Claw. She could hear Ril cooing to him. The sound vibrated through her bones as she dropped to her knees only a few feet away.

"Claw! Claw, please stop screaming. It's going to be all right, I promise!"

The battler stopped, unable to disobey, but the hysteria didn't leave his face and he shuddered uncontrollably. Ril wrapped his legs around Claw's body as he had his arms, murmuring reassurances. Solie couldn't be sure how much of it Claw absorbed, and her eyes filled with tears. She kept on talking, not even sure of what she was saying anymore, just trying to pierce the misery that consumed him. He lay there whimpering, and the sound tore at her heart.

"Oh, Claw," she mourned.

"Claw? Claw!"

Solie saw Sala pushing through the crowd, showing more emotion than Solie had ever seen from her. The young woman's eyes were wide, her brows raised as she hiked up her skirts and ran across the road and onto the lawn.

"What's going on?" she demanded, dropping down beside Claw and Ril. She looked toward the house. "What's happening? Where's Rachel?"

Claw made an inquiring sort of coo, and he stretched his head in her direction.

Sala didn't seem to notice. "Where's Rachel? Rachel!"

Solie grabbed the woman's arm as she began to rise. "Rachel has . . . passed away," she whispered. Claw still heard her and he howled.

"Oh, no." Sala bent over, her breasts against her knees. She wrapped her arms around Claw's head, and her hair fell forward to hide both their faces. Ril leaned back, not letting go but watching.

Mace watched, too. "Girl," he said, crouching down next to Sala and the blue-haired battler. When Sala eyed him, he asked, "Claw needs a master. Will you do it?"

"Of course," Sala said.

A twinge of doubt filled Solie; there was something about Sala that didn't sit quite right with her. But this was an emotional moment, and it was hard to think with all these feelings flying around. Claw had stopped wailing, though he still shook.

Mace reached out and put one hand on Claw, another on Sala. He focused, and Solie felt his energy move and interact with her own. This was the only time he ever touched her energy, but using it now, he took the pattern inside Sala and the energy that was Claw and combined them, binding the battler to the young woman forever. As long as Sala lived, Claw would be hers, and so long as she had him, Sala could never bind another sylph.

It only took a second, and Sala blinked as she felt Claw's emotions for the first time, carried to her along the patterns that bound them. For his part, Claw shuddered and lay still, his eyes wide.

Gingerly, Ril let go and rolled back.

"He needs to rest," Mace told Sala. "Take him to wherever you're sleeping and stay with him."

This was an important time for the couple, a private time, and all the sylphs moved away, giving them space. Heyou's hand under her arm, Solie rose, too. She backed away, still not sure about this, but the battlers seemed content. They would know, wouldn't they?

Solie let Heyou lead her away. Behind her, Sala stood and brushed off her skirts, watching silently as her new battle sylph finally managed to get to his feet and join her.

* * *

None of the sylphs who witnessed Claw's grief returned to their duties right away. Instead, slowly, as though there weren't anything unusual happening, they drifted to where their masters were, to see and hold them and reassure themselves that they weren't like Claw, that their masters were still very much healthy and alive. The other sylphs all did the same, and by nightfall the word had spread and every sylph was with his or her master, all of them frightened and secretly relieved that it hadn't been them to suffer such a loss, even though they knew someday it would be.

Ril went home, hearing the Petrule women chattering as he strode up onto the porch and in through the door. They were in the front room, Lizzy knitting a shawl while Betha showed Cara how to sew together patches for a quilt, and the younger girls played on the floor. Lizzy glanced up, immediately recognizing her battler's mood. He crossed the room and reached for her.

"What—?" Betha said as the blond battler silently pulled her daughter to her feet and into his embrace. His face buried against her neck, he just held Lizzy. The shawl she'd been working on tangled at their feet.

"What's wrong?" Betha demanded, rising, but Lizzy shot her a look and waved her back with one hand.

"It's okay," Lizzy whispered, holding Ril. "Whatever it is, it's okay." He just tightened his grip, still not speaking.

The others were dumbstruck. Mia stuck her thumb in her mouth and looked like she was about to cry. Nali slid over and took the three-year-old into her arms while Ralad just stared.

"What's wrong with Ril, Momma?"

"I don't know," Betha admitted.

A boot heel sounded on wood, and Leon walked in. He looked tired. When he saw his battler hugging his oldest daughter, he stopped.

Ril opened his eyes and glanced slowly toward his first master, the man who'd killed the girl used to lure him across the gate and bound him to silent slavery for fifteen years. He studied Leon and lashed out a hand, bunching up in his fist the cloth of Leon's shirt. Leon's eyes widened, and then Ril yanked him into the embrace. Lizzy giggled.

Putting his arms around them both, Ril closed his eyes again. He had other masters—the men who'd been his feeders back in Meridal, and Justin, who'd come home with him—but none of those mattered. He wouldn't care if they lived or died, would never think to come to their aid. But these two . . .

"I don't know what's wrong," Lizzy whispered to her father. "He's upset."

Leon just stood, returning Ril's embrace. "I see that. Girls, out."

The children shuffled out. Betha followed, watching her husband uncertainly. He nodded to her, so she herded the kids toward the back of the house.

Alone, Lizzy, Leon, and Ril stood in their three-way hug, their arms wrapped around one another.

"What is it?" Leon whispered, his breath warm on Ril's ear. The battler just held him closer, not wanting to speak.

Of course, with these two, he didn't have to speak. He told them silently, *Claw's master died.*

"Oh—" Lizzy started to say, but her father shushed her. They all just stood, holding one another, letting their battler draw energy and comfort for as long as he needed.

* * *

Mace returned to Lily's house well after dark. Sitting in the front room and doing their homework by lamplight, several of the orphans she fostered looked up as he walked through the front door, but Mace just strode to the kitchen. That was the heart of this home; it was where he'd find her.

She was cleaning up the last of the dishes from the day's baking, while Gabralina knitted socks. The pair had been chatting calmly, the younger of the two dropping stitches as she talked, but Lily stilled and looked past her when Mace entered.

"What's wrong?" she demanded. Gabralina stared over her shoulder.

"Rachel died," he said. "Claw had to be given to a new master."

Lily's lips thinned. Though none of it showed on her face, she was pained. Rachel had been a friend.

She looked at Gabralina. "Get the rest of the children to bed and take yourself home."

Gabralina nodded and set her knitting in the basket. She wasn't the smartest person Mace had ever seen, but she didn't lack in compassion. She hurried out to do as instructed.

Lily turned fully away from the sink, drying her hands on a towel. "That's . . ." she started to say. "That's . . ." A tear trickled down her cheek. "Oh, now I'm being foolish."

Mace crossed the kitchen and put his arms around her. "Never foolish," he murmured, his arms sliding around to press her closer against him. "Not my Lily."

It took a moment before her arms came around him as well. Lily hated weakness in herself more than others. Mace knew how lucky he was to have her. He was domineering and proud, used during his slavery to flexing the aura of his lust at any woman he wanted and having her lift her skirts. Not after Lily. She wouldn't allow it. It was just the two of them.

He wanted to make love to her, wanted to reaffirm their bond as he was sure every other battle sylph in the Valley was doing. He still had assassins to hunt down, and none of them could figure out how they'd escaped, but he needed this.

Lily pushed her hands against his chest, forcing him back so that she could look up at him. "Who's the new master?" she asked.

"Her name is Sala," Mace said. "A friend to Gabralina." He didn't know much else about the young woman, other than she was spending more and more time with the queen and her friends these days.

"Will she make a good master?"

"I don't see why not. I can't sense anything malicious about her at all."

Lily sighed and leaned against him again. "That's good. Now, take me to bed, Mace. I don't want to think about anything more. Not tonight."

He did, and she didn't.

Chapter Eleven

The exile was the only one happy to see her anymore.

In the hive, the alienation continued. It was growing worse. The nameless sylph wasn't allowed in the queen's chamber anymore, or where the food sylphs were fed and milked. Or in the chamber with the hatchlings and eggs. That last restriction hurt the worst, for she longed to see the eggs and the tiny babies coiled in their beds.

She wasn't allowed into the energy stores either, though that rule was still only loosely enforced. She managed to get enough to feed herself—and her new friend as well. Half in and half out of a storage room now, guarded by a small, sullen little battler, she scooped up balls of energy, tucking them into her mantle.

You done yet? he groused.

She grabbed a few more, tucking them inside herself with the others. Some were for her, some were for her friend, and a lot was to hoard just in case. The impossible horror of "just in case" seemed to be becoming more probable every day, and a deep, rippling itch speared her, making the nameless sylph shudder.

What are you doing? the battler demanded.

Almost done, she replied, scooping up an entire pile and hoping he didn't notice how much fatter she was with the energy hidden inside. When she backed out of the room, the battler eyed her dully. He was obviously of an inferior mating, doomed to always be small and stupid, his lightning slow and sluggish. She wondered for a moment what had happened to his father. But, she knew, didn't she? His father might well be the battler hiding on the outskirts of the field—though he'd said he'd never been with a queen.

Thank you, she said to the little battler, turning and hurrying away before he could get too close a look.

He glared after her. *Don't come back!* he shouted, making her glad she'd hoarded all she had. There were many storage rooms in the hive, but if even the dullards were picking up on her disgrace, she'd lose access to them all very soon.

The nameless sylph glanced in the direction of the queen's chambers and for a moment felt an instant of deep hatred, but she quickly suppressed it. Malice would just bring battlers. Instead, she made her way toward one of the exits, taking a circuitous route that kept her away from as many battle sylphs as possible. Not all of them were as dim as the one she'd just left.

As usual, she was mostly ignored, except for some elementals cringing away from her and a few glaring battlers. None of them said anything.

The nameless sylph flitted out of the hive and away across the fields, her back itching almost unbearably, and she finally put on some altitude so that the earth and water sylphs who tended the crops wouldn't get too close a look at her. She found the exile near where she'd left him the previous day, desolately munching on a few leaves from a purple plant while he waited.

At the sight of her, he perked up immensely, his inner lightning increasing in speed. Being around him made the itch inside a hundred times worse, but who else did she have to be with? Her kind wasn't designed to be alone.

* * *

"So, they escaped while the rest of us were dealing with the accident at the warehouse?"

Mace stood immobile at the door. "Presumably."

Leon frowned, hunkering down and lifting the edge of a blanket abandoned in the prison cell. There was nothing under it. He dropped the blanket and rubbed his jaw. "Left during, or caused the accident in order to cover their escape?"

"We would have known," Mace said.

Leon sighed and straightened, looking past the big battler to where Ril leaned casually against the wall. Solie stood next to him, alongside Heyou and Galway. With all of them there, the room was getting a bit crowded. Ril blinked at him and smirked.

"Let's back out, shall we?" Leon suggested.

They returned to the main conference room, where Heyou shut the doors. Dillon stood guard outside, currently shaped like a mix of a lion and an eagle. Leon rubbed the back of his head, kicking himself.

"I should have thought of this," he grumbled. Too many things were happening at once, what with getting Lizzy back and reacquainting himself with his family, preparing Devon for a mission to a far-off land, and then the accident.

"Thought of what?"

Leon glanced at Mace, pretty sure he'd need to demonstrate in order to prove his suspicions to the creature. The sylph was intelligent but could be tremendously inflexible. Proud.

"There's a way to outwit a battler."

Mace's expression didn't change, but his thoughts about Leon's statement made Ril growl. Heyou stepped in front of Solie while Dillon peered in, his posture tense.

Leon returned the big battler's stare, knowing that, more than any of the other sylphs, Mace hated men. He'd despised his original master, and Jasar's eventual death had been truly unpleasant. For Leon to still be alive as Ril's master was undoubtedly incomprehensible for him.

"It's how I stayed alive in Meridal," Leon explained. "You react to malice, to negative emotions. I controlled what I felt, and I was able to escape notice while they were hunting for me." He rubbed his bearded jaw thoughtfully. "I wouldn't have expected these four to be able to control their emotions enough. We wouldn't have caught them in the first place if they were."

"Someone must have helped," Solie suggested. "They must have caused the accident at the warehouse to draw the battlers off and then freed these men while everyone was distracted."

They were all quiet for a moment, chilled.

Leon rubbed his beard again. "They managed to time it for right when Wat wandered away from his post?" He let his hand drop. "We have someone we need to talk to."

* * *

Gabralina sat nervously in a chair in front of Leon's desk, Wat's hand clasped in both of hers. Wat sat beside her, looking uncharacteristically serious in a plain brown tunic and pants instead of his previous blue and gold. For once he grasped how dire the situation was, and she squeezed his hand tight as she felt his uncertainty, as well as his instinctive need to attack and destroy all that threatened him.

She tightened her grip, silently pleading with him to be still. He blinked at her and returned the squeeze before returning his stare to the man behind the desk.

It felt just like when she'd been in the Yed court, men screaming that she'd seduced the magistrate and set herself up as his mistress so that she could poison his food. That she'd altered his will so she'd receive everything he owned. She'd pleaded with them that she hadn't, that she'd innocently met him through her friend Sala and never harmed him. She'd never seen this will they spoke of. She didn't even know how to write!

They hadn't listened. Whore, they'd called her. Murderer. She'd been sentenced to death. At least this time she wasn't alone and no one was screaming.

Leon leaned forward, his hands clasped. Ril sat on the desk edge, next to the chancellor, watching, while Mace stood to the rear. Heyou was here as well, behind Gabralina and Wat.

"Are you all right?" Leon asked. "Do you want a glass of water?"

Gabralina managed a trembling smile and stared down at her lap. "No thank you, Chancellor," she whispered. Her smile faded.

Leon sighed. "Gabralina . . ." he began. "No one's accusing you of anything—or Wat. But you know what happened at the warehouse."

"I-I saw. I carried water for people."

"I know." His expression was kind. "You were a big help."

"Thank you, Chancellor." Her words were barely audible.

"Gabralina, we need you to help us. We need to know why Wat left his post."

Gabralina lifted her head, surprised. "Why don't you ask him?"

"We did," Mace growled, speaking for the first time. "His answer was . . . *unenlightening.*"

Wat actually flinched.

Gabralina looked at her battle sylph. He was beautiful even dressed in a laborer's clothing, was everything she'd ever dreamed of as a little girl growing up. Moreover he was devoted to her, loving her unconditionally. Around him, she really did feel beautiful. She also didn't think that mattered.

"Wat?" she said. He looked at her, his eyes wide. "Why did you leave your post, sweetheart?"

"Um." He blinked several times, his flawless eyes wide. "There was someone up on the surface. I could feel him, someone evil. Nobody was doing anything about him, so I went. But when I got up there, he was gone. I went looking for him. Then I kind of, um, forgot to come back."

"Why didn't you tell us that before?" Mace roared.

Wat cowered. "You were yelling at me."

Leon sighed, leaning back in his chair. He glanced at Ril, who nodded, and then back at Gabralina, who felt the beginnings of hope. "Thank you, Gabralina. You both can go."

"It's all right?" she gasped. "You're not blaming us for anything?"

"No, we're not." Leon shook his head. "It seems we were all tricked. Go home and forget about it."

"Yes!" Gabralina leaped to her feet, smiling madly. "Of course, Chancellor. Thank you so much." She reached across the desk and shook his hand, pumping it madly between both of her own. He grinned right back at her. "I'll never forget this! I mean, yes of course I'll go home and forget. I promise!"

Wat already had.

* * *

The council met several hours later. Solie sat at the head of their table, one hand on her belly as she watched the assembled men. They were sharing the information they compiled about the incident at the warehouse.

"How many people died?" she asked.

"Twenty-three," Galway answered, not looking at his notes. "Lots more wounded, but Luck has all of them back on their feet. The value of the lost goods is huge."

"I don't care about that," Solie said. "Not now. What about the assassins?"

"We haven't found them yet," Mace admitted. Solie didn't

need to be queen to be able to sense his fury. "We're still looking."

Solie nodded, her hands tightening around her belly. Heyou saw the gesture and smiled. *You're safe*, he reminded her.

Yes, Ril agreed from beside Leon.

Nothing will happen to you, Mace added. *Ever.*

Solie sighed. "Right. Does anyone know who freed them?"

"Someone from Eferem, obviously," Leon said. "We didn't exactly make their capture public, so only King Alcor and his people knew they'd come. The best guess I can make is that he sent a battle sylph master, someone who knows intimately what battlers are like and how to deal with them."

Mace frowned. "No battle sylph not of the hive could have come anywhere close to the Valley without our sensing it."

"Ril was able to travel in Meridal without being spotted," Leon reminded him. "Still, I think it was Umut Taggart, my replacement as Alcor's battler master. Bound battlers never stop projecting hate, so I think Umut came without him."

"How long can a sylph live without energy from his master?" Solie asked.

"I don't know," Leon admitted. "I've always made sure never to find out."

"A week," Mace confirmed. "Less if they use up all the energy they have."

Eferem's capital was hundreds of miles away, across the Shale Plains and through forests and farmland. A week to travel that far and back would be tough.

Mace protested, his clenched fist on the table. "We would have caught any battler master in the area. We would have tracked him by his hate—like any man."

Leon shook his head. "Someone in absolute control of his emotions won't attract a battle sylph's attention. That describes Umut completely. I've known the man for years." He grimaced. "I trained him."

Mace growled. "I think you need to prove this to me."

"I agree," Leon said.

"So, they're still here?" Heyou asked in confusion.

"Chances are they're not in the Valley anymore," Leon said. "Those five couldn't hide from us if they were, and Umut would have had to return with them—at the very least for his battler's sake."

"Mightn't he have let his battler starve?"

"Never." Leon knew the man. His tone was absolute.

Galway glanced at Solie. "The question now is, what do we do next?"

"Do?" she repeated.

"We can't condone foreign powers sending assassins here and killing our people."

"He's right about that," Leon agreed.

Solie shook her head. "What do you propose we do? Have our battlers destroy Eferem's capital? There are thousands of innocent people there."

"That would be foolish," Leon agreed. "Nothing would guarantee the other kingdoms joining forces against us like that."

"How about we just kill their king?" Heyou suggested.

Solie glanced at him, a little appalled. All this talk of killing sat horribly with her. Then again, they did have twenty-three people dead and five assassins on the loose who probably wanted another shot at her. The past week's events had to be taken as acts of war.

Mace spoke up. "I don't want to fight Thrall."

All of the humans looked at him. Heyou seemed confused, but Ril nodded. "Me either."

"I didn't realize the king's battler was special," Leon said.

"He's old," Mace explained. "Extremely old." And the older a sylph was, the more powerful.

"How strong is he?" Solie asked.

"He could wipe the Valley out," Mace replied.

"Oh, *him*. I remember him," Heyou said. He grinned at Solie. "I ran."

"I d-don't blame you," she stammered.

"There are fifty battlers here," Galway protested. "They'd stop him."

"He could wipe the Valley out," Mace repeated.

"But Alcor doesn't know what he's got," Ril said with a shrug. "Too bad for him. He's so much of a coward he's never tested Thrall in a fight, and Thrall's not going to volunteer the information. He's just standing around waiting for Alcor to die so he can go home."

"So, what do we do?" Solie asked.

The group considered for a time, tossing ideas around that didn't really appeal to them.

At last, Heyou drove one fist into the other. "How about we subsume Thrall into the hive? Then he won't be a problem for us."

Leon rolled his eyes, while Ril pinched the bridge of his nose. Mace frowned. Galway reached over and ruffled the younger battler's hair. "Think about it, boy. You'd need Solie to be right there, and there's no guarantee that Thrall would just stand still and let us."

"There's no guarantee he won't, either."

"There's also no guarantee that he won't decide he should be the lover of the queen."

"Oh." Heyou frowned. "Never mind."

"There's just not much we can do," Solie sighed. "Without those men, we have no proof Alcor tried anything. He'll just deny it. He has no envoys here we can banish, and those merchants who come through from Eferem aren't his men. He wouldn't care if we sent them away and in the long run we'd just be hurting ourselves."

"So we need to be vigilant," Leon said. "If he tries anything else, which he probably will, we have to be ready." He eyed Mace. "If there are any more accidents, we have to make sure that the battlers know not to all go straight for it. The rest of the hive still has to be protected."

Mace nodded, seeing the sense in that.

"And we need to change who's allowed to see Solie," Leon continued, staring across the table at her. "Access to you should be based on more than just how threatening a visitor feels. People need a reason to see you, and if they're not someone well-known and trusted, a battler should stay close. And by that I mean *in the room.*"

Solie nodded, not really liking this, though part of her was pleased at the idea her calendar might get a bit lighter. From the look on Ril's face, it was going to get a lot lighter. Another part of her was very glad at the increased protection for her unborn baby.

"I'm still going to want to see my friends," she pointed out.

"Well, they're hardly people we don't know or trust, are they?"

"True," Solie agreed.

From there the discussion moved to the topic of rebuilding the warehouse, and what, if anything, they could salvage from the wreckage.

* * *

Leon walked calmly into the market, making his way through the crowds gathered at the vendors' stalls, his hands in his pockets and the hood of his cloak raised to hide his face. He didn't speak to anyone he passed, just made his way in silence, his thoughts calm and peaceful.

This is never going to work, Ril told him.

Leon didn't let himself feel any annoyance. *Don't give me away,* he thought.

I won't, the battler groused. *I won't have to.*

He reached the end of the market, coming to the roadway that led to the queen's palace, the arches reaching high into the air even though the throne room itself was underground. He walked toward it, steering clear of the crowds.

A dozen battlers suddenly dropped down on him, slamming him painfully to the ground as they cheered their victory, jostling one another and shouting excitedly, laughing. Bruised, Leon lifted himself onto his forearms and looked up at Mace.

"Did you have to land on me quite so hard?"

Mace raised an eyebrow. "Yes."

"I'm getting too old for this," Leon grumbled as he climbed to his feet.

Ril appeared and helped him up, eyeing his master with an unhappy frown. "I told you it wouldn't work."

"Indeed." Mace crossed his arms. "You said you could evade us."

Gingerly, Leon rubbed his jaw and worked it from side to side. It felt like a tooth was loose. "I thought I could."

"Idiot," Ril sniffed. "They *know* you. They'd find you no matter what your emotions were."

Leon paused in checking his jaw, thinking about that, and wondered if perhaps he was losing his mind. Was it old age? He hadn't seen that likelihood. "You could have mentioned that before they all landed on me," he pointed out, grimacing at his battler.

Heyou grinned. "That wouldn't have been as much fun."

"I see."

Ril rolled his eyes and grabbed his master's arm. "Come on," he said, dragging him off. "I'm taking you to see Luck."

Disappointed but still knowing he was right that an enemy could walk past a battler, Leon let himself be dragged along like a misbehaving child. The situation amused him enough that he started smiling. The people who'd seen the sudden attack continued to gape, at last grudgingly returning to whatever they had been doing.

A basket of corn on her arm, Sala walked forward. "Was that some sort of game?" she asked.

Leon saw Mace look down at the young woman and shrug. "Not really," he said. Then he turned, likely heading back to his duties with the continuing conviction that no one could get past one of his kind.

* * *

For once in his life he had to think about Luck first. That's what *she'd* said, her tone nearly scornful even while her words were sympathetic. The people of this Valley were killing Luck, wearing her slowly out with their needs, their weaknesses . . . A lot of the injuries she healed, doctors and wise women could fix. Those injuries didn't need Luck, but no, all day, every day, people came to their cottage with the most pathetic of complaints, asking for Luck to heal them and not giving much of anything in return. True, sylphs were paid for their work, but Luck never received anything even remotely good enough to be worth the effort she put forth. The effort that she could be putting into *him*.

Zem coughed and pressed to his mouth one of the handkerchiefs he always carried. Immediately, Luck reached out to put her hands on him, and the wonderful healing energy flowed. Zem sighed, relaxing.

But the nervousness came back almost immediately as the carriage swayed and rocked up the slope that led out of the Valley. He could hear men and horses outside, shouting back and forth to one another as the caravan went on its way. Zem tried not to think too much, afraid he'd bring the battle sylphs down on him, but they reacted to malice. He was only frightened.

Where are we going? Luck asked him silently.

Zem reached out to cup her cheek, and she pressed against his palm. Her skin felt waxy but warm, soft, and pliant. He smiled at her. "We're going to where you'll be appreciated," he promised.

They were headed where she wouldn't have to heal every little knee scrape of every ungrateful child in this backward Valley, all for a mere pittance. Sala had promised them that. In Yed, healers only helped the richest of men and women, and they were paid huge sums of money in return. Sala had told Zem where to go, whom he had to see, and how he could become rich. Luck would be able to focus almost all of her attention on him, then, just as she should. Sala had even loaned him the money to pay for his passage on this merchant train.

The little man swallowed and settled back in his seat, his coat clutched tightly around himself, even though the interior of the carriage was already very warm. For now, the men he rode with didn't even know about Luck's presence. It was safer that way. It was safer overall if no one knew they were gone until they were too far away to drag back.

For her part, Luck sat across from him in silence, content and curious to follow him wherever he chose to lead.

Chapter Twelve

Summer was passing, the harvest was in and people were beginning to prepare for winter. Throughout the Valley moods were high, most people unconcerned with anything more strenuous than their families and friends.

For the council and all others in the know, things were a bit more stressful. Still, as time passed, Solie found it hard to keep worries about assassins and enemy kings foremost in her mind. Yes, battlers were around her all of the time, but they'd pretty much been there all the time anyway; and now that her morning sickness had passed, she was too mellow to care.

Her hands cupping her rounded stomach, Solie wandered down the road toward the summoning hall, smiling when she was greeted by each of the people she passed. Dillon and Heyou followed. Those two were the sylphs most commonly with her, for familiarity's sake more than anything else. Many of the women in the Valley had offered their own battlers as bodyguards, like Sala, but Solie liked Dillon's quiet and of course she loved Heyou.

Dillon wore the form of a large black cat, his head even with her thigh. Heyou was in his usual shape. Dillon only stayed during the day, spending the evenings with his own master, as Solie didn't feel she really needed two battlers with her at night. Since the warehouse incident and the escape of the assassins, nothing had happened in the Valley at all—except, of course, for Zem leaving with Luck. But while that was infuriating, it was hardly surprising. He'd always been a greedy, petty little man.

It was, however, a problem. As queen, Solie could order Luck to return, but that risked the sylph's survival if she wasn't able to convince Zem to join her, and Solie doubted the little man would ever dare show his face again after deserting them. To solve the problem, they'd been trying a different tactic.

Solie went into the summoning hall, which was a large, airy building with so many windows that the interior was lit by daylight. It was a single chamber several hundred feet across, the summoning circle inlaid on the floor in precious stones brought by earth sylphs from deep underground. The pillars that framed the windows were creamy white marble and heavily embossed. It was a beautiful place, as the sylphs felt it ought to be.

Twenty priests stood arrayed around the circle, chanting. Their words reverberated through the room, echoing from the perfect acoustics of the rounded ceiling. The circle itself was glowing, with a second circle of energy hanging directly above. This circle started to glow as well. The space inside shimmered with changing colors.

A woman with a club foot stood in the center of the circle, looking nervously upward. She was the offering; her injury, they hoped, would be attractive to a healer on the other side. Such sylphs weren't simple to find. Healers weren't common in the other world, either, and most stayed in their hives. Even when sent out to heal an injured sylph, they weren't easy to lure away. First, they had to want to come. Second, they had to get past their battle sylph guardians. No hive wanted to lose healers.

Near Petr, the head priest, was a fire sylph. She wasn't Petr's—he'd refused a new sylph when his first was killed nearly a decade before—but her master stood nearby. The fire sylph had shown a great sensitivity for what waited on the other side of the gate. She wore the shape of a little girl made of flickering flame, and Ash was her name. She liked to have a specific purpose beyond the standard role of "Keep things lit, keep things warm." Her job was to locate sylphs—or rather, to determine what sylphs were on the other side of any gate they opened.

"No healers," she announced. There never were any.

Petr sighed and made a gesture. The chanting stopped. Immediately, both gates dimmed, and the one in the air closed and disappeared. They'd wait five minutes and then try again.

The gate opened every time in a different place, though the humans were pretty sure the locations were all within a set range. There was likely some sort of corresponding physicality to their worlds. Every sylph brought through the gate here had seemed to originate from one of only a dozen or so original hives, and none of those, according to Devon's letters, equated to any of the tapped hives in Meridal.

Solie rubbed her stomach, still not envying Eapha for being queen to so many sylphs. Still, having Meridal as an ally did reduce the threat of Eferem. It was a great relief to know that within two weeks of sending a mental call to Airi she could— in theory, anyway—have an entire army of battle sylphs and their masters arriving to defend her people. Her own battlers would no doubt be unhappy, but they would obey her, and Leon had promised that Eapha was no enemy to them. She had no reason to be.

Still, they needed a healer. Badly. Human doctors could do a lot, but there were many injuries that would mean death without a healer sylph. Solie didn't want to see that happen. Eapha had dozens, she knew, so maybe if they didn't draw a healer of their own before the baby was born, Solie would ask her to send one until they did.

She stood and watched two more attempts to open a gate near a healer, both unsuccessful. Finally, she left, heading back out into the sunshine with her entourage. She felt discouraged but not really unhappy. Not with the weight in her belly.

However the child was going to turn out, Solie was already desperately in love with her.

Solie hadn't needed to ask Heyou who the biological father was; he just wasn't any good at keeping secrets. She smiled at the happy battler as they walked. Would the baby end up looking like Devon? she wondered. She hadn't talked to Devon about it except for the day he left, and Devon hadn't mentioned it in any of his letters. Knowing how he felt about battlers, she doubted it had been his idea to be a donor. She didn't want to risk embarrassing him or get Heyou feeling jealous.

"Hey, girl."

Solie looked up to see Galway riding toward her, dressed in a bearskin cape and leading a second horse. His son Nelson walked beside him, dressed in a normal tunic, which showed that, wherever his father was going, Nelson wasn't following.

"Off hunting again?" Solie asked.

The former trapper smiled. "Now that the harvest is in, I figured I'd better. Before the weather turns cold."

"Or before Mom thinks of something for him to do instead," Nelson suggested.

Solie giggled.

Heyou glared at Galway. "Hey! What am I supposed to eat while you're gone?"

Solie could feel he wasn't really angry, and Galway could tell his battler's moods just as easily. "I'll be gone for only a few days, boy, and if you get hungry, you know how to find me. Besides, that's why I came looking for you before I left. Come here."

Leaving Solie's side, Heyou went over and leaned against Galway's leg. He stared up at the mounted man, and his eyes softened as he drew Galway's energy.

Unless a battler was starved and drew very heavily, the master never even felt the loss. Galway smiled down fondly at the sylph. "Good boy," he chuckled, and he ruffled Heyou's hair.

"That always looks so weird," Nelson complained.

"Does not!" Heyou mock growled, stepping belligerently into the young man's face. His sort-of stepbrother grinned and puffed out his chest. Solie rolled her eyes.

"Oh! They're not going to fight, are they?"

Startled, Solie looked over to see Sala standing a few feet away, one hand pressed to her bosom.

Heyou grinned. "Maybe," he said.

Nelson shoved him, and the two started wrestling, shrieking and yelling, with the human doing much better than he ever would if Heyou took the tussle seriously.

Galway shook his head and nudged his horse into a walk. "I'll see you in a few days, girl. The mountains are calling, and those boys are too damn noisy."

Solie watched him ride off before returning her attention to the mock fight. Sala watched, too, and Solie felt a sudden urge to leave, though Heyou certainly didn't act threatened and Dillon remained calm at her feet. It was silly. Sala had the steadiest emotions Solie had ever felt from a woman, and the battlers weren't bothered by her. She even had a battler of her own, and Claw didn't seem to be doing badly. He'd even stopped walking around with blue hair. Still, something about Sala made Solie uncomfortable, even though Sala had managed to become part of her inner circle. Just because the girl always showed up with one of her other friends didn't mean Solie liked her.

Before Sala could try and start a conversation, Solie turned and walked away. Dillon rose and followed. Heyou continued his fight until she was nearly half a block away; then he broke free of Nelson and ran to join her, his stepbrother laughingly yelling insults.

"Silly boy," Solie said as he drew up beside her.

"What did you expect?" he asked, grinning.

She had to laugh.

* * *

Galway rode to the east, toward Para Dubh, leaving the lush greenery of the Valley and entering the sterile wasteland that was the Shale Plains. To reach any settlement would take days, but he wasn't looking to see other people. With the harvest in and the workload eased for at least the next few days, he was off to do a little hunting. He loved his family and enjoyed his job, but sometimes he just needed to get away. After decades of marriage, both he and Iyala recognized that sometimes they both had to find time alone.

The border of Para Dubh was only a few hours' ride from the Valley, and the hunting was good once the mountains were reached. To go to Eferem and its forests would have taken much longer and thanks to his affiliation with Solie he had a price on his head there. No, this was the best plan. He'd take the route he always took.

The former trapper didn't pay much attention to the landscape, dotted as it was by gray thornbushes, though he did note signs of change. The sylphs were spreading life even here. Grass was growing on either side of the road that led up into the mountains of Para Dubh. There were even a few autumn windflowers.

He reached the green forests and rising slopes that marked the border soon after lunch, and he rode through them for only an hour more before he found a deer trail and left the road. The trail brought him to a small waterfall and a clearing overshadowed by trees. He'd camped here before. It was late afternoon by this point, and he set up camp quickly, though there wasn't any rush. He'd hunt tomorrow, perhaps find a deer he could skin to make a coat for Iyala. She did love the feel of deer leather.

Content, he finished making camp and lit a fire. It burned merrily while he brushed and fed the horses. They seemed as glad to be free of the Valley as he, scarfing down the oats he'd brought. Wind stirred in the tree branches, and as the evening deepened he could hear frogs and crickets. The air was cool but still warm enough for comfort. Galway sighed deeply. He would never regret falling in with Solie, but this . . . *this* was where his heart lay.

Over the fire he hung a small pot filled with water and meat, along with some vegetables and herbs for flavor. It bubbled as he sat checking the fletching on his arrows and the sharpness of his knife blade. Definitely a deer tomorrow. If he got lucky, perhaps some mink or ermine. Iyala would appreciate a fur stole more than a leather coat for the coming winter.

The horses whickered, stamping their feet nervously and pulling at their tethers. Galway looked toward them and then intently into the woods, listening and watching the darkness. The beasts had surely scented a predator, so he tossed a few more pieces of wood onto the fire. The flames roared up. Galway kept to one side, careful not to let it blind him while he moved to soothe the horses. The beasts steadied a bit at his touch but still tossed their heads and shifted in fear. Over their racket he couldn't hear anything else.

The other animals of the night were silent now, hiding. Definitely a predator. Muttering under his breath, Galway picked up his bow, quickly stringing it and nocking an arrow. Somewhere beyond the light of his campfire, a twig snapped.

The two horses screamed, rearing up and trying to break their tethers. This time, Galway didn't try to calm them. He stepped out of range of their hooves, just watching the darkness. His heart pounded faster, but he kept his breathing calm and even, his concentration focused. He'd run into sylvan predators before; it was just a matter of dealing with whatever appeared. He had far too much experience to be overwhelmed by fear.

The horses were another matter. They threw themselves against their bonds, shrieking in mad panic. The ropes finally broke. Both horses crashed away, vanishing into the darkness through the bushes. At least they'd be easy to track, Galway mused.

There was no other sound from the darkness, but stepping out of the bushes at the edge of the light from his campfire came a huge, hunched shape. Galway swore silently. A massive grizzly bear stood there, swinging its head up and regarding him with beady eyes.

Galway started to back up. A bear might be killed by an arrow, but it usually took more than one, and this beast wasn't even ten feet away, far closer than he'd like. It had no real reason to attack him, not with his dinner sitting so conveniently close and all that horsemeat already fled. Still, Galway backed up farther, fully intending to abandon the camp to the bear.

A second beast appeared from the bush to the right. Galway froze. Both bears were male and fully adult, which was strange. Adult male bears didn't hunt together. Even stranger, the first animal lifted its head, sniffing toward Galway while the second edged around the fire. Neither paid any attention to the stew.

Behind Galway was the pool at the base of the waterfall and the stream that led away from it. The waterfall bisected a cliff far too steep for bears but easy enough for a man to climb. Galway edged toward it, retreating carefully with his bow, his feet finding purchase first on the mossy ground and then on the stony edge of the stream. He continued moving backward as the second bear trotted fully around the fire and paused to chuff at the first. It singed its fur in order to do so. Sad eyes from the first fixed on Galway.

The water was only a few inches deep, barely enough to cover the feet of Galway's boots. He splashed onward, not daring to look down, sure they'd attack if he did. The two bears followed, the second seeming almost to defer to the first.

The second chuffed again, hopping up and down on its front paws. The first hunched lower, shaking its head and stopping for a moment, apparently unhappy with the other's presence. The second just hopped more, still chuffing.

Galway stepped out of the stream and onto the bank. He continued moving for a few more feet until his back pressed up against the cliff, which he remembered as thirty feet high, rough-edged, and easy to climb. He wouldn't be able to carry his bow. Not without strapping it across his back.

The first bear turned to the second, snapping, and the second stopped where it was, stiff with surprise. Galway took that moment to drop his bow and turn, immediately grabbing the ridges of the cliff and starting to climb.

The rock was solid and dry here, which was fortunate given how much moss grew on it. In seconds he was ten feet high and rising, going nearly straight up. He'd hit twenty feet before the bears even realized he'd moved.

They roared, a sound that was nearly deafening. Galway kept climbing, forcing his breathing to remain steady as he pulled himself up, aware he was high enough already that they couldn't reach him. Hanging on tightly, he risked a look down.

The bears charged across the stream. The first hurled itself at the cliff, still roaring, and slammed its claws against the stone. Galway hung on even as the cliff shook, but he knew he was safe. Then the bear dug in its claws and started to climb.

The old trapper felt the first moment of terror. This was impossible. Somewhere deep in his mind, he felt a questioning reaction and sent out a silent scream for help.

HEYOU!

He began climbing again, frantically trying to get to the top of the cliff. From there he had no idea what he was going to do, not against bears that could follow him up vertical surfaces. He had to think of something, had to last long enough for his battle sylph to reach him. Heyou could make it here in minutes. Galway could evade for that long.

Rock crunched below, and he felt hot breath against his legs. They'd caught up! Four claws like scimitars slammed into his back. Galway screamed in agony, then was torn off the cliff and thrown down. He landed in the stream, and he felt both legs break underneath him. Unable to breathe through the pain, he stared helplessly up at his assailants. His eyes were already hazing over.

The first bear jumped down from where it had clung to the cliff nearly twenty feet up. It twisted in the air and landed heavily next to the second bear, which hadn't moved. That beast looked at him excitedly. The first shuddered and walked toward Galway, looming over him as the man coughed up blood.

Galway shook with pain. He could still feel Heyou coming and knew the battler would save him—only, the animals were closing in and all he could see was the sad eyes of the first bear. Those, and its inescapable teeth.

* * *

Heyou exploded out of the hive through one of the air vents. Lightning flashed through his cloud form as he spread insubstantial wings and shot across the sky, gaining altitude as he raced toward his master, following that cry of fear. Below, other battlers rose, roaring warnings as the rest of the sylphs fled.

Mace sent a demand to know what was happening, but Heyou didn't answer. Right now, Galway was all that mattered. It was all he'd been able to manage just to send a plea to Dillon and Blue to guard Solie, and her fright and curiosity pounded at him. His queen needed him. But his master needed him more.

Heyou blew through the Valley and across the plains, racing with the winds toward the mountains where his master had gone to hunt. They grew in size impossibly fast, for he was putting everything he had into the flight.

He felt Galway's terror, and the battle sylph screamed, forcing himself to go even faster, the plains vanishing under him and being replaced by green forest. He felt Galway's pain.

Then he felt Galway die.

Heyou wailed. Dropping down into a small clearing by a waterfall, he released his rage and pain in a terrible blast. Everything around him exploded, disintegrating down to the bare stone for a distance of a hundred feet—all but the clearing itself. The clearing stayed intact, and Heyou landed with tearless sobs, splashing into the stream and drawing up the body of his friend.

Battle sylphs couldn't weep. Heyou howled instead, hugging Galway despite the blood and the gore, howling and rocking until the other battle sylphs came to find him.

Chapter Thirteen

It had been three days. Birds sang in the garden, mindless of anyone's grief. Solie walked across her living room and into the bedroom, Dillon padding behind her in the shape of a great gray wolf. Her morning nausea was back, thanks to stress.

Heyou lay sprawled on the big bed, the sheets kicked away from his body. Solie bit her lip and went to sit beside him, leaning down to cup her battler's cheek and kiss his brow. Silently he rolled onto his side and put an arm around her, hugging her to him with his cheek pressed to her belly.

"How are you feeling, sweetheart?" she whispered.

Heyou shrugged noncommittally, and she stroked her hand down his shoulder. Under her fingers, she could feel him shaking.

"Are you hungry?" she asked, knowing he was failing. Even if she hadn't been able to feel it, Mace had told her so. Heyou had gone through nearly all of his energy trying to get to Galway in time.

He shook his head.

Solie bit her lip, her eyes filling with tears. She loved Heyou so much, and she'd never seen him in such pain. Of course, he'd never lost anyone he loved before. Sylphs, she was learning, didn't handle loss well, and she felt a moment of sadness that they were bound to such fragile creatures as humans.

"Please drink my energy," she said to him. "You need to."

It wasn't an order, not yet, and Heyou shook his head. "You might lose the baby."

"I don't care," she choked.

Heyou pulled back just enough to look up at her with miserable eyes. "*I do.*"

Solie sniffed, wiping her eyes as her lover rolled away from her and buried his face in a pillow. It wasn't fair. Two battlers had now lost their masters unexpectedly, and neither of them was handling it well. She herself wasn't handling it well. Rachel and Galway had both been her friends, and she wasn't even sure how the Valley would manage. Galway had been an integral part of the government. Solie didn't know how she could replace him.

She didn't want to even think about it right now. She couldn't. Heyou was lost in misery, starving himself in grief.

She could order him to feed from her energy, Solie knew, but . . . She put a hand over her unborn daughter and rose, stroking Heyou's hair before slipping out of the bedroom. Ril stood just outside, waiting.

"Iyala and Nelson are here to see Heyou," he told her.

Solie stopped, surprised and grieving all over again. Everything had happened so fast, Heyou's pain was so all-consuming, she hadn't spared a thought yet for Galway's family, for the woman who'd acted so much like a mother to both herself and Heyou.

"Let them in," she said, swallowing down shame and anguish.

Ril nodded and turned away. He didn't ask how Heyou was doing; he knew.

Dillon padded up beside Solie, and he sat down as the door opened to admit Galway's wife and oldest son. Iyala's face was pale, but her expression was firm and her plump arms immediately reached out for Solie. The young queen ran into them, sobbing. The older woman embraced her, whispering reassurances, though it seemed mad that Iyala should be the one comforting her. It should be the other way around. Only, Solie couldn't stop crying.

"It's all right, my duck," Iyala told her. "It's all right."

While the two women embraced, Nelson walked past them toward the bedroom. His face was white as chalk. Both Ril and Dillon watched, but neither objected when he went inside.

"Heyou?"

His stepbrother and favorite troublemaker was lying on the bed, his blue and gold uniform wrinkled and filthy. Nelson swallowed when he saw dried blood on the fabric but moved to stand beside him.

"Heyou?" he said again.

Heyou didn't answer, his face buried in a pillow. Nelson wasn't sure how he could even breathe that way.

"Come on, Heyou, I just lost my father. Don't shut me out."

Slowly, Heyou lifted the pillow. "I'm sorry," he whispered.

Nelson sank down beside him. "It's not your fault."

"I should have been with him. I should have protected him."

"You can't be everywhere."

Heyou closed his eyes. "I should have been."

Nelson puffed out a breath. His heart hurt, and he felt like someone had punched him in the gut. His father, the man who'd taken him in and given him a home and a chance at a better life, was gone. It was difficult to believe, to process that the man was dead, but seeing Heyou tear himself apart was hard confirmation.

His mother had been first to realize how devastated the battler would be. Nelson didn't know how she could deal with her own grief over her husband and still think about Heyou, but she'd discussed it with him today. Heyou was family, she reminded him, and family was more important than anything. They had to look after him.

Nelson swallowed. "Heyou," he said. "Um, Heyou, I came here to tell you I want to take my father's place."

The battler glanced up.

Nelson shrugged, embarrassed. "As your master, so you can eat. And, um, to keep you in the family."

Heyou was staring at him now.

"I mean, Dad told us what it meant to be a master and how important it is not to take advantage. You know Dad never told you what to do."

Heyou sat up slowly, leaning on one arm. "No. He kind of suggested real hard sometimes, though."

Nelson grinned. "He always suggested real hard to me, too."

Heyou grinned back. A moment later they both were pale-faced again, remembering Galway. Finally, Heyou looked at Nelson almost shyly.

"You *want* to be my master?"

Nelson nodded. "Mom and I talked it over. We don't trust anyone but family to have you. Or Solie of course, but Dad always said you shouldn't feed from her. So we decided on me, since I'm younger than Mom and everything." He blushed. "Is that okay with you?"

Heyou thought about it for a moment and then shrugged. "Sure."

In the doorway, Solie watched and sighed. She was glad that Nelson had made the offer. In some ways, Heyou had to share her with every other sylph in the hive. He loved her, she had no doubt about that, but having a master all to himself was something every sylph needed.

She turned back to the main room, giving the two a chance to talk. She'd be needed later to bind them, but for now she laid a hand over her belly and went back to join Iyala. Dillon sat by the window and watched.

"How is the baby doing?" Galway's widow asked.

"All right." Solie glanced at her. "Your son is going to be Heyou's new master."

Iyala smiled. "He's a good boy. They both are."

Solie put a hand on her arm. "Yes. They are. But . . . are you all right? Tell me there's something I can do for you."

"No." Iyala shook her head. "We'll all be all right."

The woman smiled, but with Dillon there and projecting her emotions, Solie could feel her pain. She said, "I know you'll be okay, but right now it's hard." She glanced at Dillon, who met her gaze with his golden wolf eyes. "We need another healer," she said. That wouldn't have saved Galway any more than having one would have helped Rachel, but still . . .

"We need a healer," she repeated.

Dillon nodded in agreement.

* * *

We should leave this place.

Slowly, the nameless sylph lifted her head, her six eyes swirling open as she looked around. The fields were quiet while the suns went down, the place where she lay deserted or nearly so. A battle sylph from the hive drifted along the border between field and rock, searching out threats.

Shh, she warned.

The hive battler drifted overhead, glaring down at her. Not quite hating her but not impressed either. He snorted as she pressed herself against the ground and then continued on his way.

I hate them, her companion said.

She didn't answer, though she supposed he had reason. He'd

been thrown out of his own hive, his link to his queen broken before he was chased away by his brothers. He'd spent ages living on the outskirts of other hives, eating whatever he could scavenge while avoiding predators and enemy sylphs. His only hope was to get big enough and strong enough to attract a queen's attention and be subsumed into her hive as a new mate. Until then, he hid and hated.

Slowly the nameless sylph shifted, moving along a row of plants and letting the exile free from where he'd hidden beneath her. He sighed and shook himself, his lightning flashing with repressed need. Where he'd touched her, she itched madly.

We should go, he said again.

Go where? she demanded, terrified at the very thought. This was her home, had always been her home, even if her hive mates did growl and recoil whenever she entered the hive now. No one would even let her heal them, and even this far away she could feel the queen's displeasure. But the mountains and chasms beyond these fields were alien and evil.

Where in the world could we ever possibly go?

* * *

The council's offices were located behind Solie's throne room, all of them arrayed off a reception chamber with a single desk. Ril rather liked it. To get to any of the offices, a visitor had to pass the battler chamber, go through the throne room and, finally, get past him. In a way, this was all another layer of protection for the Valley's important personages, though it took the form of paperwork.

The battler went through the week's schedule, his face impassive. He still wasn't sure how he felt about the job. When Devon was doing it, he hadn't paid much attention. Leon's office was next to the queen's, and if Ril wanted to see either Solie or his master, he'd just gone right on through. Devon hadn't stopped him; he'd been far too terrified of battle sylphs to try and stop any of them. Now that Ril had the job, he didn't let anyone through; not without a good reason. Not even battlers or Leon could just stroll in and pester the queen.

The blond battler smirked a bit. Still, Leon usually had a reason.

The door opened. Ril eyed it, even though he knew who was there. Given that he was a battle sylph, there was no one else on guard. Solie wasn't in her office, anyway, though Leon was. The queen was at the summoning hall, helping again in the search for a new healer.

Lizzy entered, smiling at Ril as she crossed the room. He immediately shoved his paperwork to one side and leaned over the desk. She laughed softly and bent down, meeting him halfway with a soft kiss. Ril relaxed into it, his eyes closing as his lips moved against hers. Lizzy braced her elbows against the desk, her fingers twining through his hair. Time stopped, all of the battler's attention focused on the woman before him.

"You two do realize this is a public place, right?"

Lizzy pulled back, blushing, and Ril glanced up at Leon, who was standing in the doorway to his office. He met his master's gaze evenly. At first he'd been afraid Leon would order him away from Lizzy, but Leon had come to accept their relationship. Right now the man's emotions were a mix of amusement and exasperation.

"Um," Lizzy said. "Hi, Daddy. I brought you lunch." She lifted a basket she'd set by her feet.

Leon's eyebrow rose. "Is there anything else you wanted?"

She shrugged and shot a quick look at Ril, who stayed silent. They'd talked over her ambitions the night before in bed. He liked her ideas, but it was up to her to convince her father.

Leon glanced over, picking up on Ril's approval. "Well?" he asked his daughter.

Lizzy shrugged, rubbing her hand up one arm. "I just want to help out with all the things Uncle Galway used to do. I know you're busy already, you and Ril . . ." Her voice trailed off.

"And you don't want to spend your life knitting afghans and helping your mother cook dinner," Leon added.

"No." Lizzy grimaced. "I'm bored out of my mind. Fields and harvests and knitting and babysitting? I don't like those. I want to deal with people. With *important* things."

"So you're looking to take over for Galway," Leon said. Ril felt both the man's interest and uncertainty. "He held a pretty important position. He handled all of the Valley's economics."

"I can learn to do that," Lizzy said. "Uncle Galway did."

"Galway was a lot older than you, sweetheart."

"But he spent most of those years in the woods setting traps! He didn't know a thing about economics when he started. Not really. And I'm good at math."

"He knew a lot about trade. He knew about haggling, and about travel to other places. He knew that—"

"Yeah, yeah," Lizzy interrupted. She eyed Ril. "Help me here!"

It wasn't quite an order, but Ril still eyed his first master. He had to obey both Leon and Lizzy, just as he had to obey the queen. But Leon's orders would hold him more than Lizzy's, which they both knew. It was a good thing that he only gave orders when he had to.

Ril sighed. "If she works here, I won't have to go running back and forth all the time to make sure nobody's trying to kill either of you."

Lizzy giggled at that. Leon's eyebrows shot up.

"I don't think either of us is in danger of immediate assassination," he pointed out.

"Two battle sylph masters have recently died," Ril replied.

"That's coincidence. Neither was murdered."

"We don't care," Ril said.

Both Lizzy and Leon were quiet for a moment, absorbing that. He was surprised they hadn't picked up on it already. Not that he gave a damn if they thought he was being silly. Two masters were dead and all his brothers were upset. *He* was upset. Every battler in the Valley was keeping his master as close as possible, and when they couldn't, they were arranging for someone else to watch them. Hector had been watching Lizzy while Ril worked, but Ril would rather she was here.

"There are also five assassins out there that we can't seem to find," he pointed out.

Leon sighed and regarded his daughter. He said nothing, just stood there.

Ril's temper flared. "Just do it, Leon," he snapped. "Teach her. You know you're overworked, and she can probably help that. Maybe she'll make it as a council member, or maybe she'll be better as an assistant to one. Either way, let's get her working here. So, just stop arguing and do it, okay?" He grabbed his papers and sullenly started shuffling them. "I have work to do."

Lizzy and Leon gaped at him; then Leon tapped his daughter on the shoulder and pointed to his office. "Come on. We'll discuss it. I'm not making any promises, but I'll give teaching you a try. You were always a bright little girl."

Grinning, Lizzy hurried into his office. Leon followed, shaking his head. Ril set his papers back on the desk, his focus on their complex mix of emotions.

The door to the entry room opened. Ril's head snapped up, and he snarled a warning that he did not want to be bothered. Sala blinked at him in surprise as his growl deepened. He wanted Lizzy and Leon working together; he didn't want anyone to interrupt them before that partnership was arranged. Besides, Sala wasn't on any of his lists.

She backed quietly away, closing the door, and Ril returned to his paperwork.

* * *

Outside, Sala frowned and adjusted her shawl. That hadn't been expected at all, though perhaps it should have been. She'd listened to Lizzy's stories about her imprisonment in Meridal. Most battle sylphs were pathetic around women, but that one had killed some. A lot of them.

She turned and walked away, not prepared for any kind of confrontation that she could avoid. She had other things she needed to do, anyway. Important things.

Chapter Fourteen

Moreena Pril had never considered herself a beautiful woman. She was too thin, her face too long, and her nose too big. She had no hips to speak of, and her ears stuck out. While her sisters were beautiful, Moreena had managed to inherit every odd characteristic of her family all at once. She'd never married, never attracted a lover, and had joined the Community, which broke away from Para Dubh, as much to get away from her neighbors' laughter and hateful looks as for a chance to make something more of her life than just being the town spinster.

Dillon had changed all of that. When the Widow Blackwell asked her to be a battler master at the age of thirty-two, she'd never really believed that anyone would come through the gate for her. Not *her*. But Dillon had. And shape didn't matter to him, not the way he flickered between forms. Sometimes Moreena thought she was making up for a lifetime of forced abstinence with a hundred different lovers.

Humming to herself, since it was a beautiful fall morning and the leaves on the trees were turning her favorite color, she made her way out the back door of her cottage and down to the end of the garden where the well stood. Dillon was away helping to guard the queen, but she didn't mind. Solie was a sweet girl, and Dillon always came back at night. He didn't sleep himself, but they both liked when Moreena used his shoulder as a pillow.

A gentle breeze blew over the garden, bringing with it the smell of the neighbor's baking, and Moreena's mouth watered as she stepped up to the rounded rim of the covered well. A crosspiece had a rope hanging from it that could be wound up or down with a crank, and a bucket was on its side on the ground. Moreena looked down in surprise, given that she'd left the bucket sitting on the well. Picking it up, she leaned against the well so that she could drop it straight down without knocking loose dirt from the walls into the water.

The rocks of the well, which had always been solid before, gave way under her hand. Moreena screamed as she pitched forward, scrambling madly for anything to stop herself, and she caught the rope that held the bucket. She staggered forward, and her legs plunged into the well and hit the other side.

Moreena screamed again, desperately hanging on and trying to pull her feet up enough to get them back on the ground. Her long skirts got in the way, and as she swung back and forth, the wooden crosspiece above her creaked at the weight. Distantly, she felt Dillon's terror and rage.

Frantic, Moreena tried to pull herself up the rope, but she just didn't have enough strength. Her hands trembled, the skin on them rubbed raw. She could feel Dillon coming, but her arms were shaky and she was weeping, frightened and weak. The crossbar creaked again, and then suddenly it splintered, dropping her another few inches. She shrieked. The crossbar broke fully in half.

A hand grabbed the rope above her, then her arm, and Moreena was hauled out of the well as easily as if she were a kitten. She stared straight into the face of her neighbor's battler. Like most battle sylphs, he was beautiful, but he also looked incredibly angry.

"Are you all right?" he asked.

Moreena shivered as he let her go, hugging herself against the sudden cold as she looked at her collapsed well. If Blue hadn't been nearby . . .

"I didn't know you stayed home during the day," she whispered, not able to think clearly just yet. "Thank you."

He shrugged. "I was watching over both you and Casi. Since Dillon couldn't be here today, he asked me to."

Moreena stared at him. He'd been guarding her as well as his own master? How strange!

A black cloud filled with frantic lightning suddenly flashed over the cottage. Down it came, Dillon shifting into human shape even before he reached the ground. He ran across the garden and threw his arms around Moreena, hugging her close. He was actually whimpering. Moreena started to cry as well.

Blue watched them for a moment, but being there was making him uncomfortable. Finally he went back across the garden wall to Casi's house, determined that nothing was ever going to happen to her. Not while he was alive.

* * *

The battlers were in uproar. After the near death of a third master, it took hours to calm them down. Even now, they still had not returned to normal. All of the Valley sylphs clung to their masters at this point, not just the battlers, and in any cases where a sylph couldn't, they arranged for another sylph to watch their master in their stead. Any master who protested just ended up with a dozen more sylphs coming to convince them to change their minds.

It wasn't quite what Sala wanted. While Dillon wouldn't let Moreena out of his sight, and therefore wasn't guarding the queen anymore, Heyou had taken over. Sala had hoped Dillon would be gone *without* a paranoid Heyou in his place. She'd have to do something about that.

Sala sat on a chair in the corner of her bedroom, watching two creatures writhe together on the bed. Neither of them looked entirely human, or anything like their normal forms, but that didn't matter to her. She liked sex and liked to watch sex, and she especially liked having the power to order these two battle sylphs to have sex with each other.

Wat was one. He was still hers, Gabralina never having rescinded that foolish order to obey her. The stupid girl had probably even forgotten. She'd undoubtedly meant for the loan to be temporary, but that didn't matter to Sala. Wat was hers now as surely as Claw, and in some ways he was even more useful. He was dim enough that he'd forget everything she directed, and now, with his banishment from the battler ranks, he had no schedule to keep. He was always free for her use.

Sala leaned back in her chair, licking her lips as she watched the entwined battlers. Wat lay on his back against the bed, that eternally confused look on his face as though he didn't understand what was happening to him. He probably didn't. He never did. He'd sabotaged the shelving at the warehouse perfectly, though, drawing Claw and Luck away so that Rachel could be poisoned successfully. Wat had then freed the Eferem assassins and carried them out of the Valley, where he'd killed them and buried the bodies, with the story she'd given him turning the council's attention toward Eferem.

Not that there would be a council much longer. Wat and Claw had worked together to kill Galway, and they'd sabotaged Moreena's well to distract her horribly protective battle sylph from the queen.

Sala's gut twisted, though her expression didn't change and she still enjoyed the show. The Valley's battlers were beginning to believe someone was intentionally killing their masters. If they managed to convince their humans they were right . . . She needed to give the battlers someone to blame so that they'd calm down and stop watching everything so closely.

Wat whimpered on the bed, Claw speeding up. Neither of them would do this without orders, which only made it more interesting. Of the two, Sala preferred Wat. She couldn't feel him. While she needed Claw, his grief and barely controlled hysteria were alien to her. They were almost disturbing. She hadn't expected that.

It didn't matter. Not so long as he did as told. Which he would. He knew she'd killed his last master, and he remembered everything she ordered him to do, and he was aware of much more that was coming. Not all of it, of course, and not yet the one thing she truly needed him for, but enough. Enough to eventually drive him completely mad so that he would do *everything* she commanded, even the thing she'd learned no sane sylph would do. That was part of why she had him and Wat together like this now. The other part was how good it made her feel.

Sala licked her lips again and slid a hand down her skirts to touch herself. Her power over the two battlers, her absolute power, was intoxicating. She smiled as she watched, part of her mind still devising plans within plans and reassessing targets.

She'd failed to kill Moreena, but she had succeeded in getting Dillon away from Solie. Once she arranged for a patsy to take the blame for everything that happened so far, she'd start again, winnowing away Solie's support until she was left unprotected. Then Sala would take her place.

Take away the queen's support. Sala shuddered delicately, pleasure swelling through her. Lizzy aside, there was only one human member of the council left. But Sala couldn't move too quickly and risk underestimating him. Not Leon.

* * *

Claw lay entwined with Wat, their bodies joined on the bed even as their minds recoiled from each other. Back in the world they came from, there were many battlers who found happiness with each other, but those weren't the battlers who risked the gate. And, both Wat and Claw had masters. Wat was unhappy here, wanting Gabralina and uselessly reaching for her despite

Sala's orders. Claw was unhappy, too, but there was no point in seeking reassurance from Sala.

He'd known what a mistake he'd made the moment he bonded to her, how she'd set him up to choose her when his dearest Rachel died. Sala had killed her. He knew that absolutely, knew it down to his core, but there was nothing he could do about it. The calm placidity of Sala's surface mind was just a mask, light sparkling on the surface of deep water that hid black mud below. Underneath was nothing, just a gaping eternity of emptiness with no love, fear, anger, or soul. Claw was trapped there, screaming inside worse than he ever had with Boradel.

He pushed himself against Wat with fake lust generated only to satisfy Sala's perverse needs and felt eternal madness push against him. It promised peace. No more need to think, no more need to feel; he could just gibber and laugh inside his own head, not caring what was done with him anymore. But he wasn't quite there.

Why not? He'd been ordered to kill Galway in the shape of a bear, knowing how it would tear one of his hive brothers apart. He'd wrecked the integrity of Moreena's well so that she'd fall in and be killed, thereby crippling Dillon's ability to be an effective guard. Sala was playing with him, hoping he would go insane. She had chosen him for his damaged spirit, needing him crazy enough that he'd do whatever she wanted. He knew that and had to obey her anyway. He had no choice.

He wanted to lose his mind, but whenever he closed his eyes he saw Rachel sitting in her chair by the window and knitting by the light of an oil lantern, or standing in front of her class, speaking about math, or reading the tiny history of their Valley. Even now when he closed them, he saw her beneath him, lying nude and beautiful, her soft gray hair spread out over the pillow, her lips pursed and spots of color high on her cheeks.

Claw groaned, his head bowed nearly to the pillow. He

moved faster, his hands clutching his lover's. Rachel smiled back at him, rocking gently and whispering.

"You're such a good soul, Claw," she said in his memory. *"Such a gentle heart. Don't doubt yourself, my sweet. Not ever. I love you."*

Claw thrust harder, rocking the bed and slamming it against the wall. He wanted this done. In the back of his mind, he felt Sala's sudden climax.

"I will always love you," Rachel whispered.

Claw cried out, stiffening, and he collapsed, lying against the warm body below him. It wasn't Rachel. His lovely Rachel.

Wat made a confused, questioning sound, and Claw pressed their cheeks together.

"I'm sorry," he whispered into the other battle sylph's ear, low enough that Sala wouldn't hear. Wat just whimpered again and put his arm around Claw's neck. The two held each other, seeking comfort for the brief moments they were allowed.

* * *

For four years Thul Cramdon had been leading a supply caravan from Eferem to Yed, then back through Eferem to Sylph Valley and then on to Para Dubh. He'd been one of the first to add Sylph Valley to his route, and as a result, he'd always enjoyed a degree of preferential treatment. He'd only had problems once, when one of his drovers got himself killed by battle sylphs for groping a girl. Thul had been careful to make sure nothing similar happened again. Not with his employees.

"I've always been agreeable to your rules!" he shouted now. "You have no right to do this to me!"

The man he shouted at, the chancellor of the Valley, regarded him impassively from across the desk. He wasn't the usual person Thul dealt with, but Thul had heard Galway died. The blonde girl on one side of him seemed a little less sure of herself, but the battle sylph on the other looked prone to violence. So, Thul took a deep breath and calmed. He wouldn't help his case by getting smeared across the wall behind him.

"It's not fair," he said instead. "I've invested thousands in coming here. I can't afford to lose that money."

"You won't," the chancellor told him, his hands clasped before him on the desk. "We're not turning down your trade. We're just setting limits on where your men are allowed to go while you're here."

"You're restricting me to the main road and a three-block area near the edge of town."

"Yes," the chancellor said. His eyes were flat. "Eferem has already sent both spies and assassins here. You're from Eferem. We don't want anyone thinking you might be a threat."

Thul hid a shudder, glancing quickly at the bored, blond battler. He didn't seem like much, but Thul knew the sylph could kill him and all of his men in seconds. The battle sylphs were the only part of the Valley he didn't like. They were usually everywhere.

The girl leaned forward. "We do want your trade," she assured him. "Never doubt that."

Thul wasn't terribly inclined to listen to a girl, but the battler looked less bored when she spoke and watched him warningly.

The girl continued. "But we do have to protect ourselves. It's for your protection as well. A wall is going up now to mark the areas to which your men will be granted access. We're making sure that all of the amenities you need will be available. But, you'll need to stay inside the trade area. Otherwise, well . . ." She glanced to her left. "The battle sylphs will react defensively."

The thought of that made Thul shudder. He'd seen what was left of his drover after the battlers were done with him. Still, he was too unhappy with the situation to keep his mouth shut. "I'm no spy. I may be from Eferem, but I work for myself.

Half my drovers sign up because they want to see this place. What am I supposed to tell them? They can come to a three-block area and if they go outside it, battlers will kill them? No one will sign up with that hanging over their heads!"

"We don't doubt that," the girl said. "Most of you traders are good men, but there have been deaths. And we're applying this to everyone, not just you. We're restricting the movements of everyone who isn't from the Valley. To acknowledge the difficulty this is causing . . . we're also willing to pay up to five percent more on previously negotiated goods."

Thul was silent a moment, considering. Given the size of his cargo, this was a significant amount of money—and he caught that he'd only see the extra five percent if he cooperated. He grimaced, reminding himself that money was money and finally nodded in agreement.

* * *

As the caravan merchant left, Leon looked down at his daughter. "What did you think?" he asked.

She eyed him uncertainly. "Can we afford to pay all this extra money?"

"We can't afford not to. By restricting traders to one area we're basically treating them like enemies. If we don't want them to start choosing other trade routes, we have to make it worth their while to put up with us."

Lizzy sighed, not really happy at the thought of walling off anyone who might be a spy or assassin. Short of starting a war with Eferem, which could result in wars with every kingdom this side of the ocean, they had no other choice. Earth sylphs were already raising a wall around the perimeter of the town. She could see it from her bedroom window.

Ril regarded them both unapologetically, just as he was unapologetic about following them everywhere they went and restricting them to pretty much staying either in the house or in their offices, where he watched the doors.

At least it was giving him time to train his daughter, Leon thought. And she was turning out to be a quick study. She definitely didn't mind Ril's continuing presence, though Leon could see that the sylphs' growing protectiveness was becoming a problem for many masters in the Valley. Already some were complaining, but Leon hadn't joined in. Ril had been his slave for decades, not allowed to speak or even choose his own shape; Leon figured he could deal with a little overprotectiveness.

Besides, he wasn't sure that Ril was being *too* cautious. Two battle sylph masters were dead and one had come uncomfortably close. Leon wasn't a big believer in coincidence. He wasn't sure what the connection between the three was— Rachel, Galway, and Moreena—and he wasn't entirely sure Rachel's death was due to anything other than old age. But he'd learned all about mistaken assumptions right around the first time he heard Ril speak.

So, they still had five assassins who'd escaped the Valley, thanks to someone who could hide himself from battlers. Leon was convinced it was Umut Taggart. He had given everyone a description, and Ril, who had seen Umut before, took the man's shape to show them. Umut wasn't walking into the Valley ever again, even without the walls. But, that had been the easy part. No one had been able to determine how the shelves in the warehouse collapsed, and Leon couldn't think of any way for Umut to have done it except with the help of his battler, Black, who would have given himself away with his hate aura.

Unless Umut had a better partnership with his battler than Leon could imagine and Black dropped his hate. That was a frightening thought. Mace's prideful refusal to believe aside, battle sylphs could indeed slip by one another. Ril had told

Leon about exiled battlers in the hive world who survived because they tricked battlers like Mace into not realizing they were there.

Still, it had to have been Umut. Alcor's other men just didn't have the subtleness to pull this off, while Umut had been working on discretion his entire life. Unfortunately, they had no clues. Rachel and Moreena might have been nothing more than an attempt to draw attention away, or a genuine coincidence. But Galway was a definite coup, and something Umut surely would have tried for.

He'd have to talk to Mace, Leon decided. Yes, Lizzy was helping and Ril was a pretty good secretary, but essentially he, Mace, and Solie were running everything, and Solie was progressing in her pregnancy. The Widow wouldn't like it, but she would have to help. They needed her mind to help keep the Valley together. There were any number of people here who could take care of her orphans, and Mace would certainly be happier with her near. Right now, he was almost the only battler still guarding the Valley as a whole, the only one relying on others to protect his mate.

* * *

It was laundry day at the Blackwell home, the fire in the kitchen built up to a conflagration. Several children were heating and hauling water outside by the bucket load, pouring it into a huge tub where the Widow wielded soap and scrubbed their clothing on a segmented board. She worked methodically, ignoring the ache in her back. Other children took the clean laundry and wrung out the water before carrying it over to the lines where Gabralina pinned it up.

Sitting cross-legged on the back porch and being pretty much useless, Wat stared mindlessly at the bees that circled nearby bushes in hope of finding late-fall flowers. Lily glanced toward him, then away. He was there to watch Gabralina, but he was watching her as well.

Wat. As her protector. Mace was furious about it, yet there wasn't much he could do if he was going to fulfil his duties. He didn't need any added stress, so she hadn't told him of the times Wat wandered off. He was just too unreliable to guard anyone, but Lily needed no guard anyway.

Wat was around today, staring at nothing even more stupidly than usual. Lily eyed him again, then turned back to her washing. The battler wasn't her problem.

Gabralina was hanging the last of the laundry, and she stepped back to admire it. The girl who'd been holding pins for her grinned.

"It all looks so clean, doesn't it?"

Gabralina smiled in agreement. "It does. It doesn't dry as fast here as it did back home when I was a girl. I did *so* much laundry."

"You did?" The girl seemed surprised.

Gabralina laughed. "It seemed I did nothing but. I was terribly poor before I met my friend Sala."

Sala. Her friend had brought pretty dresses and parties, and eventually even the introduction to the magistrate. She hadn't had to wash clothes at all. Still, it actually felt good to be doing that sort of thing again, a bit of physical labor, just as it felt good to take care of the children. Being part of something again was wonderful.

While she waited for the next batch to be scrubbed, Gabralina went over to her battler. He was staring off into space, his head tilted to one side and his mouth open, his face blank. She grinned at the sight. He looked so cute.

"Hiya," she said.

Wat blinked slowly, then turned his head, his mouth still hanging open. He blinked again, then grinned, his face coming alive as he saw her. "Hello!"

Gabralina sniggered. Sitting down, she leaned against him until he put an arm around her. "What are you thinking about?"

"Thinking?"

"You looked so thoughtful."

"Oh." He shrugged his shoulders so high that his entire body moved, and she giggled again as she was nearly knocked off the porch. "Nothing."

"Aw." She put her head on his shoulder. "You want to help me with the laundry?"

He eyed her dubiously. "Is that like chores? I saw soap. He you told me soap meant chores. He said chores are evil."

Gabralina howled with laughter. "Did he say that?"

"Yeah. Evil is bad." He looked down at her. "Is Sala evil?"

Gabralina froze. "Sala? No! Why do you say that?"

"I dunno. She scares me."

"Why?" Gabralina whispered, suddenly afraid. Sala was her friend. She owed Sala everything, and the girl had never asked for anything in return.

"I don't remember." Wat tilted his head back to one side, mouth open again. "I forget."

"Oh." Gabralina didn't know what to think.

The Widow called her name, interrupting her thoughts. "Gabralina! These sheets are ready for you."

"Right! Be right there!" The blonde girl jumped up and took a step away before turning back and kissing Wat on the cheek. He immediately grabbed for her, but she danced away, laughing, and went off to hang the newly washed sheets.

Chapter Fifteen

Thanks to the new wall and construction around the trade warehouses, the main market had moved, and the road was crowded with merchants selling their wares. Humming happily under her breath, Lizzy strode along it, stopping at a stall to look at some rolls of fabric. In her basket she already had an array of tomatoes and apples, as well as a chicken with the feathers still on.

Ril walked directly behind her, his eyes on the people crowding the square and flicking back over his shoulder at Leon, who trailed a dozen feet or so behind. Leon regarded his glances with amusement, but Ril didn't really care. He hadn't managed to talk Lizzy out of doing the shopping, and there was no one else at the moment to watch Leon, so he'd dragged the man along. Not that Leon minded. It was a beautiful day, the leaves on the trees were golden, and most everyone was outside. Dozens of sylphs trailed their masters here, some visible, many not.

A few stalls down, Justin Porter stood before a merchant selling forged spikes. Beside him, his father was haggling over the spikes with the vendor. Stria looked on with interest, but Justin didn't care. He was staring through the crowd at Lizzy.

Ril glared back at him across the distance, and Justin felt a flash of the battle sylph's disgust. It made Justin's stomach churn. It wasn't fair that he'd been made into Ril's master; it wasn't fair that the bond couldn't be broken and he couldn't be Stria's master instead. It especially wasn't fair that Lizzy had turned away from him for a stupid creature who was too crippled even to change his shape.

It was easier for her that way, Sala said. Justin shared lunch with the woman a few times a week now, and he was actually meeting her in less than an hour. *She* understood that battlers were just animals. She had one, but Claw knew his place and didn't say anything about whom she spent time with. She'd explained everything to Justin.

"A battle sylph is easy," she'd told him. "Too easy. You don't have to work at it. There's no depth there, not really. How can anyone have a real relationship with someone who has to do everything you say? Ril doesn't love her. He can't. He just follows instinct, that's all." She'd smiled sympathetically at Justin. "I feel so sorry for you. Lizzy just thinks that she has a good thing. She has no experience to know what an equal relationship really is. If she doesn't smarten up, she'll end up regretting it at the end of her life."

Justin bit his lip, thinking. This wasn't Lizzy's fault. She'd been through something terrible and Ril had come to her rescue. She hadn't seen how Justin and her father were right behind the battler, helping. She'd become overly grateful. And she enjoyed the battler sex—he couldn't forget that, much as he wanted to. He needed to be understanding, though.

Swallowing, Justin glanced at his father, still busy with the merchant. Stria was regarding him, her head tilted. He managed a smile, still bitterly regretting that she'd never belong to him. She looked away, back up at her master, and Justin took that moment to leave, crossing the road toward Lizzy at the cloth merchant's stall.

Ril saw him coming. His lip curled, and Justin felt the battler's rage, but no one else reacted. The sylph was focused solely on him. Justin forced himself to keep moving. Ril was forbidden to hurt him, and Justin could in fact order him to do anything he wanted.

Of course, then he'd have to deal with Leon. The older man was a dozen feet away, examining a bow. Leon had always been his supporter, Justin reminded himself, even if he was overly sentimental toward his battler.

Justin ignored Ril's silent warning and walked up to Lizzy. She was so beautiful. When he stopped behind her, Ril hissed. Loudly. Everyone around him jumped back, exclaiming, and Leon's head snapped up.

Lizzy glanced around in confusion before she saw him. "Justin? What are you doing here?"

He licked his lips, nervous. "Buying stakes with Dad. But, um, I wanted to say hi, see how you're doing."

Ril made a noise like fabric ripping.

"Stop that!" Justin yelped. You had to be forceful with sylphs, Sala said. They liked someone else to be in control. "I'm just talking to her!"

Ril blinked and fell silent.

"Justin, you know you're not supposed to tell Ril what to do."

"I just wanted to talk to you is all," Justin explained. "I'm allowed to, aren't I?"

Lizzy frowned. "I don't know. You said some pretty awful things about me."

Justin stared downward, willing her to feel how sincere he was, though he was bitterly aware that only Ril could. Leon appeared beside them, but he didn't say anything, just watched for a moment before he pulled Ril back. The sylph shot a look at his master, and Leon started whispering to him.

"I'm sorry," Justin told Lizzy. "I can't tell you how sorry I am. I know what I said was inexcusable, but I was upset. I know that's not good enough, but can you forgive me anyway?" He watched her hopefully.

She frowned, her lips pursed. "I don't know."

"You have to!" he said. "I said I was sorry! What's wrong with you?"

Lizzy glared at him. "I don't have to do anything. And there's nothing wrong with me. You're the one with the problem!"

Justin felt like she'd slapped him. Across the road he heard Ril's chuckle, and he could feel the creature gloating.

"You . . ." He had to make Lizzy understand. "He's no good for you, Lizzy! He's just a thing!"

She turned her back on him. "Go away, Justin." Then she moved toward her father and Ril, her head held high.

Justin's heart broke. "It's not fair!" he shouted. "You were supposed to be mine!"

* * *

"Oh, that's *terrible*."

Sala leaned against the table, her fingers laced together. Quietly, Claw poured tea into her cup and then Justin's, though his hand trembled so badly he sloshed some over the side. Sala sighed and waved him away.

"Poor creature," she remarked sadly. "Battlers are all a little crazy." She returned her attention to the problem at hand. "I'm sorry it hasn't worked out yet, Justin. But that's no reason to stop."

Justin grimaced and leaned back in his chair. "I don't think it's ever going to work out. He's got her wrapped around his finger."

"Don't give up," Sala urged, leaning over the table to lay a hand against his crossed arms. He lowered them, and she took one of his hands. "She'll come around. She has to see how false his feelings for her really are. Eventually. Battlers can't feel love. They just feel lust and think that's all that's important."

Behind her, Claw shuddered.

Sala gave a laugh and shook her head. "Honestly, Justin, I'm amazed at your control. If it were me, I don't think I'd be able to stop myself from ordering Ril to hurt himself. If he weren't around, Lizzy would come to realize how special you are."

Justin shrugged, though he'd like nothing better than to make Ril suffer the way he himself had in Meridal. Even now the memory tormented him. But: "I'd get caught if I tried."

Sala laid a finger against her lip. "Oh, I guess so. I hadn't thought of that. If I were in your situation, I'd just get so mad I'd probably do something really mean and then feel awful afterwards, even if it was the right thing to do."

"Such as?"

She shrugged. "Oh, I don't know. Order him to drink energy other than his master's? That would probably hurt terribly, and no one would think it was anything other than him being sick. Oh, wait, that wouldn't work. He'd tell everyone." She frowned. "I suppose you could tell him to forget he got the order. Can you even do that?" She shrugged again and sipped her tea. "I suppose it doesn't matter. It's good for him you're such a nice person."

Claw brought more tea at her command, and Justin was pleased that she didn't seem to notice exactly what a good idea she'd given him.

* * *

Sala had noticed Justin's expression, of course, though she didn't react. She didn't have nearly as much time to work with him as she would have liked, but she hadn't expected to need a dupe so suddenly. It was fortunate that she'd discovered the tension between Justin Porter and the chancellor's battler. Part of her just wanted to tell the bitter little coward what to do, but she had to be careful only to plant the idea. The last thing she could afford was to have anyone suspect her as the source.

Still, she'd given Justin a very effective way of dealing with his rival. Not that she cared if it got him Lizzy back. Just as long as he was caught doing it.

* * *

The entire Petrule family was gathered around the kitchen table, laughing and eating dinner. Ril sat in the living room, paging through a book. He loved the family, but he didn't need to eat human food and was feeling out of sorts from not being able to take his own form anymore now that Luck was gone. Unsettled as he was, the sight of the younger girls eating made him nauseated. Especially peas.

A chorus of ewws sounded from the kitchen, followed by Leon and Betha's protests, and Ril shuddered. Food. He didn't understand how humans could stand it sometimes.

Outside, the sun was setting. The family would go to bed soon, which would give him and Lizzy some time alone. The cottage at the end of the garden was all theirs now, but it was only a single room and the furniture wasn't as comfortable as here. It was a private place, though—provided they could ever get Cara, Ralad, Nali, and Mia not to come barging in whenever they wanted. He'd never thought he'd have to resort to such things, but he was starting to think they needed a lock.

Smirking, he flipped a page. He adored those girls, even if Mia was determined that he turn into a pony for her. She just kept begging. It hurt too much, so he'd have to bring Claw over sometime. He'd probably be delighted to be a pony. Or a puppy. Or whatever other furry animal the girls thought he should be.

Outside, Ril sensed something and looked toward the front of the house. Reaching out with his senses, he found Justin. He snarled.

The family was still eating. Leon was yelling for everyone to shut their mouths and stop trying to disgust him, it wasn't going to work, so Ril shuddered and rose, headed for the front door. He'd managed to put Justin's little conversation with Lizzy out of his mind for the past three days, though he'd been hearing from Wat and Claw that the boy was going around saying how much he hated battlers.

He went out the front door and down the walk. Crossing his arms, he glared at the boy who stood at the gate. "Go away before I kill you."

"You won't hurt me," Justin snapped defiantly, though Ril could feel his fear. "You're under orders."

Ril snorted. "Don't push me."

"Liar," Justin said, his voice low. "You can't do anything to me. You have to do exactly what I say."

Ril's eyes widened as he realized his mistake, but he hadn't actually thought Justin had this in him. The boy had always been afraid of what others would do if he tried anything.

He turned to bolt back into the house or shout for Lizzy or Leon, but Justin pointed a finger at him and said, "Don't move, don't shout, don't speak, don't call for help, don't project your emotions, don't do anything."

Ril froze, swearing inside. Leon was only a few dozen feet away, but he couldn't call for him. He couldn't even project his emotions and alert his master that way. He seethed quietly instead, watching Justin move closer.

The young man walked right up to him, features twisted with hate. "Don't move," he repeated. Then he punched the battler in the face as hard as he could.

Ril licked his lip and worked his jaw. Looking back, he saw Justin holding his fist, gasping in pain. He smirked.

"You bastard," Justin whispered. "You goddamned bastard. I *hate* you. You've taken everything from me. Do you understand that?"

Under orders not to move or speak, Ril just stared, letting his expression say everything.

Justin obviously understood. He shoved his face right up in Ril's. "I could order you to go away," he whispered. "I could order you to pick a direction and just keep going until you run out of energy and die. *Nobody* would be able to find you."

Ril went cold.

Justin grinned. "I could do it," he sniggered, poking the battler in the chest. Then the grin faded. "I tried being nice. I tried being compassionate and understanding about everything Lizzy went through, but she only wants you. She actually thinks you're some kind of person! Well, you're not. You're nothing but a slave, and it doesn't matter what kind of so-called freedoms they give you. You'll always be a slave."

The young man shook his head. "What do you think is going to happen after Leon and Lizzy die? You'll end up being property again, I promise it!" His expression of anger smoothed over. "Only, I guess you won't last that long. I love Lizzy, more than you can imagine, and I won't see her ruined by an animal. She'll be free to love me again once you're dead. *Free.*"

Ril felt a cold but impotent hatred as Justin straightened, clearing his throat and obviously thinking over a set of instructions he intended to relay. Ril watched him warily, still unable to project the fear or anger that would alert Leon and Lizzy and perhaps save him.

"You'll forget this meeting," Justin began. "You'll obey my orders, but you won't remember getting them so you can't tell anyone." He took a deep breath. "You won't feed from your masters' energy anymore. You'll feed from any source *but* them. And you'll think you're supposed to. That's my order."

Ril stared at him. Justin was ordering him to poison himself?

Of course he was.

Justin smiled. "Don't worry about Lizzy. I know she'll be

upset about your lingering death, but I'll make sure to give her all the support she needs. It'll be good for her, to learn someone real is there for her."

More than ever before, Ril wanted to kill. He wanted to erupt, to maim, to destroy. He just stood there.

Justin stepped back into the shadows. Pointing at Ril, he said, "Obey my orders, battler. Take a deep swallow. I want to watch you do it."

Immediately, Ril forgot what Justin had just told him. He even forgot that the young man was still there, standing in the bushes. He was hungry, and the world around him was full of energy, swirling in patterns he could feel tingling all over. He took a deep draught, pulling that energy into his own pattern.

His scream shattered the night air, his agony blasting out along the hive lines to his masters and every sylph in the Valley. Pain—horrible pain, crippling, poisonous agony like no sylph should ever feel—burst through him. His back arched, his mouth gaped in that ongoing scream, and shouts sounded inside the house. Roars sounded throughout the town, battlers rising as the other sylphs took cover.

Snapping forward, Ril dropped to his hands and knees and threw up, energy spilling out of him as a scattering of already dispersing sparks. He couldn't understand what had happened or even where his pain was coming from.

A few feet away, Justin scrambled to his feet. He had tripped backward in surprise at the ruckus, but now he stared at Ril in shock and fear. The battler gaped at him, trying to snarl but only gagging. He threw up again.

Justin backed away, shaking. "Don't you say anything about me being here," he gasped. "I order you—"

A blast wave of power slammed into the ground where Justin was standing, vaporizing everything to a depth of three feet.

Ril was thrown backward. He slammed into the steps leading to the Petrule porch just as the door opened and Leon ran out,

Lizzy right behind. Smeared with Justin's blood, Ril clutched his gut and threw up a third time.

"Ril!" Leon gasped, shocked in a way Ril had rarely felt. Lizzy had her hands clasped over her mouth, looking horrified. Betha held her daughter from behind, staring in fear over Lizzy's shoulder before turning back to the house and shouting that the other children shouldn't come out.

Claw landed on the edge of the crater he'd created, stared down at it with a shudder before rushing over to kneel in front of Ril. Leon crouched beside him.

Ril managed to vomit sparkling energy up all over his master's arms and lap. His ears were ringing so loudly he couldn't be sure what anyone was saying. He saw Mace drop down and land in a crouch on the nearby walkway, and other angry battlers descended as well. Pulled into Leon's arms, Ril convulsed, trying to hang on to the energy he'd consumed, afraid that if he lost any more, the rest of him would fall apart.

Mace stepped forward, his expression intense. Ril watched as the older battler knelt and abruptly slammed a hand into him. Ril gasped, and Mace siphoned out a spiderweb of energy, scattering it across the lawn with a snap of his arm.

His pain eased. Ril sagged against Leon, still not understanding what had happened.

"What?" Leon demanded, echoing Ril's thoughts. "What's going on?"

Claw shuddered. "That man. He was doing something to Ril."

"What man?" Lizzy gasped. She stared at the crater. "Oh, gods!"

Justin, Ril thought. It had been Justin. He'd seen him. Starving and miserable, he reached out for the energy in the air and the ground, drawing it into him, trying to find sustenance and relief.

"Stop!" Mace shouted.

"What?" Leon said.

Mace leaned toward Ril. "He tried to drink the wrong kind of energy. Not yours."

"What? Why?" Leon stared at Ril. "Why aren't you drinking my energy?"

Ril regarded him wearily. "Why would I?"

Everyone was silent.

The battlers and humans looked grim. Leon's arms tightened around Ril as Lizzy knelt down, staring at him. "It was Justin, wasn't it? He did something to you."

Leon stroked his hair. "Ril, you need to drink my energy. Or Lizzy's."

"Are you insane? It's poisonous."

Leon sighed. "Someone get the queen."

Chapter Sixteen

Her stomach greatly distended, the pregnant Solie waddled around the house and toward a small cottage at the end of the back garden. Small faces watched her from the window, and she smiled at the Petrule girls as she made her way through the darkness. Heyou guided her with an arm around her waist.

"They're sure it was Justin Porter?" she asked.

"I think so. Who else could it have been? Not much left to identify him, though."

Solie grimaced. She'd passed the crater in the front yard and was glad the night was now too dark to see any blood. "Has anyone told his father?"

"Uh, I don't know."

Solie eyed Heyou and cupped his cheek with one hand. "Make sure someone tells him. Someone . . . kind."

"What, you don't want us to shout it down the chimney?"

"I'd rather you didn't."

"I promise we won't laugh much."

When Solie shot him a look, he grinned. "Ass," she said.

Lizzy and Ril's cottage was a tiny thing only twenty feet wide, formed of swirling stone with a thatched roof. The windows were round and the door made of dark wood. Dillon stood outside, in human shape for once and looking moody.

"How's Moreena doing?" Solie asked.

Dillon shrugged and bowed. "Good. Blue's watching her. Mace said to tell you he and Claw went to look over the corpse's place."

"Right." Solie looked at Heyou. "Can I at least *suggest* the lot of you show a little compassion?"

"You can always suggest," Heyou replied. "Considering he tried to kill our hive mate, I'd suggest you make it an order."

Dillon opened the door. Solie rolled her eyes and went inside.

The cottage was a single room, its wooden floor covered by a patterned rug. A small couch was placed near the front, while a dresser was turned lengthwise and pushed against the back wall to create two separate living spaces, one with a small table and the other featuring a double bed. Lizzy and Leon sat on wooden chairs pulled up by the bed. Ril was mostly buried under the covers.

The two Petrules looked up as she entered, and Solie held open her arms. Lizzy hurried toward her. The young woman hugged her warmly before she stepped back.

"Ril's messed up. Somehow, Justin has him thinking that he's supposed to drink any energy but ours. Father doesn't want to risk making it worse. We don't know what else was done to him."

"Doesn't Ril know?"

"No. He doesn't remember."

Solie approached the bed. "How is he?" she whispered to Leon.

"I'm fine," Ril said loudly. He pushed the bedcovers back and sat up, jabbing a finger at his master. "He won't let me up. I'm not sick." He put a hand against his middle and made a face. "Maybe a little queasy in the stomach is all."

"You don't have a stomach," Heyou pointed out. Ril glared.

"We think Justin ordered him to drink the wrong energy and then to forget about being ordered to do so," Leon said.

Ril protested. "He didn't!"

"Well, I want to be sure anything Justin told him to do is completely gone," Leon said.

"Hey, Justin's dead," Heyou argued. "Any order he gave, Ril can just ignore now."

"Obviously he's not," Leon shot back. "Justin set him up so that he doesn't even know he's obeying an order."

The chancellor's expression was flat, but thanks to the battlers Solie could tell how utterly furious he was. Even when Alcor's battle sylphs were attacking, Solie hadn't felt him so angry. Or so frightened. He had no idea what had been done to Ril, and he had been paired with the sylph for over twenty years. She understood the intensity of such a bond.

Solie waddled heavily over to the bed, and Ril moved his legs so that she could sit down. He looked at her with exasperation before finally lowering his eyes in respect.

She smiled reassuringly and took a deep breath. "Ril, what did Justin order you to do tonight?"

"Nothing."

She waited for him to look up at her and focused. "Ril, what did Justin order you to do tonight?"

Solie wasn't a sylph. Even so, after six years as their queen she'd learned a lot. She still used Mace to help bond sylphs to new masters, but she didn't need that so much anymore, and she certainly didn't need it now, for this. She focused, and the force of her will swept irresistibly through Ril. He had other masters, more masters than any other sylph in the Valley, but, human or not, she was queen. He had no choice but to obey her first if possible.

Ril's eyes widened, locked on hers. "I . . . I . . . I don't remember."

"Tell me what Justin told you to do tonight."

He shuddered. "I don't remember!"

"Solie," Leon cautioned.

Solie frowned. If Ril remembered, he would have told her; she could feel how badly he wanted to obey. That made their enemy's plan sneaky but really smart. Ril couldn't tell anyone what had been done to him if he couldn't recall it. So, she'd have to get around that somehow.

For the moment she could only tell how hungry he was. Leon's direct order was holding him back from poisoning himself again.

"Ril," she said, making her voice as firm as she possibly could. "You will feed only from your masters or your queen. You will never feed from any other source again, no matter who orders you. Do you understand?"

"Yes," he said.

He sounded so unsure that she had to smile. "Drink some of Leon and Lizzy's energy, Ril. I promise it won't poison you."

The battler frowned, but his eyes half lidded as he drew in energy from the Petrules. She felt his surprise and confusion, but he immediately gained strength.

"What orders has Justin given you before this?" Solie asked.

"He told me to die," Ril answered, distracted.

Lizzy shrieked. "WHAT?"

Leon shushed his daughter, his face red, while Solie shook her head, silently glad that Justin was dead if he was willing to order something so awful. Heyou smirked, picking up on her anger.

"You're still alive," she pointed out to Ril.

"He left the how and when open," the battler explained. Shrugging, he added, "I figured I'd die someday, so I'd obey him then."

Solie laughed. Clever. "Anything else?"

"I really don't remember."

Heyou piped up. "Why don't you just order him to ignore anything Justin told him to do?"

Solie looked up. "That's the whole problem. How can he know what he's not supposed to do when he doesn't know when he's doing something he was told?"

Heyou looked taken aback. "Oh. Uh. *Huh?*"

"Dammit," Leon muttered. "Maybe something else? Maybe some sort of overall order not to do anything to hurt himself?"

Lizzy moaned, staring at her hands. "I can't believe Justin did this. I mean, did he really think he could make me love him by killing Ril?"

Her father put an arm around her while Ril watched worriedly.

Heyou eyed Lizzy as well, scratching his head, but then he paused, listening. A moment later he had Solie around the waist and was throwing her backward, shifting form to catch her in his mantle as he did.

Solie screamed, tumbling against solid darkness as the front door crashed open and a second cloud passed inside. Mace shifted to human form as he landed on the bed. His massive hand lashed out and locked around Ril's throat, slamming him back against the headboard.

Lizzy shrieked.

"WHAT ARE YOU DOING?!" Leon thundered.

"Claw found a diary at the boy's. He ordered Ril to sabotage the warehouse, kill Rachel and Galway, murder those assassins, and try to kill Moreena. My master was next on the list."

"I didn't!" Ril gasped.

"He ordered him to forget," Mace finished. "We don't know what else he was told to do. The queen is in danger."

Leon wore a belt knife. He had it out and against Mace's throat. "Let him go."

"That won't hurt me."

"Care to find out for sure?"

"Stop!" Solie shouted, emerging from Heyou. Awkwardly, she edged onto her feet, leaning on Heyou and keeping one hand on her belly. "Mace, don't hurt him."

"He's a danger to you."

"Sylphs don't hurt queens."

"Crazy ones do."

Leon pressed his knife against Mace's throat until the skin pushed inward, and the battler squinted at him out of the corner of his eye.

"Ril isn't crazy."

"Release him, Mace," Solie ordered. "Leon, put the knife away."

Mace slowly let go of Ril, and Leon stepped back, sheathing the knife. The two glared at each other while Ril sat up, watching Solie instead. Heyou stepped in front of her, watching him.

Solie sighed. "Ril, this is an order. No matter what you've been told, you will not harm me or the Widow Blackwell, or any other human in this Valley. Do you understand?"

"Yes."

Leon spoke up. "He won't be able to defend himself now."

"Like you were ever planning to risk him in a fight again," she snapped. Her back was starting to hurt, and the stress was making her tired. So was the late hour. She turned to Mace and asked, "Happy?"

"Happy enough," he replied. "The hive is safe."

It was. Solie turned away. Maybe now the more overprotective sylphs would calm down; she was tired of getting complaints from their beleaguered masters.

"I'd like to see this diary in the morning—and anything else you find." She walked with Heyou toward the doorway, then stopped. "Where's Claw?"

Mace paused, checking. "He went back to his master."

"Oh." Solie pictured Sala for a moment, whom she still didn't like. She hadn't seen Claw since Rachel died. Sometimes she wondered if he was avoiding her, but that didn't make any sense, so she headed out the door and back toward home.

After about forty steps, Heyou took pity on her waddling gait. Lifting her in his arms, he carried her the rest of the way.

* * *

Claw walked slowly down the underground hive passageway and past several open rooms. With the sun down and their masters asleep, dozens of sylphs were assembled for classes, lectures given mostly in the mental speech they all shared. He peered in at the assembled sylphs, most of them in their elemental forms, only a few maintaining human appearance.

He missed being in these classes, missed sitting at the cramped little desk while Rachel taught them to read, or write, or to do all those things with numbers. He missed so many things, and his walk slowed to a shuffle. He began trembling.

Sala didn't like it when he trembled. Maybe now she'd be pleased with him—though he certainly wasn't pleased with himself. He'd killed that boy when she'd said to: before he could protest his innocence for all the crimes she wanted him blamed for. Then Claw had "found" the diary she'd written, detailing all of the things she'd actually done and ascribing them to Justin. He'd accomplished these things while avoiding the queen.

He continued on, passing another class he wasn't allowed to join. He had really hoped Sala's plan would fail, but its success was unsurprising. She was too good at the details.

With the threat to the hive dead, the sylphs would settle down and stop guarding their masters so obsessively. These classes would be three or four times this size, and Sala would be able to do whatever she wanted again. He didn't know what she wanted, not entirely. He didn't want to. He just wished he could be ordered to forget, like Ril or Wat. Wat didn't have to remember a thing, and he didn't shake when he was in the presence of his master. He didn't have to stay celibate, either, though Claw was glad of that aspect. For all his instinctive nature, he didn't want Sala touching him. He was lucky that she preferred Wat.

Of course, that just made him even gladder for Wat that Wat never remembered.

He reached her apartment, the absolute last place he wanted to be, and went inside. Sala sat primly in a chair, sewing a skirt for herself.

"Tell me."

Claw closed the door and leaned against it. "The boy gave the order you wanted. Ril's pain alerted the hive, and I killed the boy before anyone could question him. Then I planted the diary. Ril and Justin took the blame for everything."

"Did they kill him?"

Claw shuddered but forced himself to stop before she noticed. "Ril? No."

Sala shrugged. "Pity. Spend time with the others tomorrow, encourage them to relax and leave their masters alone again."

He didn't want to know why. Dismissed, he shuffled into the next room and shut the door, wanting to lock it but not daring. Going to the corner farthest from the bed, he slid down and laid his head on his knees, dreaming yet again that Rachel hadn't died—or better yet, that he'd managed to die with her.

* * *

Sala felt Claw's misery, and she tried to put it out of her mind. It wasn't easy. His emotions weren't anything he could entirely banish, though he hid them well from other sylphs. That was something, but she'd be much happier if he could also hide them from her. He couldn't. Apparently that little flaw was why enslaved battlers hit their masters with a constant aura of hate. Sala would have preferred hate, but such an aura would have brought her far too much attention.

His emotions kept her from sleeping with him. Wat was

better for that, anyway, with the added bonus that knowing she slept with Wat instead of him had to be driving Claw mad. Sala certainly hoped so. She'd been investing quite a lot of time in making him insane, and he was being far more resistant than she'd expected. She wasn't entirely sure she needed him crazy, but it seemed better to be safe than sorry.

Justin had certainly turned out well, despite the limited amount of time she'd had to work on him. His public hatred for Ril had made him a perfect scapegoat.

Sala knew she'd been lucky. She hadn't expected the battle sylphs to react the way they had to the deaths and accidents she'd arranged. Killing Rachel to get Claw had made the battlers move closer to their masters. Killing Galway to isolate Solie had made them even more protective. The attempt on Moreena had made them impenetrable. Single-minded creatures. She would never get a chance to kill Solie if she hadn't given some other focus for their fear. Even so, nothing was working out the way she planned.

Despite her attempts to become Solie's friend, the woman didn't trust her. Somehow she had better instincts than her battlers. Hence Sala's work to make Claw crazy. If Sala couldn't kill Solie herself, Claw would. So long as he could mate with her afterward, it didn't matter how insane he was. Once would be enough to make her queen. After that, she likely wouldn't need him.

This time, everything was going to work out. She wouldn't be impatient, not like she'd been in Yed. She should have waited longer to kill that magistrate, used a method other than poison, been more discreet in her rearrangement of his finances so that everything went to Gabralina. She'd planned to inherit after Gabralina met with her own accident, but the magistrate's family was smarter than she'd hoped, and she supposed that she really had been sloppy.

It would be harder to stop her this time. She had to be

careful for the time being, but once she was queen, every battle sylph in the Valley would protect her, and every sylph would obey. She'd have to kill a few more people: Heyou, to see if Solie really needed him. And, she would have murdered Leon already if she didn't know it would have the sylphs even more upset. Still, he'd be the first one to die after she ascended. Once he and a few others were gone, there wouldn't be anyone else to concern herself with. Not unless she wanted to.

Sala finished sewing a button on her blouse and bit off the end of the thread. There would be others to do this sort of thing for her once she was queen. She eyed the button critically. It was a bit crooked but good enough. For now. She set the garment aside and went to find something to eat.

Chapter Seventeen

High atop the tower that marked the center of town, Ril sat on a ledge below the tallest pinnacle, his arms encircling his drawn-up knees. Claw sat to one side of him, Wat to the other. Dillon floated in cloud form before them all, regarding them through ball lightning eyes.

Ril didn't want to talk to any of them, had actually struggled to make his way up here alone. The others had just shown up. Still, Leon and Lizzy couldn't reach him here, and Betha wouldn't eye him warily for going near her children.

Gingerly, Claw reached out and put a trembling hand on his shoulder. "I know how you feel," he mumbled.

Ril shot an angry look at the other battler, but there was such misery in Claw's eyes that he was silenced. If anyone could know his pain, he realized, it was Claw. Well, Mace too, but Mace hadn't come out of his slavery broken.

His anger faded. How could Claw even speak to him? He'd been Rachel's master, and Mace had found the little bottle of poison used to kill her in Justin's cottage this morning. Ril didn't know whether to be happy that he couldn't remember lacing her food with it. Ultimately, it didn't matter. He'd killed women before, and apparently he'd done it again.

But this one hadn't been threatening him or Lizzy. She'd been nothing but kind to all of them.

"I'm so sorry," Ril said. "I don't know what to say."

Claw looked down, swallowing. His emotions felt unstable, just as they always had, and layered with a tremendous sadness that hadn't been banished even with the arrival of his new master.

"It's not your fault," the sylph whispered. "Please, I don't want to talk about it anymore."

"Okay," Ril whispered in return. He changed focus, straight ahead, and saw Dillon's sparking eyes in the shadow of his body. That was no better, given how he'd come close to killing Moreena, too. If Blue hadn't been close by, Dillon would be as miserable as Claw.

It's not your fault, stupid, Dillon told him as he sagged.

Ril glared at him in response.

Up and over the top of the steeple, another cloud appeared and dropped down beside Dillon. Ril's eyes rolled. So much for getting away.

Is he still moping? Heyou asked Dillon.

Yeah.

Ril grimaced and dragged a hand through his hair. "Look, Heyou, about Galway . . ."

The lightning inside Heyou increased in speed. *Oh. Um, it's not your fault. I know this. I understand it. I don't blame you at all.*

Really? Dillon said. *You told me you hated him.*

Yeah, but then Solie explained to me how it wasn't his fault and he had no control because Justin was his master.

Really? And that worked?

Well, not really, but then she ordered me to stand on my head all night. The young battler turned and faced Ril. *I miss Galway, I really do. I loved that guy a lot. He was the first one to get me to figure out that all men aren't evil. But you didn't kill him, Justin did. He just used you to do it.*

Alongside Ril, Claw had his hands clasped in his lap and was shaking terribly, whimpering almost silently under his breath. On Ril's other side, Wat stared in confusion. "Why did Justin do it? Why did he kill people's masters?"

They were all quiet for a moment, none of them really sure. It certainly didn't make much sense to Ril. Justin had wanted Lizzy to be his wife, but she wasn't interested. Justin hated Ril for being with her, but then why hadn't he gone after Ril directly? Why had he hurt innocent bystanders before giving Ril the order to drink poisonous energy?

Heyou finally answered. *Mace was talking to Solie about the diary they found. Justin hated battle sylphs and he wanted us all to suffer, so he went after our masters. He got a sick charge out of ordering Ril to help. Plus, that kept him safe, the bastard.*

Then why did he try to hurt Ril?

Heyou seemed a bit less sure. *Well, he still hated him, didn't he? He wanted him to suffer most of all—but he was hardly going to kill Lizzy to do it. He wanted Ril to die so that he could finally woo her.*

"I would never have hurt Lizzy," Ril whispered. "No matter what he ordered, I wouldn't have."

Wat frowned. "Oh."

He was dressed differently from the rest of them, but didn't seem affected by it. He wasn't trusted with anything important anymore, but he was still part of the hive. Claw was the miserable one; Ril didn't know what to say to him. Claw had always been damaged, and Ril felt a little too vulnerable himself at the moment to try. He simply clapped a hand on the other battler's shoulder.

"At least it's over," he said.

The other battlers agreed. But, Claw just buried his face in his hands, his heart still full of grief.

"*Ril!*"

Everyone looked down. Five stories below, Lizzy stood at the base of the building, her hands on her hips. She stared up at them, one foot tapping on the ground.

Ril stared down at her, not sure what to say. He loved the girl desperately, but what was she thinking? He knew and he didn't, and he didn't know what to do. He'd been avoiding Leon for the same reason.

At the sight of her, he felt a strong desire to go and hold her. He also wanted to stay where he was and sort through his emotions.

I think she wants you, Heyou remarked.

And she's not going away, Dillon added.

"So, go talk to her!" Wat decided cheerfully. Putting a hand on Ril's back, he pushed. Hard.

Ril pitched off the ledge. Lizzy's shriek echoed through his mind, along with his own loud yelp. Desperate, he changed shape, his form shifting liquidly, his clothes tumbling around him as he took on a body he was intimately familiar with but that was too small to hold his clothes.

Agony shot through him, damaged nerve endings igniting as the pattern of his form changed. Somewhere in the back of his mind he felt Lizzy's terror and Leon's more distant alarm, and then his wings spread. Shrieking, Ril soared above the hard ground in the form of a red-feathered hawk. It was the shape he'd worn from the day he first came through the gate until Solie gave him his freedom.

Lizzy ducked as he flew over her head. She turned, holding her hair back from the wind of his passage as he banked and swooped around, wings beating hard as he threw his feet forward. When Lizzy held up her arm, he landed on it, careful not to hurt her with his sharp claws.

"Oh, thank goodness," she breathed. She pulled him close, his feathered breast pressed against her as she wrapped her arm around him and kissed the top of his beak, right between his eyes. Then she looked up at the four battlers on the ledge, all of them looking down.

"Dummy!" she shouted. "You could have hurt him!"

The four battlers, two in cloud form and two in human,

stared back. Then Dillon formed a tentacle of solid black smoke and smacked Wat.

Lizzy bent down and scooped up Ril's clothes and boots, balancing him carefully on her arm as she did. Wings folded, Ril watched. He was stuck like this for a while unless he wanted to embarrass her by shifting and standing naked in front of half the town. There were light crowds out that morning.

Turning, she started across the square, carrying him on her arm. "You're being very stupid," she said as she walked. "I mean, really. You *know* you have to obey orders. You did every dumb thing my dad ever told you when I was growing up. Did you blame yourself for any of that? You haven't even blamed *him*."

Ril just blinked at her.

Across the square was a small building behind a stable that served as an auxiliary entrance to the hive. As if he'd heard his name, Leon appeared, looking right toward them. His expression was worried.

Of course, Ril realized. He'd felt the pain of the change.

Lizzy saw her father, and she waved him away. Leon raised his eyebrows but didn't follow.

"Justin was an asshole," Lizzy said, her mouth becoming a tight line. "I wish I'd never met him. I never loved him, but I really hate him now. I'm glad he's dead. He's the one who killed all those people, not you. Got it? I don't want you blaming yourself."

Ril cooed in response.

She peered at him, stopping for a moment and shuffling the clothing she held until she could stroke his head with her hand. "That's not an order, Ril. Daddy and I both agree we won't give you orders. That's what I hate Justin for most. Nobody should do that to anyone else. Ever. Not when they have no choice but to obey."

She carried him home. Ril let her, watching her contentedly

out of one eye. He loved this girl, had loved her from the moment she was born, was tied to her with some strange bond that he didn't entirely understand. But he knew he loved her, and he didn't want to live life without her being his master.

He'd known intellectually that Lizzy didn't blame him for what happened, but emotionally he hadn't wanted to face her. He wasn't sure what he'd say to her father, either. The man had put a knife to Mace's throat for him! That was taking his life in his hands.

Ril cooed at Lizzy again and, as she turned down their street and went past her family's home to their cottage, he chucked his head against her shoulder. Carrying him inside, she closed the door. Ril hopped off her arm, changing back to human form with another flash of pain. By the time he recovered, she was standing before him, her lips succulent and soft.

She reached for him. Ril met her halfway, his arms tightening around her body and bunching up her dress until he managed to get it off. They ended up entwined on the bed, moving passionately against each other, Ril kissing her deeply.

His hands and hips moved, lost in the moment—and in her. The danger was over, Justin was dead, and she was safe. And she was his. Ril finally let himself relax. He put the last few months out of his mind, just as battle sylphs all across the Valley were doing. Everything was good again. The hive was safe.

* * *

Leon stood in the sunlight outside the steep stairwell leading back down into the hive, leaning against the outer wall with his arms crossed. He'd felt Ril's pain clearly—very clearly. It had shocked him out of his office with the sudden fear that Mace decided to destroy Ril after all, and he'd nearly run Claw's poor master over while racing for the stairs. Ril had simply changed shape, though, for whatever reason.

He frowned, thinking about that. He'd felt his sylph's pain very clearly, and now he was noting a strange sort of block from his battler, which meant Ril and his daughter were making love. It was a considerate thing that Ril didn't want to broadcast such intimacies, and that was something Leon had certainly never complained about before, but it wasn't perfect. He could still feel his battler. He always could.

Sala came up the stairs, eyeing him curiously as she passed. Leon barely noticed. He could feel Ril now; he didn't want to, but could. He'd definitely felt when Ril changed to a hawk and back.

"Why didn't I feel him change when he killed Galway?" he muttered aloud.

Turning, he headed back to his office. Sala stood behind him, fingering her shawl and watching him go.

* * *

The itch was getting worse, drilling along the pattern to her queen and weakening it, driving her mad with the need to make it stop.

We have to go, her companion said for the thousandth time.

The nameless sylph didn't want to go. She wanted to go home, back to her hive and her hive mates; only, she felt heavy and bloated, her insides twisting around themselves, changing her.

I don't want to leave, she said.

The exile pressed against her, and though he was getting to be big for a battle sylph, he was much smaller than she, too small to stop the itching. Reduced food supply or not, she'd grown since she left the hive.

He pressed harder against her, nuzzling, and it felt good, though it also felt strange. *We can't stay here. Let me take you somewhere else*, he begged.

And then what? she wondered.

Down several rows from them, a group of earth sylphs were harvesting crops, ignoring her and not seeing him, shielded as he was by her bulk. A small battler was with them, doing the actual work of cutting the plants. It was good practice for him in using his energy. The nameless sylph dully watched them, her belly pressed against the cool soil below.

A space opened almost directly above. The nameless sylph stared, not understanding for a moment what she was seeing as the earth sylphs squealed in terror and ran, stumbling on their many legs across the field. The young battler nearly tumbled over himself, turning on it and hissing.

I've seen those before, her companion said.

So had she. They opened around the hive sometimes, never for long, but they caused whispers and discussions over what they might be. Battle sylph blasts did nothing against them, the circles just absorbing the energy, and the vortexes did nothing themselves, though sometimes sylphs vanished through them. The unspoken rule was to ignore them, but sylphs sometimes were curious. They went through and never returned.

The hive battler approached the colorless circle, hissing and lashing out with his energy. The circle, which hovered several queen-lengths above the ground, flashed whenever his power connected, but otherwise it did nothing. Both the nameless sylph and her exile watched the youngster, confounded, hissing and spitting and lunging at the thing. He didn't vanish through it, and finally he turned to flee back toward the hive, pausing only to gather up the crops he'd cut.

We have those sometimes near my home hive, her companion said. *I think they're some kind of predator.*

The nameless sylph's body itched and she felt miserable, but still she forced herself up and into the air, floating forward to see it more closely.

What are you doing? her battler gasped. *That thing is dangerous!*

Looking, she told him. She'd never actually seen one of these before, and if nothing else, it was a distraction from what was going on inside her and how her home and friends had turned her away. She floated above the circle, looking down at it, and was extremely surprised when she sensed another world on the other side.

* * *

There was a healer on the other side of the gate!

Solie stood with one hand on her hugely distended stomach, her ankles swollen and her feet aching, staring hopefully upward at the gate to the sylph home world. Half a dozen of Petr's assistants were chanting, holding steady the swirling, floating opening.

She's right on the other side, Ash was saying. *She's looking right at it.*

Solie took in a soft breath. They needed a healer desperately, needed to find her before someone else got hurt. While sabotage like the warehouse was no longer likely, accidents happened. Theirs was mostly a farming community, with everyone helping during the harvests and thereby being placed in some limited danger, and human doctors and wise women had nothing on healer sylphs' abilities.

In the center of the circle, a young man named Relig stood and looked up. He'd been used before to try and tempt a healer, with no luck, but he had a serious lung problem that wouldn't let him exert himself without ending up gasping for breath. Luck had been able to keep it under control while she'd been there, but once she'd left, it grew worse again. He needed a healer to keep him healthy.

Relig stood quietly, clutching his chest and gasping, but nothing came through the gate.

"Is she still there?"

She is.

Solie shook her head. "Isn't she going to come across?"

I don't know. There's a battler with her.

Solie cursed. A battle sylph might just stop a healer from coming through. "Offer her some other choices," she decided. "We can't let her get away."

Petr heard. He gestured, and three other people stepped into the circle, all as nervous-looking as Relig, though each with a different ailment. It was hard to say what attracted a healer, but it seemed to be deficiencies that required their talents, health crises not easily fixed. Solie hoped something in this group would coax the newcomer across.

She's still looking, Ash related silently, floating at about eye level in the shape of a rounded ball of flame. She flickered in multiple colors. *The battler is getting upset.*

"I bet," Solie muttered. "Come on, come over. You know you want to."

Apparently, the healer didn't know that. Or, if she did, she wasn't being allowed to come.

She's leaving, Ash said, sounding as disappointed as Solie felt. *The battler is, too. Not far, though. She's still close enough for me to feel her.*

This was by far the closest they'd come to finding a replacement for Luck. Solie sighed, frustrated and tired. As far as the sylphs could tell, these gates appeared in a different place in their world every time one was opened. When they next opened one, it might be nowhere near this healer.

"Petr," she called. "Can you keep the gate open? Maybe she'll come back."

Petr frowned, his face covered in scar tissue that he'd never allowed Luck to heal. Solie knew it linked to memories of how his own sylph had died years before, but she'd never asked and he hadn't volunteered the story. Now he rubbed the scar tissue and shrugged.

"We can leave it partially open. Only one of us is needed at a time for that. If she comes back, we can open it wide again."

"Yes. Good."

Solie turned and waddled out, glad this was her last stop of the day. Lizzy was taking on more duties, and of course Ril, Mace, and Leon were always around, with the Widow Blackwell grudgingly helping on a part-time basis, but there were still many duties she handled herself. While she would have to cut back soon, and even more once the baby was born, she wasn't ready to yet. Though, maybe tomorrow, she thought. Her feet ached in her shoes.

Waiting outside, Heyou grinned as she emerged. Ugly and fat as she felt, she knew he still thought her beautiful, though he'd been devastated when she'd lost interest in sex.

Loren and Shore stood with him, along with Sala. Loren said, "Wow, you're big as a house. I think you're twice the size you were last week."

"Gee, thanks. Always love to hear that."

Heyou blinked. "So, why did you tell me to stop comparing you to the cows?"

Loren laughed. "Oh boy. Nice." She shook her head. "We thought we'd stop by for lunch. Sound good to you?"

Solie hesitated. With everything that was happening, she hadn't had much time for her friends. The thought of lunch with Loren and Shore appealed, especially if they could get Lizzy to join them, but she wasn't so sure she wanted Sala around. She risked a glance at the woman, but Sala just stood quietly and Solie decided she was being silly. She had to stop picking on the girl.

"Sounds lovely," she said. "Let's go to the garden."

The women headed off, and Heyou trailed along, swinging

his arms. There was no way into Solie's chambers except for being lifted over the wall by a sylph or going in past the battler chamber, so she led the way around to the auxiliary stairs that would lead down past the throne room, thinking as she always did that they should have made the steps less steep. Someone was bound to get hurt.

Chapter Eighteen

The two other women and Loren's sylph stayed seated at the garden table, the queen barely able to reach over her huge stomach, while Sala went inside to make tea.

She glanced around. She'd been here before, but she hadn't spent much time absorbing the details. The dwelling and furniture were all sylph work, if more angular than their usual aesthetic. Too, the layout was logical, contrary to the earth sylphs' usual whimsy, with the sitting room adjacent to a hall to the kitchen and bedrooms. There was also a door to a stairway that Sala knew went down to the queen's office behind the throne room. They'd used that to get in.

The garden doors opened into a sitting room filled with ornate stone furniture. There were lots of windows and skylights, and everything seemed light and delicate despite being made of stone. There were pillows to soften the places people sat. Sala went into the kitchen, where a fire burned in a stove, pumping heat into the room but not seemingly fed by anything. More sylph work, she knew. They'd have to keep replenishing such a flame, which was why not everyone had them. Sala looked briefly for the entrance the fire sylph would use. It was under the stove, small and out of the way.

She filled a kettle with water from pipes pressurized by water sylphs and set it on to boil. While that was happening, she set out a tray with tea cups and crackers and cheese, then collected some cream and sugar. Of the three tea cups, she lightly dusted the middle one with a white powder from a tiny tin in her pocket. Then she tossed some leaves into the kettle and dawdled just long enough for the tea to steep. With that, she went back outside.

Lizzy had joined them, which gave her a moment's pause. Recovering quickly, Sala carried the tray over and set it on the table, lifting the pot and filling the cups where the women could see her but filling the poisoned cup first, before anyone noticed the powder. Adding sugar and cream, she set that cup on its saucer before the queen.

"For you," she said. "I'll have to get another cup for myself."

"Thank you," Solie said, and turned back to her friend. "Did he say why?"

Lizzy shook her head, accepting an unpoisoned cup and sipping from it immediately. "No. He just said he wanted to test something."

"Is Ril all right?" Solie asked.

"Yes. At least, he is as far as I can tell. I don't know what Dad's up to."

Solie still hadn't drunk any tea. Sala poured for Loren and sat down. "The chancellor is worried about him?" she asked.

Lizzy shrugged. "Yes, he's worried. I don't know about what. I just know he has Ril doing something."

"Great," Loren pouted. "Leon Petrule is worried. That can't be good."

Sala didn't say anything, instead watching out of the corner of her eye. Solie was picking up her tea cup and blowing on it, readying to take that fatal sip . . .

* * *

Solie was trying to hide her discomfort at Sala's presence. It was stupid, she knew. The woman hadn't been anything other than nice, and no battler was worried by her. Heyou hadn't even stayed around, finding girl talk boring beyond comprehension.

She tried to let it go and focus on what Lizzy was saying.

"I wish he'd confide in me," the girl sulked. "I mean, *I* care, too."

"Did you ask?" Loren said, her mouth full of cookie.

"Of course. He said he didn't want to worry me. Too late, I'm already worried! I think he's going to give Ril an order. I mean, we don't *do* that. We promised."

Solie blew on her tea again, preferring it cool. She could feel how upset Lizzy was. She supposed she would be upset, too, if someone suddenly took Heyou away and told her to stay out of it. She hoped this was nothing. Probably it was nothing. Things were getting back to normal.

Sala was watching her. The woman wasn't looking in her direction, but suddenly Solie knew it with an instinct that made her gut tighten; Sala was looking at her out of the corner of her eye even as she listened to the conversation.

She tried to read the woman. Except for when she spoke to the assassins, it wasn't something Solie had ever done deliberately. So long as a sylph was close by, she could read anyone's emotions—and with Shore at the table she could feel Sala's calmness. Still, she tried, looking for anything beyond the facade. But, no. Calm serenity. Beautiful, clear, inviolate. Solie had to hide a shudder. No one was that serene. It felt wrong.

Stupid! There was nothing wrong with Sala. The sylphs trusted her. She even had a sylph of her own. You couldn't fool them.

Except, Leon had done just that in Meridal when he rescued his daughter.

Solie set her teacup down, suddenly not wanting anything Sala touched. The woman's emotions didn't even flicker. Didn't that mean Solie was being foolish?

She put a hand on her stomach and stood. "I'm sorry," she lied, "but I'm not feeling well. I think I'm going to go lie down."

The other women stood, exclaiming worriedly, but Solie excused herself, just wanting to escape. The quiet of her bedroom felt wonderful after the tension in the garden, tension that she was now sure was all in her own mind.

Heyou pushed open the door and came in, crossing over to where she lay down on the bed. "Are you okay? Lizzy found me and told me you weren't feeling well."

Solie smiled and took his hand. "I'm fine. I'm just tired." For a moment she considered asking him to keep a watch on Sala but let it go. She was just suffering pregnant lady vapors. She didn't like the woman. That was all. It happened.

"Lie with me," she said.

Heyou grinned and lay down, spooning up against her back. Solie sighed, content to have him there. Minutes later, she was asleep.

* * *

Leon sent his daughter away despite her protests. If he was wrong, he didn't want her getting ideas. If he was right, he didn't want her in danger.

Sitting behind his desk, Ril eyed him suspiciously. "You want to give me an order?"

Leon nodded, leaning on the blotter on his desk. "I have to, Ril, if I'm going to be sure. I want your permission, though."

Ril frowned and finally shrugged. "Fine, whatever. Just do it."

Leon straightened. The problem wasn't that Ril didn't like getting orders, it was that, in a lot of ways, he liked getting orders too much. In Meridal, Leon had needed to take absolute control of the battler just to keep him safe from other masters.

Ril had submitted to him completely, and Leon had felt his clear contentment and happiness at that surrender. It had felt good for Leon as well. But in the long run it wasn't healthy for either of them. Not if Ril was to be a free individual.

Even crippled as he was, Ril was very likely going to survive many generations of humans. He would need the ability to think for himself. That was why Leon had given up control once they were all back and safe, unintentionally leaving Ril open for Justin to abuse. And now, to confirm what Leon was afraid of, he had to take control again.

"I want you to go to the other side of the town," Leon said, making sure to keep his tone commanding. Ril's eyes dilated a bit, in that way they did when he was accepting an order. "I want you to change shape. It doesn't matter what form you take, but I want you to hide the change from me. I don't want to feel it. Do you understand? Not one bit."

"Yes," Ril said.

"Go then."

Ril went out. It would take time to cross town, Leon knew, at least ten minutes unless he ran.

Leon stood for a while in the front reception area where Ril's desk was, and then he went back into his office. He felt restless there, cooped up in that windowless place, so he went out into the hall and crossed the throne room to the main corridor that led to the surface. He ignored the grandiose staircase for visitors and ambassadors, instead going up the steep, narrow stairs near the battle sylph chamber that most locals used when they had business with the queen. It was quiet as he did; even the battle sylph chamber was deserted.

He climbed to the top of the steep stairs, opening the doorway out onto the street. A few horses were tied nearby, outside a blacksmith's stable and beside a wagon half-full of manure. A shovel lay beside it. The sylphs hadn't been thinking about how it could look when they tossed up a stable there by the queen's palace, just that they had space for a building and a need to create. Solie insisted that it stay, liking how it reminded her whenever she went outside to be humble.

Stepping out into the sun, he waited. It was past lunchtime on market day, and so no one was out on this street, at least not close enough to talk to. The only people he saw were Loren, Shore, and Sala, who were exiting the underground by the same stairwell he'd used.

"What's going on, Chancellor?" Loren asked as she passed him.

Leon barely glanced at her. "Nothing, nothing. Just checking out a few things." He felt a distant flash of pain, the agony Ril experienced through his torn mantle whenever he changed shape. It was unmistakable. His fears had been correct. "Damn. He *can't* hide it from me."

"Sir?"

Leon looked down, realizing he'd spoken aloud. "Don't worry, Loren. It's nothing. Just go on your way." The girl looked dubious, but Leon waved her off. Sala followed.

Leon turned back toward the doorway and the stairwell, rubbing his chin as he stared into that darkened mouth. Ril couldn't hide his pain. Even with a direct order, he couldn't contain it. If he'd changed shape to kill Galway, like it said in Justin's diary, Leon would have felt it. There was no doubt in his mind now. None.

"Ril didn't kill Galway," he said, needing to confirm it aloud. The implications were horrifying.

A faint step sounded on the dirt behind him, a shuffling across light pebbles. Leon started to turn—

Something massive slammed into the side of his head. He gasped and staggered, pain blinding him. Ril's screams of outrage followed, an echo in the back of his mind. He spun, trying to focus, but stars were exploding in his vision and all he saw was a slim shadow. Something flat and hard crashed into his left arm. The bone broke.

The shape dropped its weapon and rushed him. Small hands flattened against his chest, pushing with all the strength and momentum they had, and Leon fell back, still trying to catch himself despite his spinning head and the darkness stealing most of his vision. He felt the doorjamb slip past, but his fingers wouldn't work and he still couldn't see. Desperate, he tried to regain his balance, but instead of his foot finding solid purchase, his boot slipped over the edge.

It was too late to try and grab anything. Howling, Leon fell backward. Down the steep stone stairs he fell, bones and vertebrae snapping beneath him as he tumbled uncontrollably down the long, killing length of the staircase, to fetch up finally in a bloody, senseless heap at the bottom.

* * *

The battlers were screaming. Solie struggled out of bed, frantic, rubbing sleep from her eyes and falling back before Heyou pulled her to her feet. He had his head tilted to one side, listening to all the silent shouts and explanations. Solie wasn't very good at that, not from a distance.

"What is it?" she whispered.

Heyou's face twisted with grief and anger. "The chancellor."

Leon? Solie's breath caught, and she scurried toward the door. Heyou grabbed her around the waist, his hands against her pregnant belly, but she snapped at him over her shoulder, not interested in his protective instincts. Not right now.

"Let me go!"

He released her immediately, and she went out, her unhappy battler shadowing her as she hurried through her apartments and down to her office.

It was obvious where the commotion was coming from.

Solie rushed across the throne room and into the hallway, which seemed to be full of people and sylphs. All of them were trying to push toward the stairs by the battler chamber, until a snarl like ripping fabric forced them back. An aura that Solie had banned years ago washed over the frightened crowd and vanished, then was back and gone again: the hate and rage of a battle sylph ready to kill. Her order barely held him back.

The crowd tried to flee past her, driven away by that horrible antipathy. Solie had a moment of fear that she'd be trampled, but Heyou's growl forced the masses to give them a wide, frightened berth that cleared the corridor enough for her to see. At the junction of the stairwell, Leon was lying half on the stairs and half on the floor, his body contorted into an unnatural position. His head lay on the floor, his neck bent at a gruesome angle. He was facing his battle sylph.

Ril was naked, crouched on the floor. He had to have been a hawk recently and botched his change back, for his eyes were still birdlike and his nose half distorted into a beak. His fingers and toes were claws, though he had them wrapped around Leon's outstretched hand tenderly enough. Most hideously of all, the spines of long feathers jutted out of his body, flecked with red.

Only two sylphs were within reach of Ril. Shore and an air sylph named Swirl cowered submissively on the ground in front of him, flattened into as small a shape as they could manage. The hysterical rage coming from him as he guarded his master made Solie gasp and step back, her stomach clenching. Heyou put his arms around her.

"Is he dead?" Solie managed to whisper. Leon looked like a broken doll, and he didn't move at all as Ril gave a whimpering wail.

"The sylphs are holding him," Heyou whispered in her ear. "Let me get you out of here. If Leon dies . . ."

She could feel his terrible need to take her and get her away before Ril completely lost control. The hate flowed again and was gone. Who knew what Ril would do? She could imagine. Still, Solie didn't retreat, knowing she might be the only one who could control the distressed battler.

Glancing at Leon, she saw his chest rise and fall, moving as smoothly as it would if he were merely asleep. The motion was unnaturally regular, and she realized that it was Swirl breathing for the human, forcing air into his lungs and out again. And Loren's sylph . . .

"What's Shore doing?" she whispered.

"Keeping his blood flowing—and stopping it from bleeding out. Blood's little different than water, really." Heyou touched her shoulders. "Please, Solie. Don't stay here."

She shrugged him off, terrified but determined. The stairwell was thick with battler clouds, the corridor behind Ril filled with more, as was the corridor behind Solie. The sylphs watched, their focus intent. If Ril attacked . . .

"No one hurt him," she called. "Think what it would be like if this were you."

Mace stood in human form behind Ril, looming over him. The big battler eyed Solie. *If it were me, I'd want someone to put me down before I destroyed everything around me.*

Don't touch him! she ordered.

She bit her lip as she felt Ril's hate again. The sylph was shaking, his emotions blowing fast toward madness and well past coherent thought. She'd seen him on the edge of insanity before, self-destructing right in front of her. This was so much worse. Had he attacked Leon? He'd already killed two other people.

Not unless you have to, she amended.

Mace nodded. *Yes, my queen.*

Solie shuddered and took a step forward. Ril seemed to have a territory he'd established around Leon's body, a five-foot impregnable space surrounding the man except for the two sylphs who were keeping him alive. He ignored Solie until she crossed it, and then he turned toward her, snarling a warning. His hate hit her hard enough to make her knees weak.

She forced herself to take another step. "Ril," she called out. "Ril, it's all right. It is. Let me help." She raised a hand, but he hunched closer to the floor, growling nonstop. She could feel his fury, his mindless rage, and under it all ran a desperate pain and grief.

"Ril," she whispered, kneeling awkwardly down. "Please let us help him. Leon can't be comfortable like that."

Ril stared at her and then at Leon. He made a cooing sound, his mind forcing itself to focus. To process his surroundings. "S-Solie . . . ?"

"I'm here, Ril."

"They hurt him. Why did they hurt him?" His voice was almost like a little child's.

Solie glanced around. "He didn't just fall?" she asked, hoping that he had. She could tell Mace thought Ril attacked his own master. If Ril had, he would die.

The battler shook his head, miserable, his voice distorted by the twisted beak that formed half his mouth. "Someone hit him. They pushed him. I . . . I felt it."

"You didn't hurt him yourself?" Solie asked. "Without meaning to?"

Ril looked so hurt and confused, her heart broke.

"He didn't," another voice answered. Solie turned to see Loren hunched by the wall, obviously terrified but not willing to leave Shore. "I heard Leon yell. I reached him at the same time as Sala. Ril wasn't there. He didn't do it."

Ever so slightly, the tension eased. Mace straightened.

"Ril," Solie soothed. "It's all right. Let us help."

"It's not all right! Leon's hurt!"

"RIL!"

Solie looked up as Lizzy sprinted through the clouds of battlers, her skirts hiked up. She ignored everyone and everything, including Ril's appearance, dropping down to skid on her knees into his arms, sobbing as she saw her father. "Daddy!"

Ril crushed her to him, keening. His madness vanished, replaced by miserable grief.

Solie sagged and motioned to Mace. "Go get a doctor," she ordered.

He obeyed, though none of them knew if it would be enough.

* * *

A crowd of people had gathered at the top of the stairs, whispering fearfully. They were supposed to have been safe again, Justin dead and buried, grieved only by his father. Except now the accidents had started again, and struck at the heart of their society.

Leon Petrule. Leon had been the one to lead the Community to victory against King Alcor's battle sylphs in their initial bid for freedom. He'd been the one who trained Solie, had guided the creation of the Valley and protected its continuing prosperity. He was as much a part of the Valley as Solie. Now no one was sure if he was even alive.

Sala stood nearby, not joining in any conversations. She was known to be quiet, so it wasn't unexpected; but today had not gone well. Solie hadn't drunk the poison she'd been given. If she had, Sala would be queen by now. She'd had Claw ready. He'd have consummated with her right over Solie's body if necessary. Only, Solie hadn't taken that sip and now Sala had the uncomfortable feeling that the queen suspected her—of what, Sala wasn't sure, but she was unnerved in a way she hadn't felt since the authorities suddenly started questioning Gabralina about the magistrate back in Yed.

Sala didn't like feeling unnerved, because it made her act impulsively. When she'd come out of the stairwell with Loren and heard what Leon was saying, she'd known in a heartbeat what he had Ril doing and why. She'd known she was in immediate danger, had known she would have to move.

She'd walked away with Loren and Shore and parted from them just past the blacksmith's stable. Circling back as quickly as she could, Sala had grabbed up the shovel left by a manure cart. Leon hadn't heard her coming. She'd hit him twice with the shovel and pushed him down the stairs, then ran off and circled back to return at the same time as Loren. The two of them had found the body just before Ril arrived.

Other crowds quickly gathered. Sala waited with them now, her arms crossed under her breasts as she waited to hear if Leon was dead. He *had* to be. He'd looked straight at her after she hit him, and she didn't know if he'd recognized her. If he had and he told someone, not even Claw and Wat would be enough to protect her.

If he survived the fall, she decided, Leon Petrule had to die. Solie had to die as well, soon, no matter the risk. Her time was up. It was winner take all.

Chapter Nineteen

The house was frighteningly quiet, given how many people were in it. Betha sat in the living room, miserably hunched over with a wet handkerchief clutched in her hand. Iyala sat beside her, arm around her and whispering hardly heard reassurances. The Widow Blackwell sat in a chair nearby. Mia was in her lap, shivering and silent for once. Nali sat on the floor by her feet while Ralad was close to Betha. Both girls were pale-faced and weepy, staring up at their grief-stricken mother as if begging her to make it all better.

Twelve-year-old Cara peered in from the doorway, biting her lip. Her mother was crying again, the two other adults doing their best to soothe her. The younger girls started to sob as well. Cara felt like crying, too, but she wiped her face furiously and instead crept down the hall to the stairs.

The doctor had been and gone and they'd all been told to stay away. She had to do this, though. She hadn't seen her father at all when they brought him in, had been banished to the kitchen with the other children, where the Widow kept them in their seats. She'd heard her mother weeping, though.

From the top of the stairs, Cara was careful to avoid any of the squeaky spots in the hallway. Her parents' bedroom was at the far end, overlooking the front of the house. She made her way to the door and gingerly eased it open a crack. Lizzy was inside, her arms around Ril. His were around her. Two other sylphs were in the room: one a girl made of water, the other translucent with her hair swirling in a breeze that wasn't there. The sylphs were perched on either side of the bed, staring at it.

Cara swallowed. Her father was lying in the bed, his face gray and his closed eyes black and puffy. Both arms had casts, and his head was thickly wrapped in bandages. Something stiff encased his neck, and his mouth was slack. Cara sniffled as she heard his breath, which was loud and raspy in the quiet chamber. He looked older than she'd ever seen him.

"He's so deep I can't feel him," Ril said suddenly. "I've tried, but he's not there. He's not having any dreams for me to find him in. He's only alive because we're forcing it."

Lizzy hugged him tight. "He'll be okay. It's Dad. He's tougher than anyone."

Cara would have been more encouraged if her sister's voice hadn't cracked. She wanted to go in there, but she was afraid to, afraid that if she got too close to her father, he'd die. Already he looked much worse than she'd thought.

Ril pressed his forehead against Lizzy's shoulder, then lifted his head and looked at Leon. "I'm going to find the one who did this," he snarled, "and I'm going to tear him apart."

"No!"

To Cara's surprise—ripping people apart seemed like a good idea to her—Lizzy grabbed Ril's face between both of her palms and forced him to look at her. "This is an order, Ril. Don't leave Dad, no matter what. You're going to stay in this room, and you're going to guard him until he's healthy again." Tears flooded Lizzy's eyes, and Cara felt warmth flowing down her own cheeks. "He loves you. You have to protect him."

"I will," Ril promised. She hugged him again.

Cara pulled back from the door, sitting instead against the wall. Her arms went around her knees. She cried freely, but she was going to guard her father, too. No matter what.

* * *

"She's back."

Solie stopped at the entrance to the summoning hall as she heard Petr speak. The bald man approached her, his lips tight. Behind him, three women stood in the circle, clearly trying to tempt the healer on the other side.

"She hasn't tried to come through?" Solie asked. Her feet ached horribly, and Heyou eyed her in concern. When Petr shook his head, she sagged. That would have been too simple by far. Life wasn't so convenient. "At least she came back."

"She hasn't really left," Petr corrected. "Ash thinks she's curious. She can't be sure, though. All she can tell is what kind of sylph is on the other side. She can't get anything about attitudes. I've offered up a dozen options already. I'm starting to just grab people off the street."

Solie sighed. What else could they do? Sylphs could be incredibly flaky about what attracted them. The battlers were the easiest to draw across, since all they wanted was sex. She was tempted to bring Leon here and hope his wounds drew this healer, but that was too dangerous. He was too injured to keep moving around, and he already had a sylph. The human soul couldn't handle being stretched between different patterns. According to Petr, it *was* possible for masters to be bonded to more than one living sylph, but this would eventually drain the vitality out of them, leaving such humans pale echoes of themselves who often died young. Such a strain was the last thing Leon needed.

"Keep it up," she told Petr. "If someone doesn't have a sylph, walk them under the gate. Even children. There's got to be someone she'll like." This wasn't just for Leon. It was for everyone who needed help. And with a murderer still out there . . .

"Yes, ma'am," Petr said with a bow.

Solie went back outside. There was no point in her being there, not until the healer came through, if she ever did.

It was quiet outside, people obviously wanting to come up and ask her what was going on but not wanting to brave Heyou, who stood close. She didn't mind his protectiveness for once. She didn't know what to say to anyone, and she was afraid. She was only weeks away from giving birth and her entire original council was gone. They'd stopped Justin, but was this someone else? Had Justin been implicated unfairly? Solie didn't know.

She straightened her shoulders and forced herself to appear calm and relaxed as she went back to her office. Heyou guarded her the whole way. Other battlers floated overhead, some watching many masters at once, the rest guarding against overall threats to the Valley.

Who would be the next target?

* * *

The nameless sylph studied the swirling gate, floating above it and to one side just in case it did turn out to be dangerous. It had certainly lasted longer than any other gate she or her exiled battler had ever heard of. Her old hive was universally ignoring it, avoiding this section of the field, but to her it was interesting and the only thing left that slowed the horrendous itching inside her.

Her companion pressed against her, hating them being there and convinced that the gate was evil. It didn't really seem like a trap, not with what the nameless sylph could sense on the other side. And the battler admitted he couldn't see anything through the gate; not unless he was directly underneath it. Her own senses were stronger. There was a fire sylph there, watching from the other side, though the nameless sylph doubted the little one could sense much in return.

We should go.

Behind her, almost blanketing her, the battle sylph flickered out tendrils of black smoke to shield her back and most of her sides. He was getting more obvious with his attentions, which made sense as the itch grew and she started to realize what was happening. She was beginning to know why the queen had wanted her out of the hive. She didn't blame the battler, either. She was his only real chance to be anything other than an exile.

She looked at the gate for a moment longer, wondering for the first time if she dared go through. She didn't know for sure what was on the other side, but how much stranger could it be than her future right now?

On the other side of the gate, living creatures moved, presenting themselves directly below, where they were easier to sense. To go through the gate, the nameless sylph would have to pattern her energy to theirs, *become* theirs, for otherwise that world would reject her. They seemed to want her to, offering themselves. Among them, she could detect injury, illness . . . all too easy to fix. And all expected something from her, just as the hive had in the old days. The good days.

She glanced past the gate toward the wilderness beyond the fields. The itch would drive her out there eventually. She knew that now, knew it would change her into something she didn't want to be. But going through the gate would only mean she'd be owned.

Slowly, the battler keeping his smaller form between her and the gate throughout, she turned and moved back toward where they'd been lying. She felt his discontent that they still weren't leaving the fields, but what else could she do? Actually, she knew, and soon she would have no choice at all. But still . . .

She looked toward the gate and wondered.

* * *

With the Widow at the Petrule house, Gabralina had to keep the orphan children fed and quiet. Recognizing her as weaker than their usual guardian, and wound up by the rumors that even they had heard, they were running wild.

Nearly in tears, Gabralina stood in the center of the front room and shouted for them to behave, which they ignored. Wat stood beside her, staring at the chaos with similar confusion.

"I'm scared," he whispered.

Gabralina sighed. The Widow would be so disappointed if she came back to find the children tearing the house apart. "STOP IT NOW!" she shouted. "THE NEXT PERSON TO MISBEHAVE DOESN'T GET DINNER. NOW, GET INTO THE KITCHEN AND START SETTING THE TABLE!"

Grumbling, the children moved toward the kitchen. Gabralina sagged in relief.

Wat looked at her dubiously. "Does that include me?"

"Of course not." She giggled, smiling and stepping close. Tenderly, she cupped his beautiful cheek.

He leaned down to press his mouth to hers and wrapped his arms around her body. Gabralina closed her eyes, losing herself in the few seconds they'd have together before the children started acting up again. She wound her arms around his neck and slipped her tongue into his mouth, enjoying all that he was.

Wat kissed her as thoroughly as he could, his hand rising to cup her breast. He wasn't terribly bright when it came to most things, but he knew how to please his lover. For her, he'd do anything or be anything, just as he knew she would do for him. He lost himself in the embrace, unable to imagine any other battle sylph loving their master as much as he loved his.

The front wall behind Gabralina had a long, rectangular window, a sheer, flawless plate of glass made by an earth sylph. It was still daylight out, and when Wat opened his eyes, he saw

Sala. Her pace was casual, her glance unremarkable. But when she spotted him in the living room, she swirled her hand by her side in a very specific gesture of command.

Wat's eyes widened—he was shocked as always by the realization that she could compel him—and his hand tightened on his master's breast. She gasped, rising up on her toes, and he crushed his mouth harder against hers, his hand moving lower.

The children were starting to shout and laugh in the kitchen, but the two lovers ignored them. Wat's hand was moving, stroking, his other arm around Gabralina to hold her up. He had to, as her knees went weak. She kept her mouth latched against his, shuddering with pleasure until her entire body stiffened and quivered like a bowstring.

Wat drank in her gratification and sighed, finally lifting his mouth from hers. "I liked that," he whispered.

"So did I."

A crash sounded from the kitchen, followed by a flurry of giggles. Gabralina rested her forehead against Wat's chest for a moment, then said, "I have to go."

"Yeah." He kissed the top of her head. "I have to go, too. I'll be back later."

She lifted her head to ask him his destination, but another crash sounded, accompanied by a scream. "Oh!" Standing on her toes, she kissed him quickly and smiled; then she ran out, yelling for the little devils to stop whatever they were doing or no one was getting any dessert.

Wat watched her go, smiling. She was so cute.

Still musing on how wonderful she was, he went out the front door, shifting to cloud form as he did. He rose up over the house and floated unnoticed across yards and fields, past stables and sheds, turning in a great circle and landing finally at an ordinary-sized hut only a short distance from the Widow's. It was actually one of the stairwells into the hive, one rarely used and very private. Landing there, he moved around the back and dropped to one knee, his head bowed.

"I have an order for you, Wat," said a voice.

* * *

Hating every moment, Claw flew across the square in the shape of an ordinary crow with his aura hidden so thoroughly that another sylph would have to get within a dozen feet to realize what he was. It wasn't a comfortable way to be, and it restricted his senses to the point where he felt nearly blind, but he had no choice. Sala had been absolute in her instructions. He could *not* be caught.

She was as close to furious as he'd ever seen her, and secretly, Claw was delighted. She'd made a mistake, underestimated Leon, and in attacking him she'd undone all her efforts with Justin. She was back in the same position she'd faced after Blue saved Moreena, only now it was worse because Leon could wake up and name her as his attacker. So, she was desperate.

Claw landed on the branch of a tree growing over the cottage where Lizzy and Ril lived. There he bowed his head, thinking only of Rachel. *Rachel.* Sweet, dear Rachel, who held his sanity intact even now. Barely.

Leon was inside the main house at the front of the garden, undoubtedly guarded by Ril. Sala needed Ril out of that room, if only for a few minutes. It was up to Claw to provide them. At some point, Lizzy would have to come back to her cottage to change clothes, and it was then that Claw would hurt her. He was grateful for the small mercy that he was only to do her harm. But, her pain would still bring Ril outside and leave Leon undefended for Wat to go in through the window and kill him.

It would be an easy death, he supposed. A pillow over the

face and everyone would think he'd died in his sleep. Died of his wounds. No mystery.

Glad it wasn't him with that job, Claw waited and thought of Rachel.

* * *

It had been a long day. Sitting in a chair by the window, Lizzy was sleeping, her cheek resting against her fist and her elbow on the chair arm. It slipped off and she jerked awake.

Wiping some drool from her mouth, she glanced around. Shore and Swirl were still there watching her father. They kept his blood flowing and his lungs filling with air. He looked the same as before, his face a sickly gray.

Ril lay sprawled on the rug by her parents' bed. It had been a hard day for him as well, and he was asleep. Downstairs, Lizzy heard one of her sisters shout and start to cry, and she knew her mother was down there taking care of them. She glanced out the window to see she'd slept even longer than she thought, and the light coming through the window was that of early morning. No wonder her mother was downstairs. It would be time for breakfast for the girls.

Lizzy stretched and stood up, feeling tired, hungry, and filthy, and she had a sore back on top of that. Quietly she walked over to the bed, stepping up to the side opposite where Ril was sleeping. Her father lay so pale and still. She put a hand against his cool cheek and looked at the sylphs who were helping him.

"Any change?" she asked.

The two eyed each other and shook their heads. Shore leaned forward to pat her hand. "He'll be okay." She sounded doubtful.

Lizzy smiled weakly. "I know."

She needed a bath, and it felt like something had died in her mouth, so slowly she turned and left the room, glancing back at her father and her sleeping lover for one final moment. Going down the stairs, she followed the hall that led to the kitchen and to the back door. Her mother and sisters were sitting around the breakfast table, staring morosely at their porridge.

Betha lifted her head as Lizzy entered the room. The woman looked like she'd aged decades in the past few hours. Lizzy returned her mother's regard, opened her mouth to say something, then decided she'd just start crying if she did. Instead she turned and went outside, heading across the dew-soaked lawn toward her cottage. A quick wash, change of clothes, and brushing of her teeth were very called for.

It was cold out, autumn changing steadily into winter. Her breath frosted the air and reminded her how cold it would be inside with no fire lit in the stove.

In the tree that hung over her cottage, a large crow shifted on its feet and launched itself forward, attacking her face with a scream of rage. Lizzy shrieked in response, throwing her arms up over her head. The bird flapped madly and hovered before her, pecking. Its sharp beak hurt, cutting through skin, and she screamed again, falling, then trying to scramble to her feet, but the crow continued its attack until she huddled against the ground in terror, her arms over her head to protect her eyes.

* * *

Ril's eyes snapped open. Lizzy's pain stabbed through him with the sharpness of a stiletto, causing raw panic, and he leaped to his feet and bolted out of the room, knocking the door halfway into the wall. Lizzy was screaming. But . . .

Don't leave Dad.

Ril skidded to a halt, torn by two desires. Protect Lizzy. Protect Leon.

As it always must, the full command won out. He turned and bolted back into the bedroom, Lizzy's cries still echoing through his soul. How could he ever endure?

Inside, he stopped. The window was open, Wat half in and half out. He held a pillow and was staring at the two elemental sylphs like he hadn't expected them to be there. He looked at Ril and dropped the pillow.

"Uh-oh."

Ril growled.

Chapter Twenty

Just as the sun flooded the Valley with morning light, Betha and Lizzy's sisters ran outside to defend her against a crow. Above, the window of their house's master bedroom exploded outward, and battle sylph hatred drove them all to their knees.

Wat had crashed through the window. Diving out after him, Ril flipped in midair and landed in a crouch on the ground, gasping. Using his power drained him faster than any other battle sylph and he only had a few blast waves left. He hadn't dared use his full strength—not so close to Leon—but his first attack struck Wat squarely. The battler landed on his ass in the road, his legs up over his head.

Ril charged. He didn't know what Wat thought he was doing and he didn't care. He'd felt the sylph's full intention to kill Leon, and he didn't need Lizzy's order to know a response. He didn't have to worry about Solie's command not to harm any humans in the Valley either. Sylphs weren't human.

Wat sat up, gaping in surprise. Distant battlers were screaming in alarm, but Ril had no urge to wait for them. He sent a rolling wall of power at the other sylph.

Wat was stupid but not suicidal. He rolled out of the way, moving fast, and rushed Ril with a snarl of his own. He didn't try to change his shape or use his own energy, which was strange. Ril had no idea why, unless it came from a feeling of superiority or an equally dumb desire to fight fair. Either way, the tactics gave Ril a chance.

He took it. Snarling, he lunged at Wat, painfully lengthening his fingers into claws. Wat jumped back, taking a cut along his stomach, and stared down in confusion. Ril slashed him across the face.

"Stop that!" Wat shouted. "I was just going to make him go to sleep! You're hurting me!"

Ril snarled again, hating him so intensely that he could taste it. He could sense other battlers coming but didn't want their help. He didn't need them.

"You tried to kill my master, Wat," he accused, circling.

Wat frowned. "Well, yeah. So?"

Ril lunged, slamming into the other battler. They both went down, rolling on the hard-packed dirt, clawing and biting. Now Wat did use his power, lashing out, but Ril countered with his own, redirecting the blast upward and causing himself terrible pain in the process. He thrust his head forward, biting down hard on the junction of Wat's neck and shoulder. The attack tore loose a chunk of flesh that turned into streams of sparkling energy.

Wat shrieked and threw him off, and Ril crashed into a pile of firewood in front of one of the neighbor's houses. Everyone was screaming. The people who lived in the homes around the Petrule dwelling were rushing out of them in terror, running down the street and away from the fight. Not Lizzy. She sprinted around the side of her family's house toward them, her arms and back covered in scratches.

"Ril!"

She screamed his name, running forward until her mother tackled her from behind, knocking her to the ground. Ril pushed himself to his feet, firewood clattering noisily around his legs. Grabbing a piece, he hurled it at Wat and the battler was blown off his feet again, squealing in pain.

Ril charged, growling. As he did, Wat forced himself up, reeling in confusion and pain. He saw Ril coming and took cloud form, soaring upward and trying to get himself out of danger.

Years before, Ril had fought a battle sylph more powerful than himself and been torn apart when he tried to take cloud form. The experience had been enlightening. Now, he didn't even slow, agony flaring through him as he forced spikes sharp as blades to jut out of his body at every angle. And as Wat rose into the air, lightning sparking slowly through his essence, Ril leaped.

He went right through the other battler, rolling in midair as he did. Lashing out, his claws and blades tore completely through Wat's vulnerable shape. Not quick enough to get a shield up in time, the other sylph had no protection, and Ril's blows sliced his mantle to shreds. Landing on the far side, Ril rolled and rose up to his knees, staring.

The other battler squealed in pain, shifting to human form but already dissolving below the waist. His pattern was collapsing with his shape, dissolving into a sparkling rain of energy that reeked of ozone. He fell over, still squealing, and stared at Ril in confused betrayal. The last of him disintegrated, spreading across the lawn, scattered to nothingness by the morning breeze.

Battle sylphs descended all around, roaring and shifting shape. Ril ignored them, pushing himself wearily to his feet as he regained human form. Lizzy ran to his side, throwing her arms around him with her eyes wide, and together they limped back into the house.

* * *

Gabralina couldn't stop shaking. She'd been at the Widow's house to help with breakfast when she felt Wat's confusion and pain. Then she felt his terror. Then she felt him die.

He couldn't have. He just couldn't. She'd screamed when she felt it and started crying, wailing no matter what the Widow did, but then Mace finally came for her and brought her to this windowless room. Her heart broken, she didn't care that the huge battler loomed over her now, staring through her with cold eyes. She just kept sobbing, her face soaked with tears.

Mace studied the shaking girl, looking as deeply into her emotions as he could. She was devastated. That much was obvious, and she couldn't fake it. Wat's death had destroyed her.

He felt no sympathy. Mace loved women, had taken more women into his arms and bed than even he could clearly remember. He'd certainly never harmed a woman before, but if this girl ordered her battler into the fight that led to his death, he'd break with that tradition immediately. He couldn't think what reason she'd have to tell Wat to smother an unconscious Leon, but that was irrelevant. He just needed to know if she'd done it.

Shoving the table out of the way, he knelt before her. Gabralina was blubbering at him, her lip quivering and her hands fluttering all around like little birds. He reached out and cupped her face with both hands, and she gasped for air, her expression distorted and ugly.

"W-w-w-*whyyy?*" she stammered.

Mace shook his head and stared into her eyes, deliberately searching her with his empathy. He couldn't read her mind, but he could read her heart. There was pain there, and grief, the pattern that had been Wat unraveling even now inside her. Below that was confusion, with no understanding of why her lover died. Nothing at all.

Mace dove deeper, searching the core of her, and she made no move to stop him, not knowing how and even more not caring. She wanted to die, wanted her battler back, wanted this nightmare to end.

It wasn't her first nightmare, it seemed. Old fears, old abandonment, a mind that was slower than the minds of her peers . . . She was often left in confusion when they laughed, not knowing if she was the target. Old, old fears these were. She would do anything for love, risk anything. She'd hold on to it tight and never let go. But she never wanted Leon's death.

Mace leaned back after a moment, certain. The core of Gabralina's soul was open to him, and there was no enmity inside. Part of her even loved Leon for rescuing her, albeit in a helpless, hopeless sort of way. Her pain over his attack was deep and unmistakable. She would never have tried to harm him or anyone else. For whatever reason he'd done it, Wat had acted without her.

Done with his examination, Mace leaned forward. He took the blonde girl into his arms and soothed her. "Shh," he said. "Shhhhhh, girl. It'll be all right."

Gabralina clung to his uniform, sobbing. It felt like she'd never stop crying, and he could sense how much she wanted to die. That was unacceptable, but not easy to deal with. Not for him. Mace closed his eyes, holding her more tenderly, and sent out a silent request.

He held the weeping girl for half an hour before the response came. Not from Lily, either. She was at the Petrule house, helping Betha deal with her children and grief, as well as her comatose husband. She also was back and forth to her own house, keeping the orphans under control. Instead, a tall, stout woman knocked on the door.

"Oh!" she gasped as she entered. "My poor little duck! Come to Iyala."

Gabralina looked up, saw Galway's widow standing there with her arms open and tears in her eyes, and she squirreled out of Mace's arms. She was soon wrapped in Iyala's embrace, the woman rocking her back and forth.

"My poor little dear," Iyala whispered. "We'll take care of you."

"It was awful!" Gabralina sobbed. "He can't be gone! It . . . it hurts too much."

"I know. I know how you feel, sweetheart," the woman said. "You just cry it out and eventually things will get better. I promise."

Mace nodded to Iyala, who smiled at him sadly, and went out the door. He closed it behind him. Gabralina was innocent, which was a good thing, but he still had no idea why Wat had gone after Leon.

Stupid creature. He'd been useless for the hive, and now he'd left Ril feeling guilty about having to kill a hive mate while he was dealing with all those other stresses. Wat had been a true plague on their happiness.

Mace went up a set of stairs and shifted to cloud form, rising over the town and heading toward the Widow's home. Battlers were on their rooftop perches again, guarding. Those not on duty watched their masters, and the masters of their neighbors; and elemental sylphs were taking up the slack. This would take more organization and communication, and the system was far from perfect, but it was overall progress. No master was more than thirty seconds from a sylph. This wasn't going to change until the person who pushed Leon down those stairs was caught.

Whoever it was, he was clever, like the man who'd slipped by Wat and freed the assassins. Perhaps it was even that man Umut, whom Leon told them about. Someone they couldn't sense. Such a concept still resonated in Mace as an impossibility, but Lily had given him a suggestion the day before, in the brief hour they both managed to be together and after they'd finished the more important things. It was a suggestion upon which he was just following up.

"You said that Leon told you he managed to evade the battlers in Meridal by controlling his emotions?" she'd asked, sweat still drying on her bare breasts. Mace kissed them slowly and deliberately, scraping his teeth gently over her nipple.

"He did. He tried to demonstrate, but we found him right away."

"Of course you did. You *know* him," she said. Sighing, she arched her back, and he repeated the soft nip.

"That's what he said."

Lily shook her head in exasperation, even as her fingers raked through his short hair, delicately rubbing his temples. Mace closed his eyes and leaned forward.

"I was thinking about that," she said. "When you guard, you look for negative emotions, correct?"

"Correct."

She pushed on the top of his head, and Mace went back to lavishing attention on her breasts. She shifted and sighed. "So you look for malice most of all."

"Of course." He shifted lower, sliding under the sheets. Lily closed her eyes and exhaled.

"Have you ever looked for an absence of emotion?"

Mace paused and lifted his head. "What do you mean?"

"Look for someone who doesn't feel malice, or love, or anything else. When I was a girl, they hung a man who took an ax to his neighbors and then sat down to drink tea in their kitchen. He didn't even blink when they executed him." She lifted her own head, eyeing him along the length of her body. "Would you even think to worry about someone like that?"

Mace stared. He hadn't thought of that. The concept was too alien to him. But, how else could a killer move around the Valley so easily when battle sylphs were on the alert? He'd ducked his head again and showed his thanks, and Lily gasped, shivering in appreciation.

Thanks to that conversation, he'd checked Gabralina for the absence of soul. Truly plumbing her depths hadn't been easy—it was simpler for those a sylph was patterned to—but he'd gone deep enough to feel Gabralina's soul and all the grief therein. He'd felt that very clearly indeed. No, Gabralina wasn't the enemy. That left every other man, woman, and child in the Valley who might be.

Mace flew to the top of the colored dome that covered the battler chamber. There he shifted to human form, gazing out over the roofs and fields of the Valley. This was his home as much as anything ever had been. He would die to protect it; he would challenge the ideas he'd previously held.

Battle sylphs, he sent, shouting his silent words along the hive line. *We have a new target. Watch for a person with no soul. Watch for someone* without *emotions—without compassion, without malice, without rage. Understood?*

A chorus of yeses and not a few what-the-hells came back to him.

From below, inside the dome, Claw floated up to the glass. He flowed out an exit vent and shifted to human form beside Mace. He stood slightly down the slope, his eyes downcast.

"Someone with no soul?" he whispered.

Mace eyed him tolerantly. Claw had saved him once, killing his original master when Mace couldn't, and despite his turmoil and pain, Claw had never once failed in his duty.

The smaller battler shivered, his hands clutched together at his chest. "Someone . . . *with no soul?*" he repeated.

"Yes. Someone who can do evil but doesn't feel evil," Mace clarified.

Claw seemed terrified by the concept, which wasn't a shock. It still sounded strange even to Mace.

"Someone . . . like that . . . They'd be easy to find?" The other battler stared hopefully up at him.

Mace could imagine the source of Claw's pain. With one master murdered already, he likely was horrified by the thought of another being at risk, and by such an aberrant villain. Mace had spent long hours considering his Lily being taken—and the mass violence he'd engage in as a result.

"I don't know," he replied. It was best to be honest. "I doubt it. If it were an obvious thing, we would have noticed already."

Claw sagged. "Okay."

Mace clapped him on the shoulder. "Just keep your senses open."

"Okay." The battler perked up again. "I guess it could be anyone? I mean, even someone we know?"

"It could. We'll have to be sure to check everyone."

Claw smiled at him beatifically.

* * *

Sala walked silently toward the school, her shawl wrapped around her against the cold. Classes would be starting soon, and without Rachel she was forced to do a lot more teaching than she'd planned. Still, she didn't dare quit and draw attention to herself.

The only good thing about Wat's botched murder attempt was that it wasn't Claw who'd been killed. The battlers would have been all over her if they'd known she was involved. If she was lucky, Gabralina still forgot whom she'd ordered her battler to obey. Briefly Sala considered having Gabralina killed, just to protect against any last-minute recollection, but such a plan would only make everything worse. She had to be discreet, subtle . . . and murder Solie herself the first chance she got.

She tripped past the bakery and mercantile, the small schoolhouse now in sight. Just shy of it, a battle sylph stood on the stone sidewalk, peering intently at everyone who passed.

"What are you doing?" one affronted woman demanded.

"Just checking for a soul," he answered. "You're good."

The woman sniffed and kept on going.

Sala sniffed, herself, and continued toward him. It was Blue, she saw, and she nodded to him as she approached. "Hello, Blue. Claw already checked me, naturally."

Blue blinked, caught off guard. "Oh, okay." He turned toward a group of schoolchildren running to beat her to class.

Sala kept going.

Chapter Twenty-one

Cold winds blew through the air as the residents of Sylph Valley readied themselves fully for winter. The town was quiet, the last of the leaves falling from the trees. There had been celebrations to commemorate the harvest, but they were quieter than in years past, everyone aware of the recent tragedies—and that the chancellor was dying. No one seemed to know anymore if there was an actual enemy, but tensions ran high.

Gabralina hadn't gone to work for days. She didn't know how the Widow was managing, but she also couldn't make herself care. She still missed Wat, her heart unable to accept that he was gone, and she found herself more and more just wandering through the Valley searching for him. The sight of her, more often than not without a warm cloak, beautiful and teary-eyed, long hair blowing around her, just put the town further on edge.

Not that Gabralina bothered herself with what the townspeople thought. She just kept searching, growing sadder and more fragile, wandering the tunnels underground and the streets above. Wat was nowhere to be found, so she went into the fields. Those long strips of plowed earth and grazing pastures didn't hide him, either, so she went to the summoning hall, thinking in her grief that if Wat wasn't *here*, he had to be *somewhere* and the gate was the only way to find him.

For at least a minute after she entered, Petr didn't notice her; the healer was on the other side of the gate again, and he was directing all of his helpers to hold it open with their chant.

Ash saw her, feeling the woman's grief echo like the pain she herself felt when her first master died six years before. Moved, Ash watched the small woman, her heart going out to her.

* * *

The nameless sylph had returned. She'd come mostly to look, to peer through the gate once more and satisfy some unnamed desire. The itch was unbearable, and she knew what *it* wanted from her, which was nothing she wanted for herself. She didn't want to change, didn't want to leave this place, and she definitely didn't want the attentions of the battler who stroked against her side, no matter how good it felt.

For days she'd been trying to think of a way to stop the itch, but the only method with the slightest hope seemed through this gate. If she went through, she'd be bound to one of these frail creatures on the other side. With their pattern in place of the one fraying within her, she would be able to stay herself. She'd be able to fight the change. The only problem—other than the fact that it required a great leap into the unknown— was that the creatures offering themselves on the other side wanted something from her. She didn't want to be what she was becoming, but she didn't want to be a slave either. Was that what waited through this whirling vortex of energy?

Depressed, she studied the humans being paraded past the gate until she felt the fire sylph's attention shift into sympathetic grief. Not the least bit interested in the other offerings, the nameless healer looked further . . . and saw what had attracted the fire sylph.

The female was not one of her kind, but there was a wound in her soul. The pain ran so deep it resonated through the gate and straight into the healer, making her gasp with an abrupt need to go and soothe the woman's pain. For the moment that desire was tempered by fright about what going through the gate would actually mean, but the woman's pain was endless and uncaring, a wail of anguish that demanded action.

Almost, she went to her, but there was no coinciding desire in the woman for help. The nameless sylph had been unimpressed by the other offerings because they all wanted something, but she didn't want to be tied to someone who didn't want her, either. This wounded being didn't want a healer sylph at all.

She couldn't shut out the woman's loneliness, which was making her own homesickness unbearable. Against her better instincts, the nameless sylph turned toward her old hive, just wanting to go home. She started toward it.

Leave.

She started, surprised, though after everything else that happened she shouldn't be. This had been coming for a long time after all. Still, she wailed, feeling the pattern inside her break at last, shattered by her queen.

Her battler pressed against her side, hissing. *Now. We have to go now.*

Where? This is my home!

Hysterical, the unnamed sylph darted off toward her hive, intending to return to her hive mates despite everything she knew, to deny for good what was happening inside her. Then she learned just how serious the queen's order had been.

Battle sylphs roared, smaller than she but numbering in the hundreds. They poured out of the hive and soared toward her, bellowing in attack. Her companion swept in front, his shield of energy flashing up between them, and energy exploded, sending him reeling back against her. At the sight of an exile in their territory, the battle sylphs' rage grew even stronger.

He snarled in response. She healed his wounds even as she heard his angry shout: *Run! The queen wants you dead!*

Reality came clear. She turned and fled, racing away from everything she'd ever known. Her battler, who would be just as dead as she if they were caught, flew behind her, keeping her safe with his shields. He couldn't keep them all the way around her, and hive battlers raced to cut them off, to catch them both and kill them.

If she'd left sooner, she would have been ignored and allowed to escape, but she hadn't wanted that. She hadn't wanted anything other than to be a healer, safe and happy.

A named battle sylph who might have been her own sire dove at her, lightning flaring through his form. She dodged and ducked, her battler squealing in pain as he took a blast of energy meant for her. Twisting over herself, she caught him in a tendril of smoke and barreled over the named battler, arching up to try and avoid his lashing strike. It caught her along the back and she gasped, even as she healed herself.

More battlers were closing in, cutting off escape. Her battler clung to her, matching her flight as he roared in outrage at her brothers, throwing blasts of energy at them until he was exhausted. Still their foes closed, swarming.

She shot upward between four battlers, then rolled over again and dove. It was close. She wasn't going to escape this, not now that she'd waited until her queen demanded her death—her own *mother!* At least, she wouldn't escape by fleeing into the wilderness. Even if she evaded her hive mates, the chance of finding a place to survive there were slim. Which left . . . the gate.

Desperate, she dove for it and for the female with the hurt in her soul. Not an offering, and not interested in her. A life with an uninterested party was better than death. She raced for the gate, tumbled from the pain of a blow that her battler could only partly deflect, and fell through the gate with him still in her grip. She grimly hoped he wouldn't mind.

* * *

Gabralina stared at the gate, her grief not gone but forgotten for a moment at the shock of seeing its swirling noncolor. The sight made her head ache and frightened something deep inside her. Almost, she could see patterns there, but their meaning hovered beyond her ability to comprehend.

Then she remembered the gate she'd seen in Yed and how her sweet Wat had come through. That brought back all of her grief and a surety that he must have gone back home. Was he on the other side even now, trying to find his way back?

Suddenly positive, she hurried forward, sniffling and wiping her eyes. She ran past Petr and his chanting apprentices before he realized what she was doing, and into the circle. There were three people there already, one with a missing finger, the other two apparently showing no obvious illness. Gabralina barely took notice of Cherry, one of the barmaids at the town's largest tavern, and Syl, a blacksmith's apprentice. The one with the missing finger was a cattleman. They looked curious as she joined them, and then shocked as she reached upward to touch the swirling slickness of the gate itself.

"No!" Petr shouted.

Gabralina was a short woman, and to reach she was forced to stand on her toes with her arms outstretched. Even then, despite her desperation, she only managed to brush the edge of her fingertips against the hovering circle before Syl grabbed her. Pain shocked her out of her grief-stricken stupor. The touch of the gate was electric, burning her fingertips and leaving her choking, shuddering in Syl's arms.

"What are you doing?" Cherry hissed. Her face held fear and anger.

Clearly shaken, Petr stopped just outside the circle drawn on the floor. Ash hovered behind him. She was peering at

Gabralina, who couldn't even get her breath back, let alone try to answer them.

A moment later, Ash looked up and squealed, bolting for the far side of the room. The gate bulged outward. For an instant Gabralina thought it was Wat after all, coming back to her, and she gasped, her heart pounding as she stared upward, wanting that more than anything.

"Wa—" she started. Then, "No!"

A huge white cloud came through, not streaked with lightning but streams of shimmering light. She flowed down out of the gate and kept coming. Six glowing balls of silver formed her eyes.

Wano, she was saying silently, the word echoing in Gabralina's mind.

Everyone gaped, backing away in fright—everyone except Gabralina, who stood there in shock. It wasn't Wat? How could it not be Wat? And how could she have another sylph talking in her head?

The white sylph slithered the rest of the way into the summoning hall, the gate rippling and stretching to allow her passage. Pressed to her side, the black cloud of a battle sylph glared at the humans, lightning flaring through him and sparking jaggedly in his mouth. Smaller than the healer but still larger than most battlers in the Valley, he regarded the humans as if deciding whether to destroy them.

"Name him," Petr gasped from outside the circle. "Hurry!"

Cherry goggled, glanced at Gabralina, and then pointed at the battler. "Fhranke!"

The newly named battler looked as incredulous as everyone else.

Gabralina didn't even hear Cherry bond the battler. She couldn't do anything more than look at the white sylph, feeling the creature's fear and uncertainty as strongly as her own grief.

"You can't be here," she whispered. "Not for me." Not when her heart belonged to Wat. Not when finding someone else was such a betrayal.

Wano watched her with many eyes. She had no mouth, unlike Fhranke, and she was more solid, her form only partially translucent and fluted with soft pinks and opal. Long and tapered, her eyes were reflective, and Gabralina saw her own tear-streaked face in them.

"But I don't want you!" she cried. Wano looked hurt, and her pain sent something like an itch down Gabralina's ribs.

Behind them, Petr was speaking urgently to Ash, telling her to bring Solie so that the two new sylphs could be bound into the hive. Syl and the smith were already heading for the doors. Cherry took a nervous step toward her sylph, raising a hand to touch him. Fhranke looked dubious and pressed closer to Wano, nearly pushing himself into her.

Everything happened then. A second battler dropped through the gate, his power flaring. Gabralina screamed, falling back as Fhranke rolled over Wano's back, a shield coming up between him and the incoming battler. The newcomer roared and Fhranke lashed upward, but his attack was diverted as well.

Wano streaked forward. Leaving the circle embossed on the floor, she snatched Gabralina up and fled for the doors. Held inside the sylph's mantle, yet visible through her translucent sides, the young woman screamed, tumbling until Wano formed a tentacle to hold her in place. Behind her, Fhranke hesitated for an instant, looking at Cherry, then shot after Wano, covering her retreat.

The new battler followed right behind. A third battle sylph dropped through the gate, too, and chased after them before Petr and his assistants managed to close it.

The four sylphs all shot outside and started to gain altitude, arching up over the town. Already, the local battlers were roaring, all of them rising and preparing to eliminate the intruders to their hive.

* * *

Wano was pretty sure the battlers rising around her couldn't be very happy. She'd fled through that gate in desperation, only to be rejected by the woman now inside her, and now she was in the territory of another hive. On top of that, the itch was an agony inside her, her body's intended changes fighting against her new pattern.

The two battlers from her home hive gave chase, determined to kill her despite passing through the gate. That transit had broken the link to their queen, which probably only made their rage greater. They didn't have the new bond she did with the woman inside of her, but they hadn't touched the energy of this world, either. Until they did, the world wouldn't be able to reject them. Wano and Fhranke could end up dead before that happened.

What is this place? Fhranke shrieked, turning and lashing out with his remaining energy at their two attackers. Both were larger and older than he, and they dodged his blast. *Who was that female back there? Why did she call me Fhranke? What's a Fhranke? Who are you carrying?*

My life, apparently. Wano could feel the poison in the world around her, except for inside the female she carried. The woman was full of energy that was soft and light, more wholesome and filling than anything Wano had ever feasted on. Already she wished she'd come through the gate sooner, for now that she was here, all she wanted was to protect the girl who'd named her and heal the pain deep within. Provided either of them survived the next few minutes.

Creatures like the female she carried ran in terror on the ground, minor sylphs flickering around them as they took cover. Battle sylphs raced to attack, but most were young things who would only be used as guards or harvesters in her hive.

Behind her, the first of her home hive sylphs put on a burst of speed, and Fhranke moved to shield her, bracing himself to fight.

A new battle sylph who was bigger than the others appeared, roaring in rage and slamming into her enemy from below. He drove his claws deep and tore his foe wide. The wounded sylph squealed, outmatched in size, but tried to lash back. They both somersaulted together and dropped from view as a half dozen more joined the fight.

The second battler abandoned his pursuit of her and Fhranke as twenty others flashed up after him. All of them were smaller, but that didn't matter. Even the oldest and strongest of battlers could be outnumbered.

Wano slowed to a stop in midair, fearfully but deliberately putting herself between Fhranke and the dozen battle sylphs gathering before her.

Don't do anything, she murmured.

They're the enemy! he protested.

There are too many.

She could also see what he couldn't with only two eyes and limited senses: All these battlers were originally from different hives, some even from her own, but they had been allowed to live when they crossed the gate by being repatterned. They were part of a hive where she could find a place for herself without having to change what she was.

They closed in, recognizing her for exactly what she was, and Wano twisted herself into a submissive posture. She pulled Fhranke against her side and held him so he couldn't attack.

Subsume me, she said, her new master cradled and sobbing inside her. *Subsume us both.*

Chapter Twenty-two

"She's a queen?"

Mace shook his head. "Yes and no."

Solie stared up at him, one hand on her stomach as she sat upon a chair that had been brought. Her feet seemed to be getting worse the longer her pregnancy wore on. "What does that mean?"

The big battler shrugged. He didn't look like he'd been hurt in the fight, but she could feel his pain and the Widow stood near the entrance, waiting for him with barely contained impatience. "Most healers don't become queens. Sometimes, one grows too large too fast and the queen will turn on her, which means the entire hive does. That rejection triggers a change that turns a healer into a queen. By then, she'll have been driven out and will have to found a hive of her own—or die."

"That's horrible!" Solie gasped. "The poor thing!"

Mace didn't say anything.

Solie made a face. "If the hive rejected her, why didn't Fhranke?"

"He's an exile without a hive. He was waiting for her to make the final transition so that he could become her mate."

"Oh." A thought occurred to Solie. "If she's changing into a queen, will she lose the ability to heal?"

"I don't know. Probably. I've never seen a queen heal anyone before. A healer could never order death. Queens do."

Solie sighed. It would be just their luck to finally draw a healer who couldn't heal.

She eyed their two newest additions. Both were in human shape now, the foreign battler looking like any other, except he didn't seem to have an interest in his new master. In fact, he kept leaning away from her whenever she came close. Battlers had a reputation for being all over their female masters from the moment of bonding. This one didn't seem to want anything to do with Cherry. He sat close to the healer instead, leaning against her to the point where she was about to fall off the bench.

Cherry didn't seem to know what to make of that. Like a lot of single young women in the Valley, she'd dreamed of having a battle sylph and all that entailed, and Solie had heard her argue more than once that it wasn't fair for young women to be denied battlers. Only, now she finally had one and nothing was going as expected.

The healer had shifted into the form of an average-looking woman, average except for her hair, which was dark and so short it was more like fur. Her eyes were huge and dark, flecks of gold sparkling in them. Dressed in a garment too large for her, she stared across the hall at Gabralina, who was huddled by the wall and seemed to be in shock.

Shock. Solie didn't blame her. It had to be rough having your sylph die under such horrible circumstances, and then to find yourself bound to a new sylph you neither expected nor wanted. For Wano's sake, Solie hoped Gabralina could learn to accept her. If healers turned into queens because they were rejected, Gabralina would *have* to.

But, there were other priorities. Solie levered herself to her feet with Heyou's help and waddled toward the new sylph. Incipient queen or not, if she could still heal, they needed her.

People who'd come to trust her as their leader watched as Solie crossed the summoning hall. A lot of them had come out to see what was going on, at least once the sylph battle was over and the other two battlers killed. Not that she could blame them. She hadn't dared leave her bedroom while it raged.

She saw Nelson in the crowd. He was Heyou's master now, a fact no one else knew but Heyou and Nelson, Mace, and Iyala. They hadn't been willing to take any more chances. Near Nelson stood Sala and Loren, with Claw and Shore, and what seemed to be most of the children in the Valley.

Seeing Solie was done talking to Mace, the Widow Blackwell stepped through the ranks and went to her battler's side. Mace glanced down at her even as she grabbed his wrist and led him to a corner, clearly intending to check his injuries. He could use a healer himself, Solie guessed, but not so much as another.

* * *

Wano looked up as Solie approached, then away, her shoulders hunched. Fhranke glared but seemed otherwise confused. He'd been loyal through a lot of chaos, but Wano had no doubt of the reason why. He was obeying instinct, hoping for the chance to breed in a newly established hive. She could feel that instinct waging against the bond he had now with the long-haired girl they'd called Cherry. He was torn in two directions, and she had the sad feeling that he'd be like everyone else and turn away from her.

The queen of this hive walked forward, the same species as all the other fixed-form creatures but very definitely the queen. Wano could see the lines of energy that ran from her to every other sylph, and also the life that was growing inside her. That was just like a queen of her own species, she supposed, though this would be a live birth and not eggs.

The foreign queen also didn't project disgust as she looked at Wano, or even her past queen's original indifference. The creature looked down on Wano and Fhranke with a tremendous feeling of welcome, and the itch of rejection that had been twisting Wano's insides eased. The change was so sudden as to be almost painful, and Wano shivered even as she embraced it. *Desired* it.

"Are you feeling better?" the queen asked. "I know this is all confusing for you."

"I'm all right," Wano said.

Solie smiled. "I'm sorry to do this to you. I mean, normally a newly arrived sylph is given time to be alone with his or her master, for the two to relax and get used to each other." The queen's voice trailed off, which meant an acclimatization period wasn't very likely.

Wano shot a look at the other side of the hall, at her master. The queen's welcome had made her pattern soothe, but the only reason Gabralina hadn't run away was because the surrounding battlers wouldn't let her. That made Wano's pattern shudder again, unable to decide between returning to what she had been or continuing on into the change to something new.

"My name is Solie, and I want you to heal someone," the queen said. "Can you do that?"

"Yes." It had been a long time since she'd been allowed to do so, but she had healed Fhranke during the fight and herself as well.

She stood, and Fhranke jumped up beside her.

"Hey!" Cherry protested. She'd been sitting on the very edge of the bench, chewing a fingernail while she stared wistfully at her new battle sylph. "Don't go!"

Fhranke gawped. "Why not?"

The large battler who'd killed Wano's first attacker appeared. "Let me explain."

Fhranke looked at the big sylph and hissed, his aura flaring. The other's immediately rose to match. Half a second later, the queen was ten feet farther away, her mate's arms protectively around her.

The large battler was the most powerful in the hive, but

Wano could tell that the top battler was the youngster holding the queen, odd though that was. Fhranke apparently didn't know enough to make that distinction and he was close to the larger sylph's size. The last thing anyone needed was the two fighting vainly for the top spot.

Around them, elemental sylphs were vanishing again, battlers bracing themselves for more violence. Wano tensed, ready to flee.

"Stop it!" the queen shouted. Everyone stared at her, Wano included. Back home, the queen would often allow such fights, granting the winner a name if he did well enough. Here, the queen was unimpressed. "No one's fighting anyone for any position in this Valley! Is that clear? Mace?"

The big battler turned to her, his stance relaxed. He bowed. "Of course, my queen."

Solie glared at him. "Good." She faced Fhranke. "And you?"

Fhranke looked like his entire world had turned upside down and he wanted to start ripping pieces out of it.

"FHRANKE!"

He winced and bowed his head. "Yes, my queen."

Solie nodded. "Thank you. You can stay here. Talk to Cherry. I think you might like her if you get to know her."

Fhranke looked dubious, but he didn't follow as Solie returned to Wano, putting a warm hand on her shoulder and leading her over to her master.

"I'm going to take Wano to see Leon, Gabralina," Solie told the blonde. "Is that all right?"

Gabralina looked away, her arms crossed. She shivered slightly. Her soul was a morass of pain, none of which Wano could see any way to fix. "I don't care."

"You don't care if Leon gets better?"

Gabralina winced, and Wano felt Solie kick herself inside. It was the first time Wano had ever seen regret in a queen.

"Okay," Gabralina whispered.

The three of them left the summoning hall, the queen walking between Wano and Gabralina. Heyou followed, periodically playing with her hair. The gathered crowd parted, most of them chattering excitedly, though a look from Solie silenced them.

They passed down the road. Wherever it was they were headed, it seemed far enough to cause the queen agony. Wano could feel it in Solie's feet, and she paused for a moment, debating. But, this queen had been very kind to her and she *was* her queen. So, gingerly, she reached out to touch the woman's shoulder and turn off her pain.

"Thanks," Solie managed, clearly surprised.

Gabralina addressed Wano hopefully. "Can you heal everything?"

"No. Not everything." Wano regarded her master shyly. She hadn't entirely wanted the bond, either, but now that it was made, she craved more.

Gabralina glanced down, grief spearing through her again. Wano sighed. The rejection cut deep.

The queen put a hand on her newly formed arm. "Give her time," she murmured. "She'll come around."

They arrived at their destination a few minutes later. Not knowing the names of any of these strange, solid things that made up this alien world, at least not until her master processed them, Wano let the other two women lead the way. Up the walk to the front porch of the house they went, and as they did, a larger woman came out the front door.

"There you are," she said, directing mock sternness at Gabralina. "I've been worried. Do you know how long I spent walking around this town looking for you?" She turned to Heyou. "And, where's my hug?"

The sylph promptly bolted into her arms. It was a strange act for the queen's main battler, at least by Wano's estimation, but,

hugging him happily, Iyala—that was the woman's name—
asked about her son. Wano couldn't hear Heyou's answer since
his head was buried in the woman's bosom.

Iyala next held a hand out to Gabralina. "Come here, my
duck." The blonde gave a tired sigh and went to her, and Wano
heard her start to cry.

Ignoring this, the queen led the way into the house. Instinct
said to stay with her master, but Wano knew the queen was
as absolute here as she was back home. Solie hadn't rejected
Wano as Wano's old queen had, either. That won loyalty
beyond instinct. Besides, Wano could feel the pain in the house.
Instinct pulled her as much as obedience, and she reveled in
the realization that her desire to heal still existed. She'd been
afraid her former queen had broken that.

A child stood in the front hallway, glaring. "Who's she?
Nobody's allowed in here!"

"Ralad?" a voice called. "Who are you talking to?"

A woman came down the stairs, her face gaunt and her
eyes shadowed. She was pale and eyed her visitors with weary
exasperation. "Now what?" she demanded. "Isn't it enough to
have battlers fighting overhead and Ril screaming? What are
you doing here?" Behind her, more children peered out of the
kitchen, while a young woman descended partway down the
stairs to see what was going on.

"Betha, Wano is a healer. We summoned a healer."

Betha stared, white-faced with confusion. "What?"

Solie stepped forward to take her hands. "Wano is a healer,"
she repeated. "I brought her here for Leon."

Tears started in Betha's eyes, while the children began
jabbering. Wano felt their grief whip shock into joy.

"You did? She is?" Betha threw herself forward and hugged
Wano tightly. "Oh, thank you! Come! Come!"

She led Wano toward the stairs, shushing the younger girls.
"The sylphs are working hard, but he's fading. His body's so

weak. We've been giving him water and broth by squeezing a rag into his mouth. Out of the way, Lizzy."

She led them up the stairs. The girl named Lizzy scrambled to stay ahead of them as they made their way to the main bedroom.

A battle sylph met them at the door, studying Wano silently. Wano stopped when she saw what had been done to him. She'd never seen a battler so badly damaged and allowed to live, and she reveled in what that must mean about this hive. She stepped forward, her hand outstretched.

Solie grabbed her arm. "Not him. Inside the room."

Wano glanced at the queen, curious, but Solie didn't forbid her to heal the battler later. She was glad of that.

She obeyed, walking into the bedroom but stopping. A man lay in the bed. His face was gray, and if his mate had clearly lost some weight, this human looked emaciated. The bones in his arms showed under the skin. To Wano's amazement, two sylphs crouched nearby, breathing for him and keeping his blood flowing. Bruises darkened the skin on his face and around several casts, fading to a sickly yellow color around their edges.

Wano studied the unconscious man, seeing what no one else in the room could. The two elemental sylphs had done much, unthinkable as their actions might be in her old hive, but the pattern of his life force was dwindling. His body was broken in many places, its energy twisted far from normal form. And while these two sylphs kept him alive, they had no ability to heal him.

She crossed to the bed and studied the energy flows, examined the injuries. She'd never healed a human or even seen one closely before today, but she hadn't yet lost the ability to tell how his patterns were supposed to be in order to make him whole. Even mangled as he was, his problems were simple compared to Gabralina's, whose wounds went so much deeper.

Readying herself, Wano pulled the blanket down so she could place both of her hands on his bare chest. All around, the family and the man's battler gathered, their hope distracting her until she forced herself to block it out. They were just more energy after all.

Wano focused her power, matching her pattern to her patient's and then changing it, pouring energy into him for his body to feed off. The influx was healing, reshaping his flesh and bones into the forms they were supposed to take. The man woke with a gasp halfway through the process, eyes wide with surprise and not a little pain, so she forced him back into sleep even as his family exclaimed in excitement. It was easier to do this without him moving.

The man steadily improved. Wano gave the two elemental sylphs thanks, and they retreated, slipping wearily out the window and away. Her patient's battler stayed, watching with a hungry look. The man's wife and offspring were crying, while the queen stood by the door, her hands clasped before her breasts.

Finally, Wano was done. She stepped back. The man shuddered and came awake again, blinking up at the ceiling in confusion before he lifted his head as much as the brace would allow and looked at the people surrounding him. "What?"

"Leon!"

"Daddy!"

The family piled on the bed, screaming and crying while they hugged him. The queen stood back, smiling brilliantly, as did the battler. He only watched the reunion, letting the others display their ecstatic joy first.

"You saved him."

Wano turned. Gabralina stood in the doorway with Iyala, both women having come up the stairs while she was working. The blonde woman had tears streaming out of her eyes. Her pain was still there—if anything, it was worse than before—but there was something else, too: a regret and a longing. A deep loneliness worse than Wano herself had ever felt.

She nodded. "I did."

Gabralina's lips quivered. "What about . . . what about a battle sylph? He . . . They told me he was dead, but can you bring him back?"

Wano looked helplessly toward the queen, not sure what her master meant.

"He was torn apart," Solie whispered. "There's nothing left."

Gabralina started whimpering. Wano glanced back at her, knowing there was nothing she could do. There was an old sylph pattern inside her, one she hadn't noticed before, but the edge was frayed and torn. Gabralina's last sylph was definitely dead. Now Wano knew the origin of the girl's broken heart.

"I wish I could," she said.

Gabralina buried her face in her hands, weeping again. Iyala put arms around her. Wano reached for her, too, tentatively, not to heal what she couldn't, but to comfort. Like her master's friend was comforting.

She touched her master's arm, and the girl looked up, lip trembling. For a moment Wano felt a terror that her master would turn away again, and her insides itched, twisting her in the direction of becoming a queen; but then Gabralina stepped forward and threw her arms around Wano's neck. The itching stopped.

Queen Solie watched them both, clearly pleased, and then she turned toward the happy family. The gaggle of women and the half-smothered man were all giggling and talking at once, trying to get the casts off his arms and legs, as well as the heavy brace from around his neck.

"Leon," she said suddenly, her emotions shifting. Her voice was cold. The family quieted, and the healed man nodded. "Who attacked you?"

The man regarded her evenly, but Wano could see the lines of energy that ran from him to the battler and from the battler to the queen, and all of them could feel the same thing: a tremendous uncertainty underlain with a genuine fear.

His answer was shocking.

Chapter Twenty-three

Claw perched atop a roof overlooking the market and tried to hide the growing tempest within him. He'd thought all would be found out, that this horrible nightmare would finally be done. That Sala would be recognized as the soulless creature she was, that Leon would wake and remember her as his assailant. Claw would have died defending her, but it would have been over.

It wasn't. For Leon, the twenty-four hours preceding the attack were gone. His family was happy to have him back, but he was clearly consternated. He had no idea of who'd attacked him, or why he'd ordered Ril to change shape on the other side of the town. He didn't even remember his epiphany about Justin's innocence. The new healer could do nothing about his memory loss, either. So, Sala was still unrecognized for what she was. She was still free and confident.

Remembering Rachel wasn't working as well as it had been. Already unbalanced before he was given his freedom, Claw could now feel madness digging its claws into him, that insanity gaining a stronger hold each day, like a hunter reaching inside a hive to eat everything it touched. He didn't want to fight it anymore. Wat was dead; poor, innocent Wat, who hadn't understood what was being done to him. In a very real way, he'd been the only friend Claw had. In those brief moments when Wat was allowed to remember what was going on, he'd known. He'd commiserated. He'd shared.

Now Claw was alone again, bound and gagged by commands that kept him from revealing or acting on anything. Sala never touched him, so he ached, but he was glad of that, too—and horrified, and he just wanted it all to stop.

He crouched on the rooftop and watched the marketplace, all of the ordinary people making their way back and forth, dealing with their lives, their various personal issues. Their emotions were varied, unthreatening, nothing he had to worry about. All his enemies were internal.

He had no way to win. The insanity Sala wanted for him was bearing down on his soul, and the peace that Rachel had worked so hard to instill was silently crumbling. Claw shuddered and gave up the fight.

* * *

Gabralina eyed the wide bed that took up most of the sleeping room and swallowed heavily, wondering if the pain in her heart was ever going to cease. She didn't think it could. Wat's death had left a massive hole in her, and she couldn't imagine it ever being filled. Even with a healer, she didn't think such a thing was possible.

Sniffling again, wiping her eyes, she peered toward the other room that was the rest of her tiny home. She could feel Wano there, waiting. Wano. Her new sylph.

The only thing that kept this from feeling like a betrayal was that Wano was different than Wat. Wat had been lighthearted and amorous, lustful and true. Wano was reflective and quiet, unsure of herself in the exact same way Gabralina was unsure of herself—and just as lonely. She felt something like a sister.

Gabralina clung to that idea. Wano wasn't taking Wat's place. She was creating a new place, becoming a sister instead of a lover. Gabralina could accept a sister and not feel like she was letting Wat down. Except for one thing.

She shoved the few dresses she owned into a sack and

cinched it shut, dragging it off the bed and across the floor into the other room. The healer watched her evenly, that bizarrely short hair, soft as fuzz, gleaming darkly in the lamplight.

"Do I have to call you Wano?"

The sylph blinked. "I don't think so. But, what's wrong with being called Wano?"

Gabralina shrugged in embarrassment. "Well, I didn't think it out. I mean, I didn't know you were coming or that I'd be your master and all." She looked down at her feet. "I . . . I thought you were Wat at first, coming back to me, and I started to call *his* name. I . . . I didn't m-mean to." Her eyes returned to the healer. "I don't want to call you by his name."

The last words came out on a sob, and Wano sighed and stood, walking toward her master. She hadn't been long in this world, but she had seen how the humans trying to comfort Gabralina did so, and so she stepped forward and put her arms around the girl, holding her while she cried. It was a slow and different kind of healing, but sure.

"You can call me whatever you want," she said. "I don't mind. I just like having a name."

Gabralina wept in Wano's arms for a while, and then they left the apartment, the blonde girl blowing out the lamp and closing the door for the last time. She knew she couldn't come back here, not with all the memories of Wat. Her heart ached as she turned and exited the hall, Wano carrying the bag of her possessions.

They went up the same stairs where Leon had almost died and emerged into late afternoon light. It was chill, late autumn, with the bushes mostly bare, the younger trees holding a few remaining red and yellow leaves. The sun was low on the horizon, and there weren't many people out. It was a beautiful day, crisp and fresh.

Gabralina had always liked autumn best of all the seasons, when most of the farm work was done for the year but snow hadn't yet fallen. Back in Yed it had always been too hot for snow, and she hadn't actually seen it until she first came here. She hadn't seen fall colors on the trees before, either, and she'd been awed by those—in a way she hadn't been by the freezing snow. Wat hadn't really understood that, she remembered with a familiar pain. Not once he discovered snowballs.

"Can I call you Autumn?" she asked Wano a little shyly.

"Yes," the sylph replied.

Gabralina smiled, and she felt Autumn's happiness. It bolstered her spirits. "Thank you."

They walked across town, talking quietly. Gabralina related her childhood on the farm in Yed, where they'd harvested stones more often than crops, and Autumn talked about the hive where she'd been hatched, serving as just another healer until her mother decided that she was different and had to be driven away.

"It sounds like you had a worse time than I did," Gabralina realized, "and I was nearly sacrificed!"

"I was, too, when you think about it."

Gabralina frowned. "I guess so. We both had to leave."

"That we did. And then things got better."

"Yes," Gabralina agreed. Then she looked away. "*Does* it get better?" she whimpered.

"The pain?"

"Yes. I just . . . It hurts so much that he's gone. He *can't* be."

Autumn frowned, thinking. "He's only gone from this place. Part of him still exists—his energy, if in a different pattern— and it'll be reborn someplace else as someone new."

Gabralina gaped. She hadn't thought of that. Suddenly, she felt a tiny bit better.

They reached their destination, a rambling, organic-looking house that was clearly the work of sylph imaginations. A little nervous about being there, even with the almost commanding invite she'd received, Gabralina went up to the door and knocked.

It opened so quickly they had to have been waiting for her. Nelson smiled, reaching out immediately to take her bag. Autumn handed it over without comment.

"Welcome home," the young man said. "Mom's going to be thrilled."

Gabralina blushed and stepped into the house. "It's really okay that I stay here?"

"Sure. We've got fourteen bedrooms! Stria went a little crazy making the place."

He led the way through a maze that Gabralina was pretty sure she would forget right away. She stayed close to Nelson, while Autumn trailed along behind, eyeing the walls and floors as well as the furniture that seemed to flow in and out of them. Gabralina mused distantly that, if they ever wanted to move a chair, they'd have to call Stria. The place was bizarrely homey. Relaxing.

They went into the kitchen with its huge harvest table, and the children called out greetings. Iyala, too, greeted them warmly.

"Welcome," she said, rising to hug both sylph and master. "Welcome!"

"Thanks for letting us stay," Gabralina replied.

"Say nothing of it, my duck. I'm glad you can stay and help out. It always feels like there should be more people here now that my husband is gone." Brief pain filled her eyes; then she turned to Autumn. "How are you settling in? I hear Fhranke is doing quite well."

"He is?" Gabralina said, remembering uncertainly the new battler and how poorly he'd reacted to Cherry. Autumn looked curious, too.

Iyala grinned. "I don't know all the details"—the twinkle in her eye showed that she could guess—"but it seems Cherry took him to her room and convinced him of the benefits of staying. I understand they were quite noisy. They could hear them downstairs in the tavern."

Gabralina giggled, her hands rising to cover her blushing face. Nelson shook his head ruefully and headed to the table.

Autumn smiled. "Good," she said. "Now that I'm here, I won't be able to give him what he wants. I'm glad it turned out well for him, like it has for me."

Gabralina eyed her uncertainly. "This place is good for you?" She wasn't sure how she felt about that. Pleased, she supposed. Wat's death was still hard, but having Autumn around was helping. And the guilt was dwindling. Yes, Autumn was a sylph as much as Wat, but she was a healer not a battler, and their personalities were hugely different. Autumn wasn't in competition the way Fhranke would have been. That, she didn't think she'd ever be able to handle. She felt no lust for Autumn, just friendship, and she was able to make the distinction between their relationships.

She'd never have to be alone again. That was all Gabralina ever wanted in life, at least at the start. Autumn's calm acceptance of everything helped as well.

A distant chime sounded, echoing through the house. The children started shouting, and several of them bolted out of the room. Gabralina glanced around in curiosity.

"Company," Nelson explained.

"How odd," Iyala murmured. She didn't look alarmed—not until the children came back, still shouting.

Gabralina stared in horror. Sala was there, leaning heavily against Claw and holding a cloth wrapped around her outstretched hand. Her face was tight with pain, and the cloth red with blood.

She hadn't seen Sala since Wat died. She'd been hurt by that, by the feeling of abandonment and betrayal, but she tempered that with fairness. How hard would it have been to go see Sala if it were Claw who'd been lost? What would she have said to her friend, how could she possibly console her? Gabralina tried hard to remember that and not think badly of her friend, and succeeding she hurried over, her hands fluttering before her in fright.

"You're hurt! What happened?"

"I was cutting food and the knife slipped," Sala gasped. When Iyala pressed a fresh cloth over the old one, she winced in pain. "Claw said that the healer was here?"

Gabralina started, and Iyala tapped her shoulder. "Let your sylph help her," she murmured.

Oh. "Autumn?" Gabralina turned.

Autumn stepped forward. Both she and Claw were unruffled, even as the humans in the room were frantic. She reached forward and laid her hands gently over Sala's wound, pulling the blood-soaked cloths off and trailing her fingers down the length of the wound. The long knife cut closed.

Sala relaxed as the bleeding stopped, still leaning back against Claw. Gabralina watched curiously while Autumn finished and carefully turned Sala's hand over, examining it. The sylph looked up at Claw, who stood quietly behind her, and reached out to lay a hand against his cheek. The battler's eyelids fluttered shut.

Sala straightened, stumbled a step, and forced Claw to move back, breaking the contact between the two. "Thank you!" she enthused. "Lucky for me you're here." She addressed Gabralina. "You must feel so grateful."

"I suppose," Gabralina said. "I . . . I didn't know if I'd ever see you again."

Sala hesitated. Then she stepped forward and gave Gabralina an awkward hug. "I'm sorry. I just didn't know what to say."

It was embarrassing, somehow, and still neither of them knew what to say. Gabralina cast about, trying desperately to think of a new topic of conversation.

"Claw looks good," she said at last. "He seems a lot calmer." The battler wasn't fidgeting the way he used to, instead standing motionless behind his master, staring over her shoulder at the wall.

"Yes." Sala smiled. "I've been working quite hard with him."

"Can you stay and visit for a while?" Iyala asked.

Sala shook her head. "Oh, I'd love to, but I was thinking while I came over here." She eyed Gabralina again. "How would you feel about taking—Autumn is it?—over to see Leon? Just for a checkup. I know that poor dear Betha has been worried sick about him, even with everything that's already been done. I thought it would be a nice gesture."

"Oh!" Gabralina started. She hadn't thought of that. How selfish! "Do you mind?" she asked Autumn.

"No," the sylph replied. "Of course not."

"I'll come with you," Sala said. "I'm quite eager to see how he's doing myself."

* * *

Leon slowly made his way down the stairs, one hand on the railing and Nali at his side trying to help but mostly getting in his way. Mia went ahead of them, sliding down the steps on her backside and looking back constantly.

"Don't fall," he cautioned her.

"Not gonna," she replied. "Nope. Mama said to bring you to dinner."

"I know," he said. They reached the bottom of the stairs, and he straightened wearily. "Thanks, Nali."

She beamed.

Cara stuck her head out of the kitchen doorway. "He's here!" she screamed.

"I'm not deaf, Cara," Betha protested.

Leon smiled faintly and walked into the kitchen, worn out by the simple acts of climbing out of bed, putting on a robe, and walking down the hall and stairs. The healer had removed his injuries, but he'd wasted away during his coma, losing enough weight that he suspected his daughters might outweigh him; and he had no strength left. At least he was still alive, he told himself, wondering if this was what it felt like to get old.

A circular table took up half of the room, and he and his two young daughters walked to it while Cara rejoined her mother at the stove. Ralad was already seated, carefully pouring milk into glasses, the first of which she presented to her father like a benediction.

"Thank you," Leon told her and sat.

Betha turned, a skillet of cooked ham in hand. Just the sight of it made Leon nauseated. His stomach was so shrunken he wasn't sure he could eat solid food without vomiting.

"Go get Lizzy," she told Ralad.

"But I wanna stay with Daddy!"

"Go, Ralad."

Muttering, the girl ran outside. The back door banged behind her as she raced across the garden, shouting for her sister.

Betha doled out pork along with boiled vegetables and potatoes onto plates for the family. To Leon's relief, she presented him with a bowl of chicken broth and noodles.

"Thanks," he told her. "I wasn't sure I could handle the other."

She smiled lovingly and kissed the top of his head. "There's not much point in cooking anything you're just going to bring up all over the floor."

"Eewww!" Mia and Nali both chorused. Cara just smirked.

Leon sampled his soup, enervated just by the act of lifting the spoon. It tasted good, both mildly spiced and not too hot. He felt strength start to return to his muscles.

The back door banged open, Ralad running back in, and

she was followed a moment later by Lizzy. His oldest daughter gripped his shoulder as she passed, beaming down at Leon with an expression of love before hugging her mother and taking a seat.

Her hand was replaced by a larger one, and Leon looked up to see Ril. The battler was in uniform, though the top buttons were undone. His face was impassive, but Leon could feel his emotions. Ril hadn't tried to hide them in years, and right now he projected them deliberately. They were things he would never say aloud.

Leon reached up with his free hand and clasped Ril's, reflecting his own love back.

I'm okay, Ril, he sent.

Liar.

Ril let go and went to the sink to wash the cook pots. It was one of his little ways of keeping the peace between himself and Betha, to make up some for how much she had to share.

The family chattered happily, though Betha tried to keep the volume down. Ril cleaned the kitchen around them, his emotions quietly content.

Leon ate, enjoying the broth and the company. He still felt restless, his mind turning away from his family. He'd been attacked, hit on the head and pushed down those stairs. It was a miracle he'd survived, but that wasn't the important part. Why had he been attacked? He thought everything through, spooning broth into his mouth, his eyes half-closed.

Justin had been a murderer, using his control over Ril to cause pain to other battlers in retaliation for Ril stealing Lizzy. He'd poisoned Rachel to hurt Claw. He'd killed Galway to hurt Heyou. He'd nearly killed Moreena to hurt Dillon. The Widow Blackwell had been next according to the diary, an attack on Mace. All of these were Ril's closest battler friends. That hadn't been enough, so Justin ordered Ril to poison himself and thereby given himself away.

But, Justin was dead now, so who had pushed him down the stairs? Leon wondered. The common consensus was that it had been Wat. But, why? And why *push* him? A battler could do so much worse. Which was why it was strange to think he'd tried to smother him later. He could have just turned the entire house into a crater, like Claw had done to Justin.

Why had Wat wanted him dead in the first place? And, why had Leon ordered Ril to go to the other side of the town and change shape? Why tell him to hide his pain? Ordered? He hadn't asked Ril but ordered him. Why had he given Ril an order when he'd sworn he wouldn't do that unless absolutely necessary? Leon stared at his battler's back while Ril scrubbed pots, his tired mind churning far too slowly for his liking.

A knock sounded, and Ril looked up, abruptly tense. Just as suddenly he was calm again, and he left the room to answer the front door.

"I wonder who that is," Betha said. She smiled. "We're eating a little late, but I wanted to let you sleep."

Leon smiled back. "Thanks, sweetheart. I guess people might be a little curious. Even at this hour."

She sighed. "I know, but I really didn't want anyone to bother us for a few days."

Ril returned, walking side by side with Claw. The formerly blue-haired battler gave everyone in the room blank stares. His uniform was wrinkled, the buttons at the neck undone. He moved with Ril toward the back wall, where they stood, neither sylph looking at the other. They might be talking, or equally possibly they were doing nothing. Leon wasn't sure which, but he sensed Ril was a little worried.

Behind them, Gabralina entered. She was with Sala and the short-haired healer who'd saved him.

While the women in the room greeted one another, Lizzy giving Gabralina a warm hug and Sala a nod, the healer approached and laid her hands on Leon's shoulders. He was surprised to feel better. A lot better.

"I thought you already healed me," he said.

She looked at him and shrugged.

Leon took a moment to process. No longer wearing the too-large dress, the healer now wore clothing that fit her properly, and she was a beautiful enough woman, if not when compared to her master. There was a serene intelligence in her eyes.

"There's always more that can be done gradually," the sylph said.

Luck had never subscribed to that philosophy. Her own master was the only one she healed more than once. Leon considered, ignoring the chattering women as he glanced over at his battle sylph, still standing with Claw.

"Could you heal Ril?" he asked.

She regarded the battler critically. "Not completely," she said at last. "I can't restore what isn't there. But I should be able to improve on what he has left. It'll take some time."

Leon smiled, pleased. Ril had lost much. If they could get him to the point where he could change shape without pain again, where he could go to his natural form without the help of a healer, that would be enough.

Sala stepped forward. "Good evening, Chancellor. How are you feeling?"

"Good," Leon started to say, but Gabralina darted in to hug him.

"I'm so glad you're all right!" She leaped back, blushing.

Leon smiled at both women. "I'm fine, ladies. Thanks for coming."

"Do you know who hurt you yet?" Gabralina asked. "Or why my poor Wat . . . did what he did?" Her voice cracked a bit at the end. Over by the wall, Claw looped an arm around Ril's neck.

Leon patted Gabralina's hand. "I'm sorry, but I don't know. I don't remember what happened that day."

"You don't remember *anything?*" Sala asked.

Leon sighed. "I'm afraid not. I wish I did."

She shook her head. "I'm sorry to hear that, Chancellor."

"Don't worry," he said, though he didn't have much hope. "I'm sure it'll come back."

The woman nodded in agreement, and Claw lifted his chin. His arm tightened around Ril's neck, his fist locking before the blonde battler's throat.

Ril stiffened suddenly, pulling away from Claw. Leon thought it was in annoyance, but a moment later the back door slammed open and Heyou ran in. He headed straight for Gabralina's sylph.

"Hurry!" he wailed. "Solie's having the baby!"

Chapter Twenty-four

Solie had poked with disinterest at her plate, not really interested in eating. Her back and feet ached, and she couldn't even pull herself up to the table, much as she wanted to. She was carrying the baby completely in front.

"I am so sick of being pregnant," she moaned.

Sitting across from her, Heyou nodded. "Yeah. There's not nearly enough sex during it."

Solie glared at him fondly. He had been truly shocked by her loss of desire, but how could she possibly think about sex when she felt like a bloated cow? "I gather you're hoping I don't want any more children after this."

He tilted his head from side to side, thoughtful. "Dunno. Nelson said if you do want more babies, he'll do the donating. Said it should stay in the family."

Solie blinked, surprised. She hadn't seen much of Nelson. Heyou was a little paranoid about his safety after Galway. He fed from his new master on a daily basis, but their relationship was secret. Everyone in the Valley just thought he went there to reminisce. Even the other battlers.

Heyou was pleased with the young man as his new master. Nelson as the father of her children, though, wasn't something Solie had considered. She did want more, regardless of how miserable her pregnancy was making her, but finding the donor would be tricky. Devon hadn't been given a choice, and it wasn't looking like he were coming home anytime soon. Despite all of the horrible things that happened when he arrived, he'd found a home in Meridal—and from the sound of his letters, a new love. He also showed no desire to be a father to her child, which was likely why Heyou chose him in the first place.

"How do you feel about that?" she asked him. The Galway family was incredibly close-knit. If Solie had a child by him, even remotely, "Nelson won't just stand back and leave all the work to you."

Heyou shrugged again. "I know. But it's different with Nelson. I like him." He grinned. "Besides, Iyala told me all her babies owe her grandchildren, and she won't let me be any different."

Solie laughed, her stomach tightening as she did so. "All right then, Nelson will be the father of my next child."

"No, I will," Heyou corrected. "He'll be"—he fought for a word—"the starter daddy."

Solie laughed again. Her stomach clenched, hard and painful. Solie gasped and dropped her fork, putting her hand on her belly.

Heyou was at her side in an instant, touching her arm. "Are you okay?"

"I think so," she gasped. The pain was gone, but the muscles of her abdomen were quivering in reaction. "I think I want to go lie down."

Gently, Heyou got his arms around her and helped her stand, walking them slowly toward the bedroom. The pain didn't come back while she walked, and she settled down in relief. She wasn't quite ready to have the baby. Not this instant. From the way he was rubbing his hands and staring at her, Heyou wasn't, either.

She waited, but a few minutes later nothing had happened and she started to relax, settling back in the bed. "False alarm," she guessed. "I'm not due for another two weeks."

"Okay," he said. "I can stop panicking?"

"Sure," she said. "Just let me—"

Agony tore through her, all the muscles in her belly contracting. She bent forward, unable to breathe. Everything in her was trying to *push*.

Heyou's eyes went huge, and his form dissolved into a panicked, amorphous cloud.

Solie! he squealed into her mind.

The contraction eased, and Solie collapsed back against the pillows. "Get the healer," she gasped. "Get her now!"

Hysterical, Heyou obeyed. This left her alone for the first time in months.

* * *

Three sylphs flew over the town, one massive and shimmering white, the other two smaller and black flecked with lightning. The smallest by far, Heyou flew ahead, flitting jaggedly through the sky.

Following, Claw sent out a call to the other battlers. *The queen is in human labor. She'll be frightened and in pain. Don't come to her cries. She won't want visitors.*

Cries of agreement and congratulations came back to him, and he turned his attention inward. *I've warned the battlers to ignore her.*

"Good," Sala said.

They dropped down into Solie's garden, Heyou landing in a stumbling run as he took human shape. He went to open the glass doors, and a woman's cry of pain echoed out. He ran inside with a wail.

Sala was released by Claw on the ground. He stood beside her, perfectly obedient, perfectly broken. Autumn landed, gently setting down her two passengers. The healer looked at Claw in puzzlement, but Sala stepped before him to break her line of sight. Autumn was far too inconvenient an unknown, unless she could be controlled, which Sala had a plan of ensuring.

Everything else was just background dressing. Claw's insanity, Wat's death, Leon's survival, Autumn's arrival. None of it mattered. But, it had all come to this point. She could wait no longer. Tonight, she would be queen.

Sala's mind was calm and focused, her path clear. No one would come to Solie's rescue. Not on this night, when they were expecting her pain and fear.

She followed the sylphs and the other two women inside, not paying much attention to the beautiful furnishings of the queen's private home. In her apron pocket she found the small tin of poison she'd brought, and the belt knife she'd always carried, despite how unseemly it was considered for women of Yed. Solie screamed again, a cry of pain, and Heyou appeared in a doorway, gesturing.

Solie's bedroom was large, but it held only a wide bed and a wardrobe, with a heavy, comfortable-looking chair in the corner. The window drapes were drawn, and the room was lit by an elaborate system of mirrors that redirected the light of a distant fire sylph. That light was warm, and it shone on Solie's sweating face.

The queen panted frantically, her knees spread wide, her belly huge. She stared up at them all in terror, her gaze settling on Sala in denial for a moment before next finding Gabralina, then seeing one of the very last people she'd expected.

"Betha?"

The older woman smiled. "I've had five daughters. Leon and I both decided you could use someone who knows what you're going through."

Solie sagged in relief, then reached out to the woman in desperation.

Sala crossed to sit in the chair as Betha went to Solie. Gabralina stood at the foot of the bed, wringing her hands. Both battlers stood by the door, Heyou in a panic, Claw beside him. Autumn glided up to the bed and ran a gentle hand down Solie's stomach.

Sala stood up. "I'll get something for her to drink," she said to the room. Claw was the only one who noticed that she'd gone.

* * *

Solie exhaled in relief. The pain had stopped, though her muscles continued to tighten and contract. She could think again, and breathe. Thank the heavens for Autumn.

"Don't make it too easy on her," Betha cautioned. "Too simple a birth is hard on the baby." The older woman stroked Solie's hair. "I remember how frightened I was when I had my first child." She smiled over her shoulder at the two battlers. "And how useless my husband was."

Solie gasped, trying to shift into a more comfortable position. "Hard to imagine Leon as useless."

"Oh, he was, trust me. He's still useless when I give birth. This is women's work." Betha brushed a sweaty strand of hair out of Solie's eyes and looked over her shoulder again. "Gabralina, get me a bowl of water and a cloth."

"Yes, ma'am." Gabralina scurried out.

"Thank you for coming," Solie whispered. "All of you."

"Of course, dear. You don't have to face this alone."

"Solie?" Heyou whimpered from across the room. "It doesn't hurt anymore?"

She smiled at him, her heart still pounding. "Of course not, dear. I'm fine now, thank you." He started toward her, but Claw looped an arm around his neck, pulling him back. They stood together, one battler nervous, the other impassive.

It reminded Solie of Sala. The woman was here, and Solie did *not* want that. Not during this moment. But her stomach rippled into another contraction as she tried to think of a polite way to get her to leave.

The two absent women came back into the room, Gabralina carrying a bowl, Sala a tray, both unaware of Solie's thoughts.

". . . should think about what you plan to do," Sala was saying. "I mean, you have a huge responsibility to help the Widow with those poor children, but now you have Autumn. There are so many people who are going to need her help."

Gabralina frowned worriedly, even as she brought the bowl over.

Betha took a cloth draped over her arm and soaked it in the bowl before she wrung it out and used it to wipe Solie's forehead. "I don't think now is a good time to discuss that," she chided.

Sala shrugged. "I'm sorry. I was just saying that Autumn's going to be so busy, it'll be hard for Gabralina to be with her as much as she needs. To prioritize, I mean. Autumn's going to want to help everyone, even when it exhausts her."

"I guess," Gabralina murmured. She eyed Autumn, who was sitting back on her heels, obviously unconcerned about the progress of the birth. Solie was taking her lack of worry as a good sign.

The contraction eased, the desire to push fading, and Solie sagged back against her pillows. Sala noticed and set down her tray, picking up a glass of water and holding it out. Solie took it greedily. Her mouth felt like sand.

"Try not to gulp, dear," Betha warned. "Needing to go to the bathroom while you're in labor is terribly inconvenient."

"I guess it would be." Solie laughed breathlessly, trying to lift the glass. Her hands were so sweaty, she fumbled a little.

Heyou pulled away from Claw so that he could see her more clearly. "Are you okay?" he asked.

"You better drink what's left," Sala urged.

Gabralina frowned, obviously thinking over what she and

Sala had just been discussing, and then her face brightened. "I can do it all," she decided. "I'll just order Autumn to obey someone else like she does me—like Wat obeyed you, Sala."

Solie froze, the glass almost to her lips. Just like that, she knew. Without any doubt in her mind, she knew why Sala made her so uncomfortable, even as she didn't bother the battlers. She knew why the people who died had been attacked, and why Leon ordered Ril to change his shape the day he'd been pushed down the stairs, when Sala had been one of the first to find him. Moreover, she knew why Wat had done all the things he did, from deserting his guardpost to trying to smother Leon. Most of all, she knew why poor dear Rachel had died. She knew, and when she looked up and met Sala's bland, placid, unthreatening gaze, she knew the other woman was aware of her epiphany.

"Claw," Sala called. "Kill Heyou."

Claw moved. If he'd still been standing with his arm around Heyou's neck, the fight would have been over immediately. Instead, the younger battle sylph barely had time to look amazed before his friend's forcewave slammed into his barely formed shield. Heyou was blown through the wall. Claw hurtled after him.

Dropping her tray and pulling a knife from her apron pocket, Sala threw herself at Solie.

Chapter Twenty-five

Gabralina fell back with a shriek as her friend lunged across the bed, knife upraised. Howling, Solie caught Sala's wrists with her hands, desperately holding the woman off.

"Stop it!" Betha cried. She grabbed Sala and tried to hold her back.

"Get back, bitch!" Sala shouted. She shoved Betha, and the woman gave a shout of surprise and then a scream when the knife was driven into her shoulder.

Solie rolled off the bed, tossing the blankets away as she hit the floor. She rolled again, forcing herself back to her feet with a cry of pain. Sala turned, bloody knife still in hand, and Solie grabbed a heavy candlestick off the bedtable. Sala looked down at her knife and then at Solie's stomach, and she laughed.

Gabralina cowered next to the bed. Her healer sylph, shaking, just stared in uncomprehending horror.

* * *

Heyou crashed backward through the great glass doors the earth sylphs made, continuing on halfway through the garden until he slammed into a stone wall, the rock shattering and crumbling around him as he collapsed to the ground. His shield held, but his head rang from shock and outrage, and most of all confusion.

Levering himself upright, he stared at the sylph who appeared through the ruined archway. "Claw?" he gasped. "What are you doing?"

"Killing you," was the answer. "So you better kill me first."

Claw lifted a hand, pointing at him. Heyou got his feet under himself and jumped, arching up more than twenty feet in the air as the ground beneath him vaporized. Even then, he couldn't get over the shock of it. This was *Claw*. Claw was like family!

Then he felt Solie's fear and anger.

Frightened and desperate, Heyou tried to go to her, to protect her, but Claw cut him off, crashing into him before Heyou could reach the doorway. Grabbing Heyou by an arm, Claw threw him back across the garden.

"You have to fight me!" he shouted. "You have to kill me!"

Solie's pain echoed out of the apartment, strangely ignored by the Valley battlers. Heyou stared at Claw, and his fear turned to a sudden cyclone of rage.

DANGER TO THE QUEEN! DANGER TO THE QUEEN! HURRY!

All across the Valley, battlers started to roar, their hatred flaring across town as they rose into the air, clouds of smoke as if from some sudden, hellish fire.

Claw smiled bitterly. "It's about time."

Snarling, Heyou lunged.

* * *

Sala heard the battlers roar, but that didn't frighten her. She didn't have time for panic; everything was out. She had to kill Solie immediately and screw Claw while the other battlers were confused by their queen's death. Wait too long and Claw might be killed, making it impossible for Sala herself to become queen. Worse, she could be killed herself.

If only Solie had taken a few seconds longer for her realization, just long enough to drink the poisoned water. If only Sala had kept her own mouth shut—but she hadn't been entirely positive she'd succeed today and wanted to set the groundwork for getting control of Autumn. If only Gabralina hadn't unwittingly given her away.

Ultimately, though, she had no time for such reflections.

Sala advanced around the side of the bed, watching the queen. Then again, how hard could it be to kill a pregnant woman?

* * *

Mace bolted out the door to the Widow's home, orphans scattering before him, and took to the air with a roar of rage. The queen was in danger. He'd felt her fear, felt her pain, and ignored it. Now at last they knew who the enemy was, and he cursed himself for not recognizing Claw's warnings.

Lily hurried out onto the porch behind him, calling the children back while she watched him race toward the center of the town. She didn't know what had happened; he certainly hadn't had the time to tell her. But she knew there was something wrong, and he felt her well-wishes as he joined the clouds of other battlers rising up, all of them abandoning their homes and masters. This was a threat to the queen.

* * *

Like Mace, Ril bolted out of the house. One of Mia's toys was lying on the walk, and he tripped on it, nearly falling.

Lizzy ran out the door behind him, her skirt hiked up. "What's happening?" she gasped.

Ril looked up at the clouds of battlers racing toward the queen. All of them were screaming; their hatred and fear was blanketing the Valley. He wanted to go with them, but pain held him in the form he was in.

"Ril!" Lizzy shouted.

He looked back at her, loving her but not having time. Leon came out of the house, still pale but improved since Autumn's second visit. They were both so fragile, so easy to hurt.

"Stay here," he told them. "Don't follow me."

"Ril—" Leon started to protest.

"DON'T FOLLOW ME!" he bellowed, and they both jumped. Turning, he ran, the road blurring under him as he sprinted toward the queen, listening to the silent screams of what was going on, and who was doing it, and why.

Claw, he thought. Oh, poor Claw.

He forced himself to run faster.

* * *

Solie backed toward the center of the room, her focus on nothing except the woman advancing on her. There was help coming; she could feel them in the back of her mind and hear them, but it would take time. Only seconds, but seconds right now were an eternity.

To prove it, Sala lunged with her knife.

Solie brought her candlestick around. It glanced off Sala's arm instead of breaking the woman's wrist as she'd intended. Sala's eyes flashed in pain, but she drew back for a moment. She knew as well as Solie that she had almost no time.

Sala advanced again, and Solie readied herself, ignoring her thundering heart, her fear, the pain in her stomach, and the water that suddenly poured down her legs. If she was going to live, she could do nothing else.

* * *

The two battlers came together high in the air over the garden, blasting each other with energy and lashing out with sharp and fiery tentacles.

Heyou, younger and smaller, struggled to keep his shield up against Claw's passionless attack. Claw didn't want to fight him. Heyou could feel that, and it was confusing, but Solie needed him; no matter how much Claw might not want to win, this battle was for keeps.

Stop this! Heyou shrilled, desperate to get back to Solie, barely able to think through his fear for her.

You know I can't, Claw returned. He lashed out, energy rippling from the tip of his tentacle. It tore through Heyou's weakening shield and into his body, throwing him back. He shrieked and retaliated, but Claw dodged. The energy blew past him, arcing down into the town. There was an explosion, and a group of buildings was obliterated, the roof of one lifting up into the sky.

Careful, Claw cautioned, mad laughter in his voice.

Enraged and horrified, Heyou lunged. He was knocked aside, tumbling, and tried to right himself before Claw could hit him again—which was when Dillon slammed into the underside of Claw, both battlers reeling from the impact, squealing.

With his assailant engaged, Heyou's first priority remained unchanged. He turned and darted toward the house, flickering across the garden to the gaping hole where the doors used to be. He could feel Solie's focus and determination, her pain and fear underneath. He felt Gabralina's terror and Betha's agony; but from Sala, all he felt was her usual calm. Even in this, she felt nothing. Heyou raged that none of them had realized.

Ahead, the doorway grew closer, while behind, Claw rolled over Dillon. Obeying orders, he released a burst of power. It slammed into Heyou, who, squealing, crashed into the garden, plants and paving stones tearing up around him. He trailed ozone and pain.

The other battlers swept in from all directions. They were led by Mace. Claw saw them coming and shot upward, trailing enemies as he raced for altitude, leading them away. Heyou howled, shifting to human form and clawing at the ground to pull himself upright, trying to shout at them not to follow Claw, to come to the queen, to Solie, but he couldn't speak through the pain, neither aloud nor through the hive line. He could only feel Solie and had to go to her.

One battler recognized the real enemy. High above, Mace dropped away, letting himself fall until he was under the raging cloud that formed the Valley sylph pursuit. Ignoring Claw and everyone else, including Heyou, he blew straight toward the queen, and Heyou felt a moment of great gratitude. Then something changed, and everything inside him thundered to a stop.

* * *

Autumn was bent over Betha, cooing to the woman while she healed her. Betha stared upward in weeping terror, frightened to her bones by what had happened and wishing for once that her husband's battler were there. A few feet away, Gabralina cowered in fear, watching her friends fight and listening to the screams of battle sylphs outside. She didn't understand any of this.

"What's going on?" she wailed.

Autumn looked over at her, reached out to lay a hand on her shoulder. Some of Gabralina's fear eased. "She wants to be queen."

But she *was* queen, Gabralina thought for a moment, thinking Autumn meant Solie. Then the truth hit her and she gave a horrified gasp. *Sala* wanted to be queen? But there was only ever one. They'd told her that, even kept her from making love to her sweet Wat until after he'd been brought into their hive. They'd done that to prevent him from turning Gabralina into a queen.

Another truth came to her then, though from Autumn's

touch or her own sudden realization Gabralina never knew. With an abrupt pain, Gabralina saw all of what her so-called friend had done, what she'd been able to do, thanks to Gabralina stupidly telling Wat to obey her.

Wat.

Her Wat. Dead. Killed for trying to murder the chancellor. For doing something that made no sense, except that Sala told him to. Only, Gabralina hadn't meant for Sala to be able to do that. She'd only meant for Wat to help her carry some luggage. Not this. Not any of this. He'd *died* because of this.

Guilt flooded Gabralina's broken heart, making her new sylph eye her in concern; but more than that, rage filled her. Pure, blinding hatred. Autumn drew back in shock.

Gabralina shot to her feet, hiking her skirts up out of her way as she clambered onto the bed. She threw herself at Sala with a howl. Her friend. Her confidante. Her betrayer.

Sala half turned, surprised, but Gabralina slammed into her, knocking her to the floor and landing on top. Solie backed away, gasping, one hand to her stomach. Her skirts were soaked, and she slipped on the puddle she stood in, falling against the wall with a groan.

Gabralina didn't notice. She struggled with Sala, trying to get her hands around the woman's neck, thinking of Wat, screaming for Wat. Sala just pulled her hand back and plunged the knife she'd been holding deep into Gabralina's chest.

Gabralina gasped in shock, her limbs suddenly useless and weak. Sala shoved her away, and Gabralina fell onto her back on the floor, soundlessly moving her mouth, gaping at the ceiling.

Autumn threw herself over the bed toward her master. Since she'd come to this place, she'd seen battle sylphs associate with non-hive males, elemental sylphs try to heal the injured, and her own biological imperative turn back on itself. The absolutes of her origin hive didn't exist here. So, landing atop her master, she flattened one palm against her, healing the damage the knife had caused—and with the other, she punched Sala square in the face.

The woman shrieked in surprise and pain and fell back, tripping over her long skirts and falling onto her backside, her hands raised to her bloody face. Only a foot away, Solie grabbed a heavy porcelain jug off a small table and brought it down as hard as she could. The thick porcelain didn't break immediately on Sala's head, but she kept hitting Sala with it again and again until it did.

The scream of a single battle sylph outside was long and echoing. Its tone of gratitude was somehow worse than any sound of despair.

Solie dropped the broken handle of the jug, her face white. It landed in the blood pooling on the carpet. Pain rippled across her expression and she swallowed hard, both hands on her belly. Mace flew into the bedroom, shifting to human form. He barely looked at the body on the floor. Instead, he went to the queen and lifted her, bearing her out of the room.

Gabralina reached up to grip Autumn's arm. The healer looked down at her, bemused.

"I actually *hit* her," Autumn said.

"You did." Gabralina laughed, half sobbing as she sat up. Her dress was bloody and torn, but there was no pain, and Autumn tossed Sala's knife next to the shattered jug in the pool of blood.

"Is she dead?" Gabralina whispered, not daring to look at the body lying sprawled so close to them.

Autumn glanced at Sala and shrugged. "I don't think she was ever alive."

Shivering, Betha stood. She made her way around the bed, her own dress cut and bloody while the skin underneath was smooth and untouched.

"Are you all right?" she whispered, helping Gabralina to her feet. Autumn rose beside her. Gabralina didn't know how to answer the woman, but Betha didn't seem to need a response. Leaning on each other, shaken by what happened, the two women left the bedroom. They were careful not to touch anything of what lay in the center of the puddle that was even now stopping its spread.

Chapter Twenty-six

Solie was crying as Mace carried her into the sitting room and over to a chaise near the window. "Why didn't you know?" she wailed at him, hitting his arm with a trembling hand. "Why couldn't you tell what she was?"

His sorrow echoed through her. "Forgive us, my queen."

Solie sniffled sorrowfully. "Where's Heyou?" she sobbed.

"Solie!"

Mace laid her on the chaise, and she saw her beloved, Heyou, limping badly and hanging onto the broken frame of the doorway to keep from falling. His shape was as perfect as always, but he held himself wrong, flickers of smoke rippling across his skin. He stared at her and nearly collapsed, but she felt his relief at seeing her alive.

Dillon caught him, holding him up and helping him over. Solie sat up on the chaise, reaching for Heyou and sobbing. The entrance was suddenly full of battle sylphs staring in at them.

Heyou fell to his knees beside the chaise and into Solie's arms. She hugged him tight and wailed as another contraction shook her, this one worse than any before.

"You're in pain," he whimpered, holding her.

"I'm supposed to be." She laughed and started to cry again.

Autumn stepped up beside them, one hand on Heyou to heal him while she lifted Solie's skirts with the other. The healer checked on Solie, tapping her belly, and Solie sagged back against the chaise in relief as the pain vanished. The sensation didn't: she felt the baby coming.

"Wait!" she heard suddenly. "Wait!"

Startled and afraid of what might happen, Solie looked up to see Sala's other surviving victims.

* * *

Unsurprisingly, Ril arrived later than anyone else, sprinting across town as fast as he could. The energy inside him burned. It was all Lizzy's, Ril not being willing to take any from Leon that the man might need while he was still in recovery. He was fueled by Lizzy's love instead, staring up at the swirling cyclone of battle sylphs rising high over the ground, all sweeping upward after one of their own.

He felt their rage and confusion. Claw was a hive mate, and there wasn't one of them who couldn't feel how badly he wanted to stop fighting them. Everything he felt was in the open now, all the secrets he'd been ordered to keep revealed.

She'll be queen! Claw screamed, sobbing. *She killed Rachel to have me! She'll kill the queen and make me take her. She'll be queen of us all!*

They would kill him. Ril had no doubt of that. He'd kill Claw himself if that was what it took to protect the queen, just like he'd killed Wat, and he'd live with that grief as well. Claw rose above them all, still fighting even as he screamed out his master's confessions and begged them to finish it before she did.

Then his scream became different.

Ril couldn't feel the death. None of the battlers could, not with the strange soullessness of Sala that hid her nature from them for so long. Claw did, and lightning flashed through him, turning him bright white for an instant before he fell, dropping back into the swirl of battlers below.

Ril sprinted across the wreckage of a building destroyed during the fight, past a hysterically barking dog and up to the wall that circled the queen's garden. He jumped it, one hand slapping down against the top of the stone as he vaulted over and landed on the grass on the other side. Claw and the other battlers were there.

Don't kill him! he shouted, running straight into the storm of battlers, their cool mist gentle against his skin even as their lightning made him ache to join them in his natural form.

He threatened the queen, Fhranke hissed.

He didn't, Ril retorted. *His master did, and she's dead.* This close, he could feel it now, through Claw. *If all of you didn't know that, he'd be dead already.* With the death of the master came the freedom of the sylph. Claw would only be a danger now if he lost his sanity.

He found the battler lying in his human form in the center of the storm cloud, shaking, his hair blue again but his eyes wide with madness. Ril knew exactly how Claw felt. He'd lost his own sanity when he came through the gate and Leon killed the girl who'd drawn him. They'd made peace, but first had been the madness—and it hadn't been Leon who pulled him out of it.

Inside the building, Solie wailed in pain. Her child was still coming.

Ril hauled Claw upright, pulling the other battler back against his chest and locking arms around him. Claw didn't help, but he didn't resist, either, hanging limp in Ril's grip as he was dragged across the garden and into the house.

"Wait!" he shouted. "Wait!"

Solie looked toward him in fear. Her feet were drawn up on the chaise, her knees spread and her skirts pulled up. Ril could see her clearly, and the crowning head that was already emerging streaked with blood.

Ril grabbed Claw's chin, forcing his head down to watch. "Look!" he gasped. "Look at her! *See* her!"

Solie screamed, bearing down, and Ril looked away, afraid

to see the birth. That was how he'd regained his own sanity. In seeing Lizzy born.

He looked away and found himself staring at Betha. The woman stared back, eyes wide. Ril just watched his masters' wife and mother, and he closed his eyes against her understanding, not knowing what to say.

* * *

Claw was lost.

Rachel was dead. Wat, Galway, and Justin were dead. Even Sala was dead. He'd felt her die and been able to do nothing about it, and even as he'd reveled in that, he'd shattered. No, there was nothing left of him; only the dying remained to be done. Darkness. He'd welcome that.

Ril was shouting, telling him to look at her. What her? It didn't mean anything.

"Claw," Solie gasped suddenly. "Look, Claw."

Orders were absolute. Claw focused, even as he didn't want to. Solie's hair was soaked with sweat; tangled, plastered to her face. She was gripping the sides of the chaise hard and gasping, all of her muscles tight and trembling. Between her legs, between her legs . . .

A baby was sliding out from between her legs, a filthy, slimy baby girl with a face already screwing up into a scream. Claw looked down at that perfect, untouched spirit, and she blew through him, bringing light like a massive, sun-drenched diamond dropped into the pool that was his soul. She took him and made him hers as surely as the girl for whom he'd first come through the gate. Except, this was so much more powerful. Claw stared, rapt.

Ril whispered something in his ear about her being his, or him being hers, but Claw didn't really hear. The other battler let him go, and he thudded to his knees, staring at the shrieking baby as she was wiped clean and handed to her mother.

Heyou stared like he'd never seen such a thing before and didn't know whether to smile or run screaming. Claw didn't care. He looked at the queen, who stared back at him with contented exhaustion.

"Can I call her Rachel?" he asked.

Epilogue

Solie walked past the window that overlooked her kingdom, glancing idly out at the fresh snow that fell during the night. It was warm inside, heat piped in from a central location the fire sylphs took turns making as hot as they could. The entire downtown core of the Valley was riddled with such vents, and those living farther out could relocate if it became too cold in their own homes.

It was peaceful, even with the late afternoon dim and cold. Solie hadn't fully appreciated how tense she'd been over the last few months, afraid of an enemy she couldn't even identify. That was over now. Before he'd stopped talking entirely, Claw told them all what Sala had done. Unlike Wat, he hadn't been ordered to forget, all in the hope that when the time came, he would be insane enough to kill his own queen. Solie wept when she learned what had been done to him.

She left the window and walked past the newly repaired doors to her garden. A big bull mastiff slept before them, his ear twitching as she passed. The garden itself was still devastated, but Shore and Loren would need to wait for spring to fix it.

Since the attack, Solie hadn't stepped into what had once been her master bedroom. She went into one of the smaller rooms instead. In a corner, a crib stood against the wall, Heyou looming over it with his jacket off and a wondering look on his face. He really hadn't realized what he was getting himself into, Solie reflected with amusement.

Heyou looked up and returned her smile. "She's about to wake up hungry," he said.

That little trick was going to be convenient, Solie thought. There was no chance that this child was ever going to complain that her parents didn't understand what she was feeling. Or that she would ever feel alone.

Solie stared into the crib at the sleeping little girl and at the blue-furred puppy that lay beside her.

"Hello, Claw," she whispered, and he shuddered, his wounded gaze never leaving the baby. Beside him, Rachel shifted and screwed up her face, getting ready to scream.

"Aw, it's all right, sweetheart," Solie promised, lifting her up and carrying her over to a chair to nurse.

When Claw started whimpering, Heyou picked him up and brought him over as well. Claw didn't speak to him, but Heyou didn't seem to mind. He just cuddled the puppy as the two of them settled down to watch.

At least Rachel would always have a protector, Solie thought as she nursed the infant. Claw would always be there for her, and someday, Rachel would be his master. Eventually, she would be his queen. Until then, Claw's master was asleep in the other room.

It had been an experiment, binding him to an animal, but Claw was too damaged to take orders from anyone. The mastiff was working fine.

Solie nursed her daughter, her thoughts turning toward the maintenance of the Valley. She'd heard from Devon Chole again. He was content in Meridal and planning to stay there as a permanent ambassador. Solie had written him a letter in return, congratulating him and telling him about the daughter he couldn't ever acknowledge. There would be other children for him, she hoped.

Mace continued to work directing the battlers. Leon was back as chancellor, with Ril as Solie's majordomo and Lizzy still learning how to keep track of the Valley's finances. She was a surprisingly quick study, and the Widow helped out on a part-time basis, when she wasn't working with her orphans. Nelson was starting to help Lizzy, too, brought into the council on a trial basis. He and Heyou had made their status public. Things were safer now, though life in the Valley had changed forever, thanks to Sala. They knew their vulnerabilities more clearly. They lay in the people who were also their strengths.

She felt the emotions of her people. The Valley was at peace, everyone settling down to bear the winter. In the Petrule house, Ril lay on the couch in the living room, his head in Lizzy's lap and his tunic undone. Autumn had her hands pressed against his chest, working slowly to try and repair old damage, while his masters both watched hopefully and Betha chatted with Gabralina. Children played and argued all around them, making a happily chaotic noise that no one really minded.

In the Blackwell home, the chaos was far less controlled, the orphans playing loudly with a big battler who didn't often deign to do so. Mace tickled the girls, sending them giggling hysterically while they squirmed to get away. The boys piled on top of him, trying to wrestle him to the ground. The Widow watched all this from the doorway before shaking her head in patient tolerance and turning to go and finish dinner.

Meanwhile, at the Galway home, Nelson headed into the basement while his mother shouted for him to get back in time for dinner. In a corner, he found and unlocked a door that led to a stairwell down into the underground corridors of the hive. Stria had made this connecting corridor for the house, and he was very glad of it as a way to avoid the cold snows whenever he went to the queen's quarters and his hungry battler.

Solie didn't know those actual activities, but even with her limited empathy, she could sense that the Valley had breathed a sigh of relief. Winter was here, but it was a cleansing cold, the snow a blanket that would cover the horrors of the past year and freeze them away. Once spring returned, the Valley would be like new.

She kissed her daughter. For now she had no other worries than making sure Rachel was fed and clean. She settled back in her chair with her eyes closed and her child feeding contentedly at her breast. Heyou grinned, and she returned his smile. The future looked good.

About the Author

L. J. McDonald was born in 1970 in Canada and has a bachelor's degree in Anthropology from the University of Victoria in British Columbia. She grew up reading horse books until Christmas day when she was twelve, when her parents gave her a book titled *The Elfstones of Shannara* by Terry Brooks. It was the first time she ever read fantasy, and from that point on she was hooked. L.J. started writing when she was fifteen, but she didn't try very hard to get published until she was in her later thirties. L.J. works in the Canadian military and also spends her time drawing, knitting, and reading as many good books as she can get her hands on. Visit her Web site at www.ljmcdonald.ca for more details on upcoming releases.

INTERACT WITH DORCHESTER ONLINE!

Want to learn more about your favorite books and authors?
Want to talk with other readers that like to read the same books as you?
Want to see up-to-the-minute Dorchester news?

VISIT DORCHESTER AT:
DorchesterPub.com
Twitter.com/DorchesterPub
Facebook.com (Search Pages)

DISCUSS DORCHESTER'S NOVELS AT:
Dorchester Forums at DorchesterPub.com
GoodReads.com
LibraryThing.com
Myspace.com/books
Shelfari.com
WeRead.com